BRITTANY ACKERMAN

The Brittanys

Brittany Ackerman's debut memoir in essays, *The Perpetual Motion Machine*, was the winner of Red Hen Press's Nonfiction Award. She has a creative writing MFA from Florida Atlantic University and has attended the Writing By Writers Methow Valley Workshop and Mont Blanc Workshop in Chamonix, France, as well as a residency at the Wellstone Center in the Redwoods. *The Brittanys* is her first novel.

The Brittanys

The
Brittanys

BRITTANY ACKERMAN

Vintage Books

A DIVISION OF PENGUIN RANDOM HOUSE LLC

NEW YORK

A VINTAGE BOOKS ORIGINAL, JUNE 2021

Library of Congress Cataloging-in-Publication Data
Name: Ackerman, Brittany, author.
Title: The Brittanys / by Brittany Ackerman.
Description: New York : Vintage Books, 2021.
Identifiers: LCCN 2020044125
Classification: LCC PS3601.C545525 B75 2021 (print) |
LCC PS3601.C545525 (ebook) | DDC 813/.6—dc23
LC record available at https://lccn.loc.gov/2020044125

**Vintage Books Trade Paperback ISBN: 978-0-593-31173-8
eBook ISBN: 978-0-593-31174-5**

Book design by S. Walker

www.vintagebooks.com

Printed in the United States of America
10 9 8 7 6 5 4 3 2 1

For Carl

The Brittanys

· ONE ·

*B*rittany Rosenberg's lost her purse. She's laughing, though, not crying, even though her pink Coach bag could be floating around the fairgrounds, where teenagers are paid to dress up like zombies and pop out from behind maze walls. This is the ticket. We want to be scared. We begged our parents to let us go. We've paid for this, folded-up twenty-dollar bills in our little plush wallets. This is the kind of occasion we wear jeans to, tight Brazilian jeans decorated with holes and embroidery that lace all the way up the thigh, with a nice top, our hair straightened by our regulation flat irons. We can never get the back straight, and there's always one lumpy wave from the crown of our heads to the base of our necks. In pictures, it appears as though we are wearing hats made of our own hair.

There are five Brittanys in the group: Brittany Rosenberg, Brittany Jensen, Brittany Gottlieb, Brittany Tomassi, and me. There is also a Mackenzie Bedner, aka Kenzie, and a Leigh Cotner, but we just call her Leigh. The seven of us: linked together, traversing the darkness of fairgrounds filled with haunted houses for the month of October. It's eighty degrees in Florida, even though it's fall. Winds are strong, the telltale sign of a storm approaching, but we persist. Brittany Jensen's parents lead us around, chaperones, and tell us to hold on to our things. Our hair blows into our lip gloss, and our bare arms dampen in the ever-present humidity. I'm the only one who brought a zip-up hoodie, and I've loaned it to Jensen, who wears it unzipped and loose around her shoulders, pointless.

When Brittany Rosenberg screams, "My Coach purse! Where is it?" Jensen's parents immediately identify the nearest attendant, a ponytailed teen in bloody face paint sporting a straw hat and wielding a flashlight. He looks for the purse on his hands and knees while we all laugh, because he's kind of cute.

"What color is it?" he asks.

"What's your name?" Kenzie, the slutty one, asks back. She was the first of us to get felt up: in the seventh grade, at Adam Leibowitz's bar mitzvah. She's also the only one who doesn't stuff or wear a padded bra, because she actually has boobs somehow.

The ponytailed attendant shoots Kenzie a smile, and Brittany Gottlieb, the know-it-all, wants to know, "What was in the bag, anyway?" To which Rosenberg replies, "My permit! I just got it two weeks ago! And some tampons and my Hard Candy lip gloss. Oh, and fifty dollars for tonight."

Brittany Tomassi gets on all fours, too, says, "We'll find it, don't worry!" Leigh twirls Rosenberg's long black hair into one big knot, then lets it loose on her baby-blue tank top, an attempt to comfort her, I guess.

Brittany Jensen, my best friend out of all the best friends, butt-bumps me and turns me around to the Ferris wheel. When we were twelve, we rode one together at her church's annual fair. Without speaking, we grabbed each other's arms and thought to ourselves, *I hope we stop at the top, I hope we stop at the top.* We closed our eyes and hoped so hard, and when we felt the car shudder to a halt we opened our eyes and saw we were right smack-dab at the apex. It was then we knew we were magic, witches, fairies—whatever you want to call it— but we could do it, make things happen just by thinking.

For the last two years, we've used this power at school to get the fire alarm to go off or to get hundreds on our social studies tests. Now we are fourteen, it's two weeks before the real Halloween, and we know we can find Brittany Rosenberg's purse if we use the magic. We turn away from the group, and I grab Jensen's arm as she grabs mine. We think, we hope, we drown out the loud music and flashing lights. We concentrate on that pink purse. We focus on Brittany Rosenberg's face, her blue eyes, her black hair frizzing up in the humidity, her pale, flat tummy showing from underneath her top, her wedged sandals, her shiny, glossy lips.

"*I found it!*" the ponytailed guy calls to our group. We run and see he's actually found her bag, the pink Coach purse with interlocking C's all over it.

Kenzie writes her phone number on a used gum wrapper, using Leigh's bony back as a flat surface to compose the note. She hands it to him, and he asks, "How old are you, anyway?" and she says, "Sixteen," and he walks away, laughing at the obvious lie. *He ended up calling her the next weekend, and she gave him a blow job in his truck. I remember how she didn't want any of us to know except Leigh, but then Leigh ended up telling everyone during an eating-disorder-themed assembly. It's ironic, because Jensen always thought Kenzie might really have an eating disorder since she always went to the bathroom right after lunch and her teeth were kind of yellow. But I remember Leigh, how she kept giggling while some blonde teenage girl who must have weighed all of eighty pounds told us about how she'd overcome her friend ED, which stood for "eating disorder," and how ED would always be in her life, like a true friend, but how he could never hurt her again like he had in middle school. Leigh kept laughing until Rosenberg made her say what was so funny. Finally, Kenzie told us. She said his "thing" tasted like nothing but his "stuff" tasted like crushed-up SweeTarts. SweeTarts—that's why Leigh couldn't keep it together. For the rest of the year, whenever someone brought them up, we all lost it.*

Rosenberg reunites with her purse and checks inside for all her belongings. She reapplies her lip gloss, and it makes her mouth bright pink.

"You smell like a cinnamon bun," Jensen tells her.

"It's Creamsicle," Rosenberg says, and I remember debating between that shade and one called Confection, which I ended up getting.

Our group migrates to the snack stand, and Brittany Jensen and I split a blooming onion, dipping the fried strips into the ranch in the middle. Brittany Gottlieb wants to share, but we're adamant that no one gets involved except us. Jensen's parents also buy us two Cokes, and we feel like we own the place because we're the ones with the big cups of Coke, the snack and refreshments, the matching Guess watches. She has a lime-green Kate Spade, and I have a small, classic Burberry bag. My mom gave me the twenty-dollar bill that I folded and ended up not needing because Jensen's parents paid for me.

We look forward to Fright Nights every year. Usually, the fairgrounds are home to the Expo Center, which hosts concerts and conventions, but it is mainly known for the South Florida Fair. You can eat a burrito made out of cotton candy, you can pet an emu and have it nip at your fingers, you can win a stuffed bear the size of an armchair. But we much prefer the place at night, when the moonlight makes us appear older than we actually are and we become unafraid of the things that are supposed to scare us.

We do a few haunted houses, scream and laugh so hard our voices will be gone tomorrow. Tomassi and Gottlieb sit these out: they don't like the fake chain saws and the way a guy dressed as a psychotic clown gets too close to their legs. The rest of us move through the houses, pushing Rosenberg up front, watching her buckle in fear, take every corner with a squeal, and eventually fall down onto the hay that covers the ground. Tomassi gets a Diet Coke and drinks it out of the bottle like a model. Rosenberg takes a sip and snorts so hard it comes out her nose. We take a group picture on Jensen's digital camera. Kenzie keeps asking me for gum, but it's my last piece. I break it in half, and Jensen slips her half into the pocket of her jeans.

At the end of the night, everyone is having a sleepover at Kenzie's house, but I have to be somewhere in the morning, so it's been arranged that Brittany Jensen's parents will take me back to their place, where my parents will pick me up. No matter how late it is, I'll call and they'll come. I say bye to my friends when Kenzie's mom arrives in her Range Rover and all the girls pile in. Brittany Jensen is laughing at something that Brittany Tomassi said, and I worry I'm missing out. I feel good in the car, though. Jensen's parents drive a white Mercedes-Benz, "Old Mercy." Ironic, because the car is brand-new, but I think Jensen gets embarrassed by the money her parents have.

The back is spacious, and I put my purse on the open seat where Jensen sat before, earlier today, when her dad picked us up from school. He brought us Subway sandwiches with extra pickles and two half Sprite—half Cokes. Up front, her mom calls my mom, and I hear them talking. Jensen's mom says it'll be forty-five minutes or so, that it got a little crazy with all the girls around and then the whole mess about the bag, and something about how they'll never do it again, they'll never volunteer to be the chaperones.

I drift off while they drive, and I'm out by the time we get to the highway. I don't think about the girls in Kenzie's room teaching one another how to use eyeliner on the inside of their eyelids. I don't think about how Brittany Gottlieb has her period and a boyfriend and I don't even know what a "thing" looks like yet. All I've ever done is kiss a boy, and it's only been for truth or dare, nothing real, nothing out of love.

The first time happened when I was at my friend Anika's house for a birthday party in fifth grade. Her older cousin, whose name I don't even remember, something boyish and proud like Nate or Jonah, was dared to kiss me on the trampoline. It was about to rain, and I heard the beginning of a drizzle drumming on the tight canvas below us. His lips were so big, like gummy worms, and he smelled like the inside of a tree. If my name comes up tonight, I hope Jensen will recall this story for everyone, because she was there that night and saw it all go down. I miss her. I smell her cucumber-melon perfume on my arm. Maybe I could grab my own arm and hope, but she isn't here with me to make the magic happen.

When we pull into the driveway, I wake up and see my parents' car already waiting. I take the stick of gum out of my purse, the one I broke in half for Jensen because we only had one. This way, we each got a piece. This way, we could share what we had.

TWO

*O*ne week after the fair, we decide to dye our hair. Mine will be red, since I want to be the Little Mermaid for Halloween, and Jensen will do a streak of blue in solidarity. I've asked my mom many times if she'd take me to a salon to get a red tint, and every time she said no it only made me want it more.

Tonight, my dad is coming home from his weekly commute between New York and Florida, so we're going out to dinner at this hibachi place where they cook on the table and make flaming onion towers. Jensen was supposed to come with us, but she's grounded because she didn't walk her dogs and they made a mess on her mom's new sofa.

Jensen almost never gets into trouble. Her mom is an interior designer and her dad is a lawyer. They're rarely home, and her older brother, Matty, who's a senior like my brother, Brad, is usually out with friends. Jensen and I like having her house to ourselves, to watch movies and go in her pool and paint our nails and walk to the park. One time, we stumbled across a bounce house in the park that had been left up after a kid's birthday party. No one was around, and we bounced in it for hours until we got tired and sat inside talking until dark. It was one of the best days of my life. When we're at the Jensens', it never matters what time we come home or how late we stay up, since her parents and Matty are usually back way after us anyhow.

But the one thing her mom is strict about is keeping the place clean and orderly. Jensen's mom never makes the bed for me when I stay over. Instead, Jensen has to take out the bedding, and I help her stretch the sheets over the pullout. In the morning, I have to fold everything back up, and Jensen assists me, our arms wide to open the sheet and then meeting back in the middle to clasp the edges together, corner by corner. Jensen knows how to do things that I don't, because she has to take care of the house when her parents are working. My mom still does most of that stuff for me, but I really am eager to learn certain chores, like how to clean dishes and bake cookies and mop a floor and take out the trash. I think Jensen enjoys coming to my house more because those things are taken care of. My house is a luxury, an escape, a more comfortable home away from her home. But I envy how grown-up she is.

Still, despite the couch blunder, she's sure that she'll be able to fix it so she can come over tomorrow for our hair-dyeing adventure. But now I have to endure a family dinner alone.

"Why do they have to put mushrooms in the soup?" Brad complains, and passes it off to me. I had to forgo my appetizer since I'm sharing the teriyaki chicken with my mom and she loves the salad with ginger dressing. So I am happy to obtain this small prize.

"It wouldn't kill you to eat a vegetable," Dad says, and winks at me, proud of his daughter for being a vegetable eater, a noncomplainer in the land of food, but really I'm just starving and I'll take what I can get. If Jensen was here, she'd have ordered her own meal and gotten soup and salad and refused to share with me, even though we always end up taking most of the food home because it's so much. She'd take chopsticks and carve JENSEN into the Styrofoam package so no one would eat it from our fridge.

"Actually," says Brad, "the pesticides they've been using on produce have proven to cause a lot of serious diseases and long-term illnesses, so they actually *could* kill me."

I get nervous and move the mushrooms to the side of the soup bowl and eat around them.

"But not organic ones, right?" I ask.

"Those are even worse!" Brad says. "Those are the produce you always see crawling with all kinds of insects and mites and covered in dirt."

"Well, I'm thinking of becoming a vegetarian," I say. "It's so inhumane, what they do to animals."

"So you don't want to share the chicken teriyaki?" Mom asks.

"No," Dad says. "You need the protein. Eat the chicken."

"Why are you so worried about animals all of a sudden?" Brad asks.

"I saw this video in school, and all these chickens were in cages and could barely move and then their heads just get chopped off one by one, and it's horrible!"

"Oy." Mom puts down her salad fork.

"This is what they're showing you at school?" Dad asks.

"It was for biology. It was really sad. I want the chickens to live full, happy lives and be free . . ."

"Chickens?" Brad laughs. "You should be more worried about the magnetic fields collapsing and our Earth's core rotting and solar storms that could send us back to the Dark Ages . . ."

"Brad!" Mom yells. "Don't scare your sister like that."

I notice in my periphery that a few people at the surrounding tables have craned their necks to hear our dinner conversation, and I'm mortified.

"Apologize to her," Dad says, pointing his fork at Brad and then at me.

"Look," Brad concedes, "none of this will happen in *your* lifetime, so don't worry about it. Maybe your children or grandchildren will have to endure the demise of society and the world as we know it, but most likely not you."

Our hibachi chef rounds the corner of our table right then and introduces himself. He confirms everyone's orders, including the surf and turf for my dad and brother, and the chicken teriyaki to be shared between my mom and me. I nod my head yes when the chef speaks to us and decide there are bigger things to worry about than one little chicken for dinner. Anyway, it's one of my favorite meals, and maybe I'm not ready to give it up just yet.

The food is served with a flourish, but we eat most of the rest of the meal in silence. Brad just sits there, peeling the lobster shell away from the body. He doesn't look up from his plate.

I've already decided I'm not going to tell Jensen about what happened, the raised voices and the way everybody turned and stared. I figure some things are just private, things other people, not even Jensen, would understand.

Jensen is off the hook the next day, as expected. Her mom and dad are going to a wine mixer in Naples, but she still credits her early escape from being grounded to her wit. We decide to bike to CVS to buy temporary hair dye in a box, the kind we've seen on commercials and in magazines, the products that women scrub onto their heads in the shower and later shake out in voluminous waves for the camera. That will be us soon.

Whenever we ride to CVS, we always stop at Subway for a kids' meal, even though we are fourteen. We like the circular buns and our choice of cookie. We both always get white chocolate macadamia nut. That day, when we pull up at Subway, we see Joey Fratinelli and Mitch Parker inside. Joey is in our grade; he's a punk kid. He kind of looks like Steve-O from *Jackass* and is in all remedial classes, a step below Jensen's regular classes. He doesn't live in my neighborhood, though. He lives out in Coral Springs, and Jensen and I are both confused as to why he's hanging out with Mitch Parker, who lives one neighborhood over from me.

"He's probably selling him weed," Jensen offers as an explanation.

"So they just met up at Subway to do a drug deal?"

"Druggies gotta eat!"

We laugh our asses off before gathering ourselves and heading inside.

"Don't talk to them," Jensen whispers. "You *always* want to talk to guys."

"I don't even think Joey Fratinelli knows who I am."

"Then please don't talk to him."

"Why?"

"It's embarrassing. I just want to get our sandwiches and go."

As the door dings its traditional ding, we realize we're still in our uniforms. Our school has a pretty strict dress code: you can only "dress down" and wear your own clothes on select days, like on your birthday or for various school events, and even then only if you donate a dollar to charity. I'm wearing a regulation red polo with a khaki skirt, and Jensen is in a navy polo with a khaki skirt as well. Joey's in a black T-shirt and his school khaki pants, and Mitch is in his striped navy-and-white polo. When you get to sophomore year, you're allowed to wear the striped shirts. Another year until we can wear the blue-and-white-striped polo with a khaki skirt, straighten our hair, and adorn ourselves in the same Tiffany choker with a heart charm and the Birkenstock slides that every sophomore wears. We can't wait.

The boys are ordering their sandwiches. Jensen and I peruse the cookie selection from afar, and I can already see they're fresh out of white macadamia. This day can't get any worse.

"You girls go to our school," Mitch says suddenly, pointing his foot-long plastic-wrapped sandwich at us. I stay quiet, since Jensen told me not to speak. She nods. I place my hand on a promotional sticker of a teriyaki-chicken sandwich. I attempt to peel the edges with my pointer finger and eye Joey looking at me.

"Are you in middle school?" Mitch asks. It's the worst question, because we are not in middle school, but we must look like we are, even though we're freshmen. We're small and are always at the bottom of height and weight for our age at our yearly checkups. Our doctor points to the chart. He points below the pink arch for girls where we should be but are not. Maybe next year.

"They're in my grade," Joey finally says. I thought he'd gone mute. I know he's embarrassed that we're in his same grade and that he has to introduce us to Mitch, even though we already know who he is without really knowing him. That's the crazy thing about our school: you pretty much know everyone since it's so small. When my brother graduates at the end of the year, there will be twenty-seven kids at his graduation ceremony. The school is growing more and more each year, but not much, since it's a prep school. There are about three hundred kids in the whole upper school, 106 in ninth grade, and five of them are Brittanys.

"What are you doing for Halloween?" Mitch asks, handing the cashier money for his and Joey's subs.

"We're dyeing our hair," I blurt out, nervous. I realize too late that Mitch meant what are our plans for the actual holiday, and not who or what we are going to be. "That's why we're here now. We're going to get hair dye. I'm going to be Ariel, the Little Mermaid."

"That's hot," Mitch says. "Are you going to have a coconut bra or whatever?"

"Shells?" I suggest.

"Yeah, shells. Damn, that's hot. Are you gonna do that?"

"I'm making the costume myself, so probably," I say, even though I hadn't planned on it.

"What are you gonna be?" Mitch asks Jensen. Last year, Jensen and I stayed in and watched *The Others* even though we had both already seen it—together, in the theater, actually. We bought a tub of popcorn from Blockbuster and some candy-corn pumpkins and drank Cokes. We wore black Soffe shorts with orange T-shirts to appear festive to no one.

"I don't know yet," Jensen says.

"She's doing a blue streak, though. And I'm doing red."

"Joey, these girls are pretty cool; why don't you hang out with them?" There's a pause while Joey and Mitch look us up and down. It feels like Joey is trying to figure out the answer to that very question while Jensen and I wonder, *Yeah, why don't you hang out with us? We're girls and we want what girls want, have what girls have, do what girls do.* Joey begins to smile, and it gives me hope, a light at the end of this teenage tunnel.

"They don't smoke weed," Joey says, and elbows Mitch. They laugh.

When he says it, I feel like dying. I can feel how badly Jensen wants to kill me for having started all this. It's true that we don't smoke. We've never even tried it. We haven't had the opportunity. I'm not really as against it as Jensen is. Our ex-friend Christina Kirkland started smoking weed in seventh grade and Jensen refused to speak to her, so I don't speak to her anymore, either. Sometimes she smiles at me in the hallway. I know she still hangs out with Kenzie and Gottlieb because they all live west of the Turnpike, but it's not the same. We were never super close anyway. I slept at Christina's house once, after a bar mitzvah, and in elementary school we bonded over our love of

SpongeBob SquarePants, but that was about it. Jensen played club volleyball with Christina over the summer and their dogs got along, but otherwise we could do without her.

But, no, we've never tried the stuff, and it separates us from the "cool kids." The thing is, we had been "cool" once. When Jensen took me under her wing in fourth grade, we ruled the school. Everyone was afraid of her, so, therefore, everyone respected me as well. We were equals. Jensen was blonde, I was brunette. Jensen's favorite color was blue, mine was purple. Jensen was Christian, I was Jewish. Jensen liked sports and video games, I liked boys and makeup. We evened each other out. Neither of us went anywhere or did anything without the other. We were a team, a duo, an unstoppable force of girl-hood. But something we had decided on long ago was that drugs were "bad."

Weed is questionable, though. Is it really *that* bad? "It's a plant," Jensen argues sometimes, late at night, when we can't sleep. "It comes from the ground, like a tomato or a carrot." Jensen's brother, Matty, does it all the time, but we've never partaken. We're scared of being out of control, I guess, of becoming bad kids, because we're so "good." Dyeing our hair will be the first thing we do to explicitly go against our parents. It's been fun to plan it, talk about it at school all week, and research shades that will go best with our eyes. But in all actuality it feels bad not to have our parents' approval. Jensen doesn't care as much as I do, mostly because we're doing it at my house, so, naturally, my parents will find out first.

Sometimes it feels like she isn't as worried as I am about things. I've always had this deeply rooted fear that if I did something bad I'd be shunned, or my parents would hate me, disown me, send me to jail. It manifests as sharp pains in my stomach, killer headaches that take three Advil to remedy, or sad naps that can last anywhere from twenty minutes to a few hours. But Jensen sort of likes living on the edge, the very edge I stay far away from. She lies to her parents all the time. She takes money from their wallets, even though they would give it to her if she asked. She uses cheat codes for her video games and gets extra lives, extra coins, extra chances to win. No matter what I do, I still feel a general desire to be "good," to be liked, to be loved. I want to fit in, be accepted. I want to play the part. And maybe it's because Jensen's parents both work full-time and can't see her as much as she would like, or maybe because her older brother is a "hoodlum," or maybe because her grandparents essentially raised her and their old-fashioned Greek Orthodox ways didn't translate, but Jensen just wants to rebel, to live a life that stretches some invisible cloth of the world. The more she stretches, the greater the reward for her. She can decide her own fate.

The boys laugh and exit Subway. A guy in an apron asks us what we want, and we proceed to order our kids' meals. I get turkey. Jensen gets tuna. Both on round rolls. Both with extra pickles. The cashier tells us there's a fresh batch of white chocolate macadamia cookies being made if we want to wait a few minutes. Things are looking up.

"Would you ever smoke?" I ask Jensen while we wait for our cookies.

"Not with Joey Fratinelli."

"Why not? He's cute."

"He's not cute! His eyes are too big for his head. He smells like hamster food. And he's emo. Why do you like him?"

"I think he volunteers at a PetSmart. But I don't like him. I just think he's cute."

"You think everyone's cute."

"No. I don't think Mr. Zuppurdo is hot, and you do."

"Alan Zuppurdo is a man. He's like a silver fox. He drives a sensible van. That is hot."

"I'd smoke weed with Joey."

"I feel like if I'm going to smoke, I'd want it to be with someone I'm really close with, just in case I trip out or something. I'd want to do it with you, I guess."

"Where would we even get weed?"

"And we wouldn't know how to, like, roll it up or whatever."

"Well, that's why Joey's good. 'Cause he can do it with us— like, show us how to smoke."

"Joey thinks we're losers. Thanks for butting in, by the way. We probably could have gotten invited to a sophomore Halloween party if you didn't ruin that for us."

"Mitch said we were hot. And you weren't saying anything!"

"Sometimes it's best not to say anything in the presence of guys."

We eat our sandwiches and head to CVS, a couple stores over. I save my cookie, but Jensen eats hers right away, fresh out of the Subway oven.

"It's so good," she says. "How do you not want yours now?"

Inside CVS, we make our way to the hair-care aisle. We're not entirely sure what we're looking for, but asking for help is out of the question. I just need red and she needs blue. I find a box that shows a girl with super-shiny red hair, almost the color of our uniform's polo shirt. Not so much a ketchup red, but a bit deeper, like the wine Jensen's mom drinks. Jensen comes over to me with her box.

"I think I might just do a lighter blond."

Her hair is already whitish blond. It was definitely lighter when I met her, but it's pretty damn light now.

"You're chickening out! That's, like, getting clear!"

She laughs so hard she drops her box, then picks it up and shows it to me.

"No, it'll lighten it. See how some of my hair is, like, orang-ish? This will make it all one color. There'll be a noticeable difference."

"Whatever. I'm still going red. I can't believe I'm the bold one here."

We pick up some Nerds Ropes and pay for our boxes. We're so happy that you don't need to be eighteen to do this stuff. Anyone with a bicycle can pick up hair dye and change their look. We've got that small freedom, and we're riding with it, until we both, inevitably, get into trouble.

We decide to do it at the same time. This way, we won't have to wait patiently for one result, then the other: the big reveal can come all at once. We run upstairs to my room and wrap our-selves in the shittiest towels I have. In our hair-coloring boxes, we are equipped with gloves, plastic dye bottles, powdery mix, and instructions. We're supposed to mix the dye in the bottles and squirt it strategically onto our hair in sections, let it sit for thirty minutes, then rinse out, and ta-da.

For the most part, my mom seldom comes upstairs. Instead, she yells from the first floor that dinner is almost ready, tells me to do my homework, asks if Jensen is staying the night. Now she yells up that a bad storm is coming and we should use the electricity while we can, and that Jensen's mom called and they are stuck in Naples for the night, so Jensen will need to stay over. This is okay with us. We hurry with the hair dye.

Jensen's super-blond mask looks like nothing on her head. She didn't do sections, like the box said, but simply scrubbed the dye all over and twirled her hair into a bun to let it sit. I let her do my dye job, and she sections my hair into a middle part, with two portions in the front and two in the back. After a while of dividing the liquid diplomatically, she eventually squeezes the bottle haphazardly onto my head and rubs the dye all over, trying to get it even.

"What happens if we leave it on too long?" I ask.

"You'll just be really red."

"And you'll be clear."

"I think it's better to leave it on longer than not long enough."

"Yeah, I don't want it to do nothing."

While we're waiting for the dye to set, we notice a stain on the bathroom rug, the one with a pattern of yellow roses around its border that I begged for and that was very expensive. I wanted it so badly and then I got to have it, and now there's bright red hair dye on one of its corners. We try wiping it off, scrubbing it, soaking it in hot water, but the stain remains strong. There is no way to tell my mom about this. There wasn't even a plan for telling her about dyeing our hair, aside from just coming downstairs sporting a new look.

It nears the thirty-minute mark, and we press on. We lay a towel over the stain and proceed to wash our hair dye out in the sink. Jensen goes first so my red can sink in a bit more. With a shower cap covering my hair, I can't quite tell yet if the dye is doing anything. Jensen's looks the same after she washes it, but she promises that once she blows it dry it'll be shiny and white.

She washes out my hair in silence, which is concerning to me.

"What does it look like?"

"Ariel. You're definitely Ariel."

I look in the mirror, and with my hair sopping wet, I can see how red it is. It's *Little Mermaid* red, all right. My mom is going to kill me.

We both dry our hair, Jensen first and then me. It becomes obvious that Jensen's dye in fact did not do anything at all and that my dye did everything. I look completely different. Especially in the fluorescent bathroom light, you can see the fractals of red bombarding my light brown hair. It worked too well. I should have left it on for less time. I like it, though. I think the red looks sexy, like Jessica Rabbit, cartoonish but cool. I think the guys in my grade will like it. I can't wait to show up at school next week and look different.

My mom yells from downstairs that she's ordering a pizza and that we should come down and tell her what we want. It's now or never. Jensen follows me down for support.

"Does mine look different at all?" she asks.

"No."

My mom's in the kitchen, leaning on the island next to the telephone. She's reading the menu for Nino's Pizza, and when she looks up at us she does a double take.

"What did you do?" she yells at us, but mostly at me— probably all at me.

"It's temporary!" I try to calm her down.

My mom asks Jensen to go back upstairs and in the same breath asks her if cheese is okay. Jensen nods and runs. I know she wants pepperoni, but she's taking one for the team.

"I thought I told you I didn't want you to do this," my mom begins. She stands with her hands on her hips. I note her hair, the blond she has a colorist highlight in every six to eight weeks, and remind myself how unfair this all is. Why can't I get my hair colored, too? Most girls in my grade have highlights or dye their hair, get it chemically straightened, even shave the back of their necks so you can see a field of fuzz when it's up in a ponytail or a bun during PE. It goes against our school's dress code, yes. We're not supposed to have crazy colors or styles, piercings, or tattoos that might distract from our studies. But it's only hair. It'll fade or grow out eventually. I know my mom probably just wants me to stay the way I am, to always be her little girl, but I want to look *different*. I want a change.

"Yeah, I just really wanted to do it," I say. "I don't get why it's such a big deal. It's my hair. It's temporary. It won't last forever."

"If it doesn't wash out in a week, we're going to the salon."

"Fine!"

I go upstairs and tell Jensen the news that I'm not in trouble. She asks when the pizza will arrive.

We decide to look for a movie on HBO to watch after dinner. Our neighborhood started getting free HBO a few months ago, and it's been a godsend. One night, we stumbled upon a movie about a couple who goes to a hotel and there's all these murders in the middle of the night and you think the butler did it but it ends up being the maid who seduced the husband, and also the movie is a porno but you only see tits and ass, no frontal lower regions. We watch it because it's good, and laugh during the sex parts, because they're overly dramatic and too passionate, very unreal, or what we assume is unrealistic in bed.

The storm gets a lot worse, and the TV goes out a few times. Eventually all our power goes out and we can't sleep. Jensen suggests we talk about what we'd buy if we won the lottery. She says she'd buy her own boat and go sailing all over the world, but I remind her she gets seasick, so then she says she'd just buy a plane ticket to London and meet a British man and fall in love. I say I'd want a mansion on Star Island in Miami, with a huge pool and a waterfall and a private chef, and then I realize Jensen is fast asleep. I close my eyes and think about Joey's eyes and what it'd be like to smoke with him. I wonder if he'll like my hair.

• THREE •

*W*e wake up later than usual because of the storm. Usually on Saturday mornings we get up early and eat breakfast and beg our parents to take us to the mall, but this morning it's dark outside, even though my watch reads 12:00 p.m. The sky is still swirling, but there's no more rain. The clouds are the color of bone.

"It's a hurricane now," my mom says, as we realize we can't make Eggo waffles in the toaster because the power is still out. "No one flush the toilets unless it's an emergency."

Jensen uses her cell phone to call her parents and says she's going to stay with us until the power comes back. Jensen and Tomassi are the only Brittanys with cell phones. Tomassi has a BlackBerry because her mom has a BlackBerry, and Jensen has a Nokia flip phone with a camera. Not even Kenzie has a cell, but she steals her mom's sometimes. My dad said I can't have one until I turn sixteen and start driving on my own. He thinks that's the only reason a "kid" should have a cell phone. My mom's on my side and thinks I should have one in case of emergencies. We're both working on slowly wearing him down.

My dad lays out old towels in the dining room next to each of the large windows. He's prepping for water damage. His flight back to New York for next week already got canceled because of the weather. None of us are really sure what to do if things get bad here, but my dad has confidence that we'll be okay. We don't have hurricane shutters, but our neighborhood association assured us the windows were hurricane-proof. The first year we lived in Florida, my dad was out of town when a hurricane warning was announced. My mom drove my brother and me up to Orlando and we went to Disney World for a week. But this time we haven't had enough warning to escape and will just have to ride it out. Jensen keeps bringing up Hurricane Andrew and how this is nothing compared with that.

"You were, like, two," I argue. "You didn't know your ass from a hole in the ground!"

"Excuse me," Jensen replies. "I can assure you I was a very intelligent toddler."

"What the hell happened to you then?" my mom chimes in, before giving Jensen a kiss on her forehead.

Our neighborhood is usually quick to get power back after a storm. It'll probably be another day until it all gets fixed. It just sucks that the storm is being wasted on the weekend and we can't miss school for it instead.

"Let's play N64 with Brad," Jensen suggests. I know she has a weird crush on him, even though he's kind of nerdy and not really interested in girls yet. Or maybe he is but doesn't make it obvious. Jensen gets crushes on the most random guys: teachers, our pediatrician, Jude Law. She never likes guys in our grade, or even in our school, unless they're teachers.

"Brad has to study for his math competition," I say. "And the electricity doesn't work. We can't do shit."

"Crapulence."

"I guess we can see if he wants to take a break and play a board game," I suggest.

We gather the courage to go upstairs and knock on my brother's door. He keeps it closed most of the time. Since he's a high school senior, I try to respect his space. I've been closing my door, too, lately, slamming it when I'm mad, locking it when I want to be alone. But my dad threatened to take the door off the hinges if I keep locking it, something I'd let happen just to watch him do it. A lot of my parents' threats are empty, but I do worry about my hair dye not washing out.

I motion for Jensen to knock on the door, and she puts her hands behind her back and shakes her head no. I go ahead and knock, and Brad calls for us to enter. He's at his desk, which is covered with a bunch of textbooks and notepads. He holds a graphing calculator, something I am still afraid of, even though I know I'll have to learn how to use one eventually. His blue quilted comforter is haphazard on his bed, and there are a few empty cans of Red Bull on the floor. There's a leather jacket in a frame on his wall.

I remember the story my mom always tells about when we lived in New York. Our family went to see the musical *Grease* on Broadway with a few family friends. Before the show started, Rosie O'Donnell, who was playing Rizzo, got onstage and asked if any kids wanted to come up and participate in a dance competition. To my parents' surprise, my brother, age eight, jumped up and threw himself onstage. He was always shy, like me, but something in him just made him get up and want to dance that day, right there in front of everyone. There was a group of about fifteen to twenty other kids who got up onstage, and "Greased Lightnin'" started to play in the big theater. My brother started doing karate kicks and splits and spins and wowed everyone in the audience. In the end, he won, and a stagehand ran from the wings and handed Rosie a kid-size leather jacket. Rosie placed it over Brad's shoulders. I was there when this happened, but I was so young I don't remember it—only the story.

Brad's become introverted since those days. Sometimes I think the move from New York to Florida was harder on him. He's still made friends and excels in school, but he seems so far away from the kid who let loose on that Broadway stage.

"What?" he says, not looking up at the two of us hovering in his bedroom doorway.

"Do you want to play Monopoly or something?" I ask.

"I'm studying, and Monopoly's the worst game in the history of the world."

"What about Life?" I ask.

Brad lets out a cackle. Jensen starts to laugh, too.

"What?" I ask. "I love that game! I love the little car and picking up all the people."

"I always end up with, like, fifty kids," Jensen says.

"Last time we played, I had to be a cosmetologist," Brad says.

"We're bored," I say. "We're desperate."

"Why don't you go outside?" Brad suggests. "The neighborhood probably looks cool as shit now, with all the trees and garbage everywhere."

As usual, Brad is right. We go to the garage to grab bikes, but Jensen wants to use my old Rollerblades. They're bright purple and babyish-looking, but she argues that probably no one will be out anyway. She's much better on them than I've ever been. I once rode over a patch of gravel and scraped up both my knees so bad that I couldn't fully bend or extend my legs for a month. I'm okay on a bike, though.

We ride around my neighborhood surveying the damage. The sidewalks are a mess: trees blown down, leaves everywhere. We step over dirt and debris, random mail, letters and newspapers strewn about the streets. There are no cars out. It feels like the end of the world.

It's easier for Jensen to maneuver the Rollerblades through the wreckage. I notice that she flexes her left foot and pivots when she wants to slow down or stop. I never knew that technique existed. I just rolled forward until I could grab on to a mailbox or a tree trunk to stop myself.

"Do you think school will get canceled?" I ask Jensen. She slows down and turns back around toward me on the bike, a move I didn't know was possible, either.

"I hope," she says. "Maybe the school blew away."

We see Florida Power & Light attempting to fix a power line up ahead.

"Thank you! We love you!" I yell.

"We love you, FPL!" Jensen screams.

"We'll suck your dicks if you get our power back!" I scream

at the top of my lungs. One of the workers looks down from his post. We wheel away quick.

When we return to my house, we discover two bicycles slumped in a bush out front. I haven't been friends with anyone in my neighborhood since Mike Lipski moved out last summer. I had my first sip of alcohol with him. He poured all the alcohol he found in his mom's liquor cabinet together into a "Magic Juice." He hid it under his bed, and we drank it in his room, pretending to get drunk off one or two sips. It tasted terrible. Then his mom remarried and they moved to Miami. Otherwise, Jensen and I know the twins, Daniella and Danny Albertson, from school, but we don't like them very much. We hope to God it's not them, because we have literally no excuse not to hang out now. There's no power, nothing to do, but we'd still rather do nothing alone than with them.

We walk inside and hear the voices of my mom and a couple boys.

"I told them all we had was cold pizza," my mom says. "They rode all the way from Coconut Creek."

It turns out the boys are Brody MacIntyre and Fred Weitz. They're both sophomores. I know Brody because I went into the library once during seventh hour and he was in there for study hall. I had to get copies for a teacher, and Brody told me I was cute. Brody has curly black hair and is pale, very pale, with piercing blue eyes. He's got a boyish frame but is tall and has full lips. I heard he was dating a sophomore, Hannah Abrahams, but I guess she's out of the picture if he's here in my house. I'm in love with him, and it's a bit unnerving to see him sitting at my kitchen table.

Brody hops up and gives me a hug. He wipes his mouth with the back of his hand while his arms are around me. Jensen is in shock. Fred I don't know too well, aside from that he's neighbors with Brody and doesn't go to our school; I've only heard about him from Brody. He just sits there and continues eating his slice.

"Did you dye your hair?" Brody asks.

"Yeah, it's for Halloween. It's temporary."

"It looks hot. I mean, good. It looks really good. Crimson."

"What are you guys doing here?" Jensen asks, and I wonder if she's annoyed or feigning interest.

"We were bored, so I figured we'd ride our bikes as far as we could, and we got all the way here." He leans over to whisper to me, "And we had to pick up weed from a kid who lives a few subdivisions over."

"Anyway," says my mom, "as I was telling Bodie—"

"It's Brody," Brody interrupts.

"Oh, sorry, *Bro-dy*, Jensen's mom called my cell and said that she has to go pick up her new dog today at four o'clock. She's coming to get her at three thirty."

Jensen lights up.

"What dog?" I ask.

"My mom's coworker's shih tzu had puppies and we were promised one. They're giving them up for adoption."

"We gotta head back anyway," Brody says. "I just wanted to stop and say hi."

"How did you know which house is mine?"

"The school directory. My mom still orders one of those

each year for some reason. It finally came in handy." Brody
smiles.

It's only now that I can tell Brody is high. Maybe I can get
high for the first time with him. He must like me, or want to
do stuff with me, if he came all the way over here. But, then
again, he was already coming to my neighborhood in order to
get drugs. Brody and Fred leave, and Jensen and I run upstairs
to discuss plans for the rest of our lives.

"If I choose the girl pup, I'm going to name her Lucky, or
something girly, like Baby, but if it's a boy, I want to give it a
real boy name, like Jack or Franklin. I think that's so cute, to
have a boy dog named a real name like that."

"Yeah, but what about Yacko, Wacko, and Dot?" I ask.
"How are your parents even letting you get another dog at this
point? And won't they be jealous of Lucky or whatever?" I ask
these questions as if I care about the dynamics between her
dogs, but really I'm hoping she'll bring up Brody soon, so I can
talk about him forever.

My mom yells for me, and I tell Jensen I better go down
alone. I hurry downstairs and brace myself.

"Did you buy drugs from Brady?" she asks.

"It's Brody. And no, Mom! Why would you think that?"

"Those boys smelled like marijuana."

"Oh my God, Mom, no, they didn't."

"You're crazy if you didn't smell it on them. They were
stoned."

"Okay, well, I didn't. Can I go now? Jensen is leaving soon."

"I need to ask you something."

"You just did."

"When you girls dyed your hair, like idiots, what did you use to clean up?"

"What do you mean?"

"What towels did you use? I assume you put towels around your necks and on the floor. They must be covered in red dye. Do you think I'm stupid?"

"I used *old* towels."

"When Jensen leaves, I want you to show me."

I run back upstairs, and I tell Jensen that my mom wants to see our towels, and she laughs and tells me I'm screwed.

Jensen is getting her school bag together. She never actually packs but simply shoves all her things into her navy-blue JanSport and calls it a day. I have a red JanSport—we bought them together before sixth grade. It was a whole ordeal, picking them out at Target. I obviously wanted a feminine color, but Jensen wouldn't let me get purple or pink, and she wanted brown, the worst color ever. We decided on red and navy because they both would go with our uniforms for high school. We were proud of ourselves for thinking about our future. And we like that we match but aren't exactly the same.

When I first moved to Florida in fourth grade, Jensen hated me. My arrival meant there was another Brittany in town, and Jensen was afraid that her boyfriend, Jonathan D., would fall in love with me because I was new and had lots of colorful butterfly clips that I wore in my hair—though I never knew how to style them properly, so they sat on the top of my head, having landed there unfashionably. Jensen was a tomboy with beautiful platinum-blond hair. I had buckteeth and a unibrow, but a boy named Billy Millman said he loved me, wanted to marry me. These things happen when you're nine. He was the only one who talked to me, who showed me any attention. Then one day at recess, Jensen pulled me aside.

Her icy-blue eyes were serious. "Do you want me to 'take care' of the Billy situation?" she asked.

"What do you mean?"

"Don't worry about it. I just need to know if he's *bothering* you."

She told me that she didn't like Billy, either, but never really explained why. I assumed it was more of the same. Maybe he'd harassed other girls before; maybe he used to bother her and she didn't want to admit it, didn't want to show what was underneath her toughness. Anyway, Billy wasn't really *bothering* me, it was just annoying, the way he followed me around and tried to touch me with his fat hands. But I said yes because I wanted her to do me a favor. I wanted to be her friend.

So she punched Billy in the stomach and got sent to Principal Sherry's office. Billy left me alone after that. And I got to play basketball as a "package deal" with Jonathan D. and his best friend, Jonathan Z., and Jensen, of course. We stood side by side on the playground until the boys asked us to play with them, and they always did as long as they got both of us. When I told her I didn't know how to play, she said all we had to do was have the ball tossed to us and then gently bounce it back to whoever passed it. Easy enough.

I never wanted to be "cool" until I met Jensen. The way she wore boys' basketball shorts and never blow-dried her hair, it was clear she didn't care what anyone thought of her. She knew how to bake cookies and how to run fast. She understood her dogs' feelings better than her own. She was the only person I knew who could beat *Donkey Kong* on Nintendo 64. Jensen was the one who realized we could use the Brittany name to our advantage, to confuse teachers in class. We became inseparable and unstoppable, answering at the same time when "Brittany" was called, fitting into one PE T-shirt because we were the same person, talking in a backward language that no one else could understand.

A part of me feared Jensen, too, but it was more like respect. From the moment we met, I knew it was her schoolyard, her turf. Principal Sherry didn't even care about the punch on the playground. She agreed with Jensen that Billy Millman was a pain in the ass. Instead of getting suspended, Jensen spent the rest of the day in Principal Sherry's office doing homework and eating candy. From that day on, I knew I had to listen to Jensen, learn from her, try to become like her. She would always be the leader, and I would always follow.

FOUR

A few days later, when the Internet comes back, I see that Brody sent me an instant message, *You're pretty*. I die over it and call Jensen to tell her. I can hear Lucky barking on the other end of the line. Jensen can't talk much, because the new puppy requires a lot of attention. I lose the nerve to tell her, and instead of talking about Brody, I say we still need to figure out what we're doing for Halloween. We agree to let each other know if anyone gets invited to anything. We only miss one day of school because of the storm, and I spend most of it taking pictures of my red hair in the mirror on Jensen's camera that she left at my house.

When my hair hasn't faded by the end of the week, my mom takes me to her salon to get it washed out. It doesn't come out fully, and for months afterward I have a red tint, the kind I always sort of wanted. My mom hates it. She also finds out about the carpet when she's in my bathroom to look at the towels and calls me an asshole. Sometimes she'll call me a bitch or an idiot, but she's never called me an asshole before, and it feels comical, but she doesn't laugh. She's really upset with me for a while. I don't get in trouble, though; she just says I'm not allowed to get nice stuff for my room anymore.

Since my hair isn't Ariel-red anymore and Jensen just looks like she always did, we decide to go as sexy babies for Halloween. The only plans we manage are to hang out with the dreaded twins, Daniella and Danny. Their names are so stupid it makes us sick. But they have a huge house a few subdivisions over. All the neighborhoods in Boca look the same: a string of homes and pools and well-placed palm trees. Our neighborhood, Woodfield Country Club, has twelve subdivisions, smaller areas of our community with similar-style houses. I live in Bay Creek, where all the houses are beige with Spanish-style architecture, rounded doorways and windows, and coral-colored roofs. The Albertsons live in Cascada, which is much larger, with much bigger houses that are modern and simple. There's one subdivision, Briarcliff, that has houses so expensive, they have their own guard gate. Woodfield Country Club is always really busy on Halloween, so we figure at least we can hang out with other people this year instead of just ourselves. Also, my mom won't let me go out unless it's in a group, and Jensen doesn't count, so this gives us a way in.

For our sexy-baby idea, we're both wearing baggy men's sleep pants from Target (mine are SpongeBob and hers are Batman) and tight black spaghetti-strap tank tops with major push-up bras. Our hair is in pigtails, hers low and mine high, and we have pacifiers that we got from Babies R Us. I think we look sexy. Jensen wears Crocs that I hate, and I'm wearing Nikes.

We get to the Albertsons' house around 6:00 p.m. We're

sleeping over, so my mom says she'll pick us up tomorrow at 9:00 a.m. She tells us not to do anything stupid. Daniella and Danny are both wearing all white and going as Miami Heat fans, which we think is dumb. They're always doing dumb stuff we don't understand. Daniella is wearing white eyeliner and it looks scary. Danny has a secret spot in his room called "the cave" where he watches porn and masturbates, and when we're over he lets us sit inside and watch some of his movies. Before we go out trick-or-treating, he shows us one of a German girl losing her virginity to her boyfriend that he's shown us before, but we watch it again. Their mom made us red velvet cake, but it's cooling and we can't eat it until later.

I really just want candy. I love Halloween. It's always been my favorite holiday since I was a little kid and dressed up as a different Disney princess each year. I loved collecting candy in my orange pumpkin basket and dumping it out on the floor at the end of the night, sorting it into chocolates and fruit-flavored candies. I always gave my mom all my Whoppers and Bit-O-Honey. My favorites are Twix, Twizzlers, and Reese's Peanut Butter Cups. Jensen loves chewy candy, like Starburst and anything caramel, so we make a good team.

Daniella and Danny give us pillowcases to carry our candy in. Before we head out, Nick Morano comes by to say hey. He's our age but doesn't go to our school. He knew Danny and Daniella when they were in sixth grade together at another school. Even though Nick is way cooler than them, he has some kind of camaraderie with them that won't ever go away. Nick rides over on his moped and gives each of us a turn. I can't balance on it, but Jensen impresses Nick with her athleticism.

Nick says he'll ride next to us as we walk but he doesn't want to ask for candy. Nick's definitely not my type: brown hair and green eyes with a muscular build. He's wearing basketball shorts and Nike slides with a tank top. For some reason, Jensen is really into this kind of look. She likes athletic guys, and I can tell she's into Nick. She doesn't say anything to me, though, doesn't even eye me when he's not looking. I wish she'd be honest with me. I don't understand why she never tells me when she *likes* someone. I always know anyway, but it's frustrating that she can't just be normal and talk about that stuff.

We make our way around the houses in their subdivision and get a good amount of candy. Girls in the neighborhood are dressed in variations of slutty: Little Red Riding Hood in short shorts; witches who've simply donned black leotards, witch hats, heavy makeup, and kitten heels; angels and devils but mostly devils; and other even sexier babies. All the boys are wearing basketball shorts and bandannas and calling themselves gangsters, but really they just look like they're ready to play basketball or go to sleep. My pillowcase gets heavy, and I have to sling it over my shoulder between houses. Nick wants to go to the house of this one kid he knows, Devin Kempler. We all agree and follow him to the next subdivision. It feels weird to leave the safety of Daniella and Danny's area and move into the night with God knows what else out there. There's a thick fog in the air, and the shrubbery is cut differently. For the first time tonight, I feel cold. I can see Jensen shivering, too. Nick gives her his flannel, and she throws it on. It's oversize, but I can tell she loves the feeling.

We get to Devin's house, and he has some people over, all guys. They're watching a scary movie about a clown who kills people. Devin is sitting on a big leather couch, rolling a blunt. Nick asks Jensen if she wants to smoke, and she asks if I can smoke, too. He says yes, and Jensen and I reconvene in the bathroom. We decide that we'll do it and that she'll go first, since she was offered and pretty much got us to this point. Good job. I think about Brody and how happy he'll be that we can smoke together now. I think about Joey and how I'm finally going to prove him wrong.

Daniella is knocking on the bathroom door and crying, so we pull her in.

"I . . . don't want . . . to be . . . around drugs!" she whimpers.

"You can leave if you want to," I offer as consolation.

"Yeah, you're not, like, a prisoner here," Jensen adds.

"You guys are sleeping at my house. You need to stay with me," Daniella says. "Don't you want to get more candy? We've barely filled one pillowcase. Last year, Danny and I got, like, three whole full ones."

"I mean, we're just a little old to be worried about candy, don't you think?" Jensen says.

I'm torn, because, although I agree with her, I also still love candy. I kind of wish we could just keep trick-or-treating and dump our bags out and share our treasures, but we have to grow up at some point, and maybe this is that point. We're fourteen, and even though we're dressed like babies, we aren't little anymore. We're young women, and we want to smoke weed with Nick Morano and Devin Kempler.

"We'll meet back up with you later," Jensen offers.

"Yeah, we want to sleep over and have red velvet cake," I add.

"If you guys don't come with me now, then you can't sleep over, and you can't have any cake," Daniella says firmly.

"What the hell, Dani? You're such a cockblock," Jensen says.

Daniella leaves the bathroom, and we know we have to stay with her: we can't go back to my house high at midnight. It's not an option. We follow her out. Nick comes running outside after us.

"Where are you going?" Nick shouts, but we're too embarrassed to turn around and answer. Jensen runs to Nick to hand him his flannel and then returns to us. We walk the whole way back to their subdivision in silence.

Once we're back, though, we hit up some more houses, houses that Daniella and Danny were saving for last because they're the best. These houses give out king-size candy bars or have bowls outside that say TAKE ONE, so you take a fistful.

I'm looking inside my second pillowcase for a sucker to eat while we walk when Jensen pulls me aside. We let the twins walk ahead a bit, and she tells me she needs to take out her tampon.

"We were *just* in a bathroom! Why didn't you do it there?"

"I don't have another one with me. These pants don't have any pockets. I was going to just wear it the whole night, but I'm scared of toxic shock syndrome because Amy Hershel in math got it from wearing hers for, like, six hours."

"I'm sure we'll be back to their house soon, and you can just wad up some paper towels in your underwear or ask Daniella for a pad."

"I *doubt* she's had her period yet," Jensen says, and realizes I don't have mine, either, and that she's hit a nerve with me. "Well, even if she has, it doesn't matter. I need to take this one out, pronto. I'm not bleeding that heavy. I'll just stick leaves in my thong or something. Or go au naturel for an hour."

Jensen gets the idea to run behind a house and throw her tampon as far as possible. I hold her pillowcase while she rushes behind a fence, squats down, and then chucks her feminine product across a yard. We hear the tiniest splash, and Jensen runs back to me, grabs her pillowcase, and says, "*Run!*"

"What! What?"

"I think it landed in their pool!"

We die laughing and run over to Daniella and Danny, who are clueless to the situation.

"Don't you dare say anything!" Jensen yells, and I can tell she's kind of embarrassed.

"I swear," I say, and reach out my pinkie finger to meet hers. We kiss the ends of our hands and solidify the promise.

"That guy's gonna have fun cleaning his pool tomorrow," Jensen says.

"So gross!"

"What?" Daniella asks.

"Nothing, oh nothing," Jensen says.

We get back to the twins' house, and their parents are still up, drinking wine and watching a movie. We each cut ourselves a hearty piece of red velvet cake and sit at the kitchen table eating in silence. The cake is so good and rich, and the cream cheese icing is my favorite. This cake is one of the only reasons we hang out here. It's that good.

Their dad comes over and explains that if we have to go to the bathroom in the middle of the night, we shouldn't flush for number one, pee, but we can flush for number two, poop. I don't like it when their dad says "poop," especially because we're eating, and also because it's just weird. Now I know if someone flushes the toilet in the middle of the night it's because they're going number two. It just makes me feel like a little kid, being told what to do with my bodily functions.

We get ready for bed, and Danny asks if we want to go to the cave to watch another movie. I kind of do want to watch one. I like the pornos because everyone gets what they want. If a girl says, "I want you so bad," the guy lets her have it. If a guy says he wants to do something dirty to a girl, they do it. It seems so simple. I wish I could ask someone to kiss me and then they'd just do it. In real life, I freeze up and get quiet. In real life, no one ever kisses me like I want them to. But Jensen thinks the pornos are weird. She always laughs at the actual sex parts, so I have to, too. She says she only agrees to watch them for the story lines, the stuff leading up to the sex. I like the plots, too, but I'm much more interested in the sex scenes. It's the closest I can get to real sex.

We say no, though, and go to Daniella's room, where Jensen and I have to share a cot. We're not sure why we wanted to sleep here so bad. We probably could have just stayed at Nick's or even at Devin's, but then my mom would come here at 9:00 a.m. and get mad.

Daniella falls asleep fast, and Jensen and I talk to each other in whispers.

"Do you like Nick?" I ask her.

"Nick's hot, but he's kind of a pothead, you know?"

"Yeah, but do you like him?" I prod.

"How can I like someone I barely know?"

"I don't know. But I wish we could have smoked with him tonight. I feel like that was a good chance."

"Same. And I doubt he'll ask us to do it again, because we just ran off like idiots."

"Brody messaged me that I'm pretty," I finally confess.

"Brody is a weirdo."

"Why?"

"He just showed up at your house, and he was only there to buy weed, I'm sorry to say it. Maybe he does, like, like you, but I think he's definitely a pothead."

"So what if he is?"

"You don't want to be with a pothead. You want to be with someone who has, like, other interests and stuff and doesn't just smoke and get high and buy drugs and sell them. He's not good for you. You need to be with someone good. And I think he's dating Hannah Abrahams."

"He's not anymore, I think."

"Shhhhhh!" Daniella whisper-yells from her bed.

"Sorry!" we whisper back in unison.

"It's impossible to find someone who's all good at our age," I say.

"Yeah, that's why I like Mr. Zuppurdo."

We laugh. Daniella shushes us again. We apologize.

Jensen turns on her back to face the ceiling, and I do the

same. We realize that this position gives us much less room. We laugh again through our noses and try to be quiet about it. She rolls to her side and lets out one last whisper: "This sucks."

When I wake up the next morning, I call my mom from the house phone. I try to be quiet in the kitchen and wrap the cord around the corner to speak. The twins' parents are up at 8:00 a.m. Their mom is doing a load of laundry, and their dad is doing some work on the computer in the office. My mom answers and asks why I'm up so early. I tell her to come get us sooner: we want to go home. She asks if we want McDonald's for breakfast, and I say yes. I wake up Jensen and she's reluctant because she loves to sleep in, but I tell her about the McDonald's and she gets up. We throw our stuff into our backpacks, grab our pillowcases full of candy, and head downstairs without waking Daniella to say goodbye or thank you for having us. We don't bother knocking on Danny's door, either. I realize at some point we'll have to return the pillowcases.

Jensen became exempt from this nightmare, because the pillowcases stayed at my house, not hers. Most people would have forgotten about something so small, but Daniella brought it up a couple of times in our history class. When I gave them back to her a month later, she actually inspected them in front of me. It only made sense that someone so anal would, years later, end up landing a job at the United Nations. Meanwhile, Danny never made it out of Boca Raton. He still sells cars locally, and once, when we were both in our mid-twenties and single, he asked me out on a date. We caught up over chicken fingers and beer, but nothing happened beyond that. He said he was trying to be more positive about his life, trying to find happiness in simple things. I've always kind of felt sorry for him. His sister is such a smart and successful person, and it reminds me of Brad, how I've always felt pressure to live up to his genius.

We slip out of the house unnoticed and wait by the mailbox. Candy wrappers and streamers cover the streets, like a Halloween hurricane came through the neighborhood last night. More foreign objects, like the butts of Swisher Sweets and broken bottles, lie in the driveways and on the sidewalks, too. I imagine Jensen's tampon floating in some stranger's pool, the blood-red cloud surrounding it, the limp string sinking toward the bottom. I feel like Jensen's forgotten it already; it's become another bad thing she did that didn't really matter.

My mom pulls up and takes us to McDonald's, where we order egg and cheese on biscuits with orange juice. Jensen gets an iced coffee, and I think it tastes like the smell of smoke. She loves it, though. We keep looking at each other, because we know we have a big day ahead of us.

My cousin Liza works as a receptionist at our pediatrician's office and gave me a bunch of earring starter kits a while back. They're these little punch machines that shove an earring into the desired spot. It doesn't really hurt, and it's mainly used on babies. I told her I needed more studs, and she just let me have a whole bunch of these kits. Jensen and I both have our first and second holes pierced, one on top of the other, both somehow approved by our parents, but we want more, of course. Jensen wants to do one more hole above her second, and I want to do the very front part of my ear, the little piece of cartilage called the tragus. After much research from Katherine Bennington on the varsity volleyball team, who is a grade above us and has piercings all up and down her ears, this seems like the

best plan. And today feels like the perfect day to put the plan
into motion.

When we get back to my house, we start sorting candy,
making a small pile for my mom. My dad gets back from New
York early this afternoon, so I make a stack for him as well,
but my brother doesn't eat candy so I don't worry about him.
After we eat a sufficient amount of after-breakfast candies, we
sterilize our hands with Dial soap and water. We pull our hair
into tight buns and clip back any pieces that might slip out
during piercing. I go first, to show Jensen how to use the piercing mechanisms. I draw a tiny dot in permanent marker on
the spot where the earring will go, then line up the sharp end
of the earring with that dot, and squeeze the plastic until the
earring and stopper click together. I aim for the center of my
ear and end up going a little too close to the edge, but it still
goes in. It hurts like a bitch. The tragus is thick toward the center, and I have to keep pushing, because it's cartilage. There's
a sense of control, but I'm definitely going to need to ice it
after.

I remove the plastic, and we can see the piercing's a little
off-center, but you can't really tell unless you're up close, so
I'll just have to show people from far away. It's going to take
time to heal anyway, but it's fun to show people right when
you first get it. Jensen begins working on her third hole while I
go grab ice from downstairs. I make sure to cover my ear with
my hair so my mom won't see it if she's in the kitchen. She's
not, so I grab a paper towel and wrap it around a few ice cubes
and run back upstairs. Jensen's already done and admiring her
new piercing.

"It was so easy!" She beams. "I squeezed it just to line up the earring and it went right in."

We're both happy and in a little bit of pain. We watch a movie and take a nap, careful to sleep on the opposite sides of where we just pierced so nothing catches and tears.

Jensen leaves later that afternoon, because I have to go to some party for my brother. He'll be off to college next year, and a family that lives in Margate is having an open house for the University of Miami. Brad's already pretty sure he wants to go there, but my mom wants him to meet some other kids who might end up attending, too. He's applied for a bunch of scholarships, and my parents are convinced he'll get funding because of his good grades—he's got a 5.6 GPA, which isn't even possible, but he got an award for it. They have all the faith in the world in him when it comes to his schoolwork and his genius.

It's Sunday, and I don't have anything better to do, so I don't object to coming along. I like being driven around by my parents anyway. In two years I'll get my license and be free to do whatever I want, but there's something nice about listening to my iPod in the car and staring out the window, watching the Florida scenery drift by. Jensen and I already have plans for the day she gets her license, which is about a month before I'll get mine. She's going to pick me up and take me to the mall, and we're going to listen to *NSYNC on the way. We made the plans back in fourth grade, when *NSYNC was really popular, but we want to stick to it, because it's what our nine-year-old hearts wanted. It's our dream to go to the mall and find a parking spot and go inside all by ourselves, without one of our parents waiting at the entrance of Bloomingdale's, without walking around the mall in fear or embarrassment that we might run into them.

I get overdressed for some reason. I feel like looking nice, even though it's not my event. There'll be older boys there, juniors and seniors, maybe even some college freshmen, so I wear a navy-blue dress from Abercrombie & Fitch and straighten my hair as best I can. I wear small wedge heels that aren't too bad to walk in, but the lady who owns the house insists on no shoes inside, so they come off anyway. My mom drags my brother around to talk to other parents and kids of those parents who are going to the University of Miami. My dad finds a seat on the couch and talks to another father about something I have no interest in. I try to find a phone to call Jensen, but the only one I see is in the kitchen, and it's too out in the open, even if I stretch the cord. Any others must be upstairs, which is off-limits. There's a big sign tacked to the wall telling people not to go up, which makes me want to, badly. Instead, I go to the bathroom and examine my ear. It's not doing so well. When I pierced my second holes, the area was itchy, which meant it was healing. But this time it's pulsating red and hot. I think it might be infected. I decide to take it out, and luckily the hole doesn't bleed. I wrap up the earring in tissues and toss it into the trash can next to the toilet. I take a hand towel and wet it with cold water. My tragus is on fire. I feel stupid for trying to pierce that part of my ear, something that probably needs to be done professionally. I also feel stupid because now Jensen will be the only one with a new piercing tomorrow at school.

I wet my ear and there's a little relief. It needs time to heal.

Back in the living room, I beg my dad to let me use his cell phone, and he agrees. I go out back, to the pool, where some older kids dressed in shirts and ties are eating chips. I feel cool with my dad's cell phone. I dial Jensen, and she knows my dad's number when it comes up on her phone, so she answers.

"I had to take out the earring," I say. "So don't tell anyone we both have piercings tomorrow. Or before tomorrow, if you talk to anyone before then."

"I took mine out, too!"

"Why?"

"I think those kits are defective. Mine was hurting so bad."

"Was it hot?"

"On fire. That means it's infected, right?"

"I think so."

"I showed my brother, and he said you're supposed to leave it in if it's infected, but I already took it out. It feels better already."

"Mine too. I didn't tell my brother, though. He'd probably tell on me." I look around the party for a minute. In a few years, this will be me and Jensen in someone's backyard, getting ready to venture off to another place, somewhere bigger and better than Boca.

"How much candy do you have left?" I ask.

"Too much."

FIVE

*O*ur school is supposed to be beautiful, with its big lake and many breezeways, statues of eagles perched at various elevations, all the buildings painted canary yellow. There are neatly trimmed hedges lining the pathways to air-conditioned classrooms, palm trees that wrap around the perimeter of the campus, a stable full of horses for the equestrian team nestled behind the senior-class parking lot. There's a whole room with semicircular stadium seating dedicated to the student government's meetings, called Town Hall. We have everything we don't need, and we hate telling outsiders that we go to a prep school. I often walk in on girls doing lines in the bathroom or upperclassmen receiving blow jobs in the stairwell of the building where I have history. Everyone smokes weed in the parking lot. Everyone buys and sells pills there, too. Plus our lockers are a rusted red color and clash badly with the navy-blue tiled floor. All our classrooms have popcorn ceilings, just like every other place in Florida.

I'm in all honors classes. I was proud to see the big capitalized *H* next to each course when they mailed us our schedules at the beginning of the year. I love English, and history is okay, but I've always struggled in math. In pre-algebra, I sit behind Eddie Bernstein, who smells like chocolate and knows all the answers all the time. I never understand the material, so he lets me copy his homework. Kenzie isn't in my class, but sometimes she tutors me during free period and I pay her back by checking her English homework for her. I have a hard time listening to Kenzie, though, because we sit at the new café they just put in by the lake, which sells cookies and Rice Krispies squares. It's hard to focus with all those snacks. I'm always so hungry. I eat a ton, but I don't gain any weight. Jensen's grandparents, Yiayia Thea and Pappou Christos, tell me I need to eat more or they'll give me the *pantófla*—some Greek joke about a slipper.

But since the tutoring didn't help, the first week of November I'm told I'm getting switched out of honors pre-algebra and into regular. The dean says they want to see if I fare better in a "slower-paced environment." My mom is concerned about how it'll look on my transcript, and I know she secretly wishes I could be in all high-level classes, like Brad. Last year, my mom even had *him* try to tutor me, but he got so frustrated with my not understanding that we had to stop. So, even though I know it will ruin my GPA, I can't help but feel a little relieved—maybe this way I'll actually be able to understand the math and not have to feel so behind, like everyone else gets it except for me.

After my demotion, Jensen and I go to her grandparents' house for the weekend, like we do sometimes. Pappou Christos picks us up from volleyball practice and brings us cheese pies, phyllo with cheese and butter. We always want to stop at 7-Eleven, even though we've already had a snack, and he takes us. We get Coke-flavored slushies and play floppy doll in the car, which until recently I thought was called "floppy dog." It's when we let our bodies change with the movement of the car, our positions often resembling those of a rag doll. This is fun until we spill our slushies. We don't have the heart to tell her grandpa, so we leave the slush pile in the back seat. I wonder if he'll ever notice.

At Jensen's grandparents' house, I take in the oddly comforting sight of the big pile of shoes by the front door, the rugs on top of the carpet all over the house, the bowls of dried chickpeas and yellow raisins out on the kitchen counter. We go from room to room and admire the antiques and family heirlooms. Jensen claims certain pieces for herself to inherit before her brother can, and she tells me they always argue over the black-and-gold vase in the icon corner. I remember when Jensen told me about the corner in their house that was meant for prayer, how her yiayia Thea kept an oil lamp burning at all times. I'm always jealous that our house doesn't have anything like that, a special sacred area where we can go and talk to our ancestors. Our menorahs and candles sit in the closet, gathering dust.

"It's yours," Yiayia Thea promises Jensen, then says, "Let me fix you a snack," even though we've had so many already. Warm pita, more phyllo and cheese, lamb and potatoes and orzo, baklava with raisins and nuts, and butter cookies with ice cream. The cookies look like little braided challahs. Jensen gets mad when I don't finish all my dessert.

"It's, like, rude to refuse food from an elderly Greek woman," she says.

"I can't eat that much. I'm going to die," I say. My stomach has expanded over my shorts, and I feel sick. I guess Yiayia Thea finally found my limit.

"You're literally breaking her heart."

We go to bed full, and I want to do my homework for math, but Jensen promises it's an easy class. She's in regulars, too, and already failed her first two tests.

Jensen's different at her grandparents' house. First of all, it feels like we're in another world, all the way out in Boynton Beach, in a retirement community where some people can still take care of themselves, like Jensen's grandparents, and other people have live-in assistance. There's a clubhouse in the middle of the development that has a pool and an air hockey table and has sweet tea and lemonade out for grabs at all times of the day. Jensen always pockets a few sugar cubes and sucks on them at random throughout the rest of the weekend. But mostly it's that Jensen was raised by her yiayia Thea and pappou Christos because her mom and dad worked so much. These are like her *real* parents; she doesn't ever want to do anything to upset or offend them, whereas with her *actual* parents she's a total brat. I'm not close with my grandparents at all. I only have one grandparent from each side of the family still alive, but one of them remarried and lives in a retirement community in Deerfield Beach, and the other is still in New York, and I haven't seen her since we moved to Florida. I don't understand how someone could be so close to a grandparent, but Jensen's are funny and quick-witted. Her grandma can even do the splits.

It's hard for me to fall asleep when we stay there, though, and I always regret agreeing to spend the night. That night, I get up and go to the bathroom. There's a night-light that glows aquamarine and the toilet seat has a pink plush cover and a matching pink rug. When I come out, I see her grandparents sitting on the couch in the living room, watching TV. It's well past midnight, and they are watching QVC. I try to stay quiet, but Yiayia Thea hears me.

"Are you hungry?" she asks.

"No, I just had to use the bathroom," I say.

"There's more lamb if you change your mind. I can heat it up for you!"

"Leave her alone!" Christos shouts.

"*Fýge apó edó!*"

They start whisper-yelling at each other in Greek, and I creep back to bed. I can still see a hint of the blue night-light shining into the room. It doesn't seem to bother Jensen, though. She's fast asleep, and I stare into the darkness. I always worry about something bad happening in the middle of the night, or even that I won't ever be able to fall asleep. I do end up sleeping, though, just like I always do, and I wake up when it's morning, still not having done any homework.

The regular class is much slower than the honors. They haven't even gotten to finding slope yet. They're still on defining x and y as variables. The teacher, Mrs. Alonzo, gives out Airheads candy for no good reason and keeps stepping outside to make calls to her husband from the hallway.

Ben Weiner has the desk behind me and says, "Welcome to the jungle," when I sit down on my first day. He has a pointy nose and bright blue eyes and really gelled hair. He's chewing on a blue-raspberry Airhead and his tongue is dark. "Want the red one?" He gestures it toward me, and I accept, but I'll end up giving the candy to Jensen at PE, our only class period together this year.

"All right, everyone," Ben announces to the class when Mrs. Alonzo is once again out of the room. "At exactly ten thirty, we will all drop our pencils directly in front of our desks. Got it?"

No one responds. We continue our horizontal drawings of x-axes and vertical y ones. I let Ben borrow a piece of graphing paper from my binder even though it is a class requirement to have your own supplies, so I worry he will need one every day for the rest of the year. His excitement builds every minute the clock nears the specified time. Mrs. Alonzo returns, in her long denim skirt, big lavender sweater, and white sneakers, and coughs up a ball of phlegm when she sits down at her desk. At 10:28 a.m. we all look at one another and telepathically decide that Ben's plan will work, whatever that means. We will appease him because Airheads aren't enough and we want to learn something, or maybe it's because we want to rebel, or maybe it's just because we can so we will and it will be a story to tell the other kids. The honors kids appreciate the antics of us regulars. We may not be wise, but we sure are funny. We create chaos where we lack genius. Our older brothers and sisters set such high standards, big shoes to fill, and we just can't live up to them.

10:29 a.m. We pick up our pencils.

10:30 a.m. *Drop.*

"*Ben Weiner.* Conditional!" Mrs. Alonzo yells, and Ben stands up, gives a peace sign to the class, and leaves the room. His parents will have to sign a conditional form, a green piece of paper saying that Ben did something stupid, and the next day he will be back in his seat, behind me, telling us to inch our desks forward every minute on the minute for the entirety of our class. *I would never learn algebra correctly, but at the end of the month we had a placement test that I passed with flying colors. I got back into honors pre-algebra, where I would stay this time, because I knew I could do better.*

Ben Weiner was still nice to us, though. He was one of those kids who always gave Jensen and me hugs in the hallway. He was one of those people who understood the suffering of life, how hard things are, and to deal with it he simply made fun of it. I saw pictures of him online years later. He'd joined the Peace Corps and was smiling in a distant land. He looked happy. He looked like he'd ended up where he was supposed to.

The seasons don't change in Florida. When November hits, the skies don't grow gray or cold. People can still go to the beach on the weekends or days off, or when they just plain feel like skipping.

In the "winter months," the student government stands outside the 300 Building and serves hot chocolate for free. It's not that great, but it feels nice to walk around holding something, a sort of conversation piece that makes young adults feel

older. Around this time, we take our PSATs. Standardized testing leaves us with a lot of half days, days off, early dismissals.
There's only one way to get off campus.

You have to get a parent to sign a letter that you must hand
in at the beginning of the day. Then the office calls your parent
to confirm, and you're free to go when their car shows up. If
you drive, same process, but you get a yellow pass you show
the guard at the gate. Sometimes, if you really want to leave
bad, you can type up your own note, print it in a classroom,
forge the signature, call your mom from the bathroom, and
tell her you feel sick, sad, depressed, overwhelmed, want to
spend time with her, and plead to have her confirm the note,
go to the office, tell them you forgot to hand the note in before
first period, then look down at their desk, not up at them, just
down at the eagle-shaped paperweight. Then the office assis-
tant will ask how your family is doing as she dials your mom's
number, even though you don't know her that well and your
mom definitely doesn't know her that well. So you sit in a blue
chair next to the desk and wait to be okayed and confirmed,
and then you go back to class and wait to get called to the
office, where your mom is poised to take your backpack off
your shoulders, but you insist on holding on to it because it's
yours. These few minutes between the office and the car are
some of the only moments when you truly appreciate your
mother. She's been cleaning all day, paying bills, thinking about
you, and now here she is to save the day. She is so warm and
beautiful in jeans and a T-shirt and Asics sneakers. Her purse,
filled with more paperwork and a book to read in case she had
to wait for you, sags at her shoulder. She asks where you want

to go, and you always say the mall. She asks if you're hungry, and you say yes, very.

I get Chinese food from the food court, usually sesame chicken with fried rice, and a Coke. My mom grabs a handful of fortune cookies, which I open and read and throw away unless she wants them. "These would be great with some vanilla ice cream," she always says. We walk around the mall for a while, and I ask to go into Bloomingdale's, try on a pair of Hard Tail pants, show my mom how good they look until she buys them for me. She asks if I need anything new, and I say I don't know, but then we end up in Abercrombie & Fitch and I get some new stuff: a few tank tops and denim shorts, something floral, lacy, girly, a color and not black or gray. My mom says that she likes these clothes better than the overpriced Hard Tail pants. We stop at the candy store and fill up a plastic bag with Swedish Fish and dark-chocolate-covered almonds and a few malted-milk balls for Mom.

When we get home, Jensen calls and asks where I was and I tell her my mom picked me up to leave early and she says I'm lucky. Her grandparents won't bend the rules; they don't believe in early dismissal. She calls me a truant and then asks if I know about Kenzie and how she's dating Charles Bates from the junior class. She also says that Brittany Gottlieb slept over at Leigh's house last weekend, and they all smoked weed with some freshman boys.

I'm still too high off my mall purchases and getting out early to care, so it's not until later that I think about our conversation and start to long for these types of things. I want a boy to like me, to want to date me. Kenzie's got it made if she's dating a junior, because that means he has a car and can take her home from school and go out on the weekends without parents around. I also still can't believe Jensen and I are almost the only ones of our group who haven't smoked yet. Kenzie's tried it, obviously, and now Gottlieb and Leigh. We know Rosenberg hasn't. Her parents are the strictest of all, and she rarely even gets to leave the house. She lives all the way out in Weston, and if we want to see her we have to make the pilgrimage there. She never comes to Boca. And Tomassi is new. For all we know, she tried it at her last school, a public school, and it's old news to her to get high. She seems innocent, though. We make a plan to ask her the next time we're all together.

My main motivation for showing up at school now is Brody. Every day during last period, I ask to go to the bathroom and sneak outside the library to meet Brody at exactly 2:45 p.m. School gets out at three o'clock, so we can talk for four or five minutes before anyone notices; then I still have enough time to slide back into my art class, put away my supplies, and pack my bag.

I barely talk when we see each other. He always gives me a big hug and a kiss on the cheek and tells me I'm pretty. I started getting up at 6:30 a.m. instead of 7:00 so I can do my hair and makeup to last the whole day. I have a mirror from Sephora that Jensen's mom got me last year for Christmas. It came with a gift card. I use it to look at myself before meeting up with Brody each day. One day, he gives me a CD that he made for me. I have to hide it in the waist of my skirt until I get to the art room and can slip it into my backpack. I listen to it when I get home. The first song is "Maps" by the Yeah Yeah Yeahs.

When I was little, I used to watch *Grease 2* and dance around my room when the "Cool Rider" song came on. I pretended I was Stephanie Zinone, with red lipstick and sultry stares at nothing, no one. That's how I feel when I listen to Brody's CD. I feel wanted, and it feels good to pine for someone. Jensen doesn't know how much we've been talking and seeing each other. We instant message late into the night, and he says he really wants to come over one day. He keeps talking about wanting to make me come, and I'm not sure what it means.

I get the courage to ask Katherine Bennington at volleyball practice one day. Junior varsity and varsity practice at the same time, so I'm in luck. Katherine has long blond hair that she pulls up in a ponytail and thin legs with a slim waist; everyone says she looks like Kirsten Dunst. She has abs and eats a lot of Taco Bell. She's a sophomore, and her boyfriend, Anthony Damon, is a junior. He's on the baseball team and hates that she smokes weed. But they have a lot of sex, apparently. I find time to ask her when Jensen's out of practice for a doctor's appointment.

" 'Come' means, like, an orgasm," Katherine says.

"Oh, okay."

"Do you know what that is?" Katherine is setting a ball to herself. She sets it up really high once and then spikes it at another girl on the team. She laughs.

"Not really," I say.

"That's okay. I didn't know *anything* until Anthony. He was my first *everything*. He's the first guy who ever went down on me. That's the most amazing thing ever, by the way."

"What does it feel like when you have an orgasm?"

"Flying."

I look around the gym, girls in blue and white and yellow with their hair in messy buns and high ponytails. I get hungry all of a sudden, and tired, overwhelmed with all the things Brody wants to do to me. Maybe I'm not ready.

"Who do you want to hook up with?" Katherine asks.

"Brody MacIntyre."

"I thought he was dating Hannah Abrahams?"

"He gave me a CD last week."

"That's so cute. Well, whatever he wants to do, you should let him. Everything feels good. Trust me. Just tell him not to use his teeth."

Katherine runs back to the varsity team and I make my way to the locker room. *That was the only time I ever really talked to Katherine Bennington. Even later, when we saw each other at parties, it was sort of understood that she was above me because of her age, her coolness, her way with people. She got along so easily with everyone, in a way I could only dream of. I needed to think about everything all the time, and it drove me crazy, but she seemed like the type of person who "goes with the flow," as my mom says, who could let life happen to them and not make a big deal of it. It's no surprise that she dropped out of college to travel the world and follow her favorite bands. Her profile picture: her in a neon-pink bikini with a flower crown and Hula-Hoop, smiling ear to ear—a free spirit.*

As I take off my socks and change into flip-flops, I feel like I could let Brody do whatever he wants. I want to feel like I'm flying. It sounds nice. It sounds like what should happen.

My parents are taking my brother to a math competition in Jupiter, so I have the house to myself for a night. They trust me on my own, because I'm a good kid. I have an essay on *The Scarlet Letter* due Monday, so they must assume I'll be writing, writing, all day and all night. They leave Saturday morning and are staying in a hotel for the night, so they won't be back until the next day.

I eat a bowl of Apple Jacks and wander around the house. I start in my parents' room, the master bedroom, and take the Thigh Master out of my mom's bottom drawer. I lie on my back and do a few exercises with it until there's a burn. I put it back and move into the den, which is what we call my dad's office, in the very front of our house. I sit down on the brown leather couch in there and put up my feet. I pretend I'm in a therapist's office and talk to myself for a minute.

"Well, yeah, like, I know my family's crazy, but what am I supposed to do about it?" I say to no one.

I go upstairs and into my brother's room, a room that's forbidden without permission. But he's not here, so it's fair game. There's a CD player on his desk, and I open it. The words *Underneath the Fruitless Mulberry* are written in Sharpie on the burned disc, and I shut the lid and put on the headphones. I listen to a few different tracks, most of them wordless, sad songs. But I like them. I look in his desk drawer, and there's a stack of printed papers with the same title as the CD. Brad would kill me if he knew I was in here, so I try to memorize the way the pages were placed inside the drawer before I take them out to read. It's a script about a family, our family. The main character goes to a prep school and falls in love with a girl from his class, but she doesn't know it. Unrequited love.

Listening to the CD as I sit on the floor of Brad's room, reading, I remember something I've forgotten, which is how similar we are. We were always really close growing up, but lately I feel like we're drifting apart. He's become so quiet, staying in his room and playing video games, preparing for his tests and competitions. He got a perfect score on the PSATs, but he has the most terrible handwriting, so bad he almost didn't finish in time because he had to write so slowly to make it legible. My mom says that's just what happens when you're a genius, that social things and common sense fall by the wayside, but he can ace any test and memorize the periodic table.

I wish I was as smart as him. I have to study so hard to get good grades, and to him it comes so naturally. I wonder if he wishes he was better with people rather than textbooks. I think I'd rather be a genius, though, and just make a bunch of money and outsmart everyone. Maybe that's his plan.

I put the papers back where they belong and place the CD player in the same spot where I found it. I look at the LEGOs he's built that are displayed on shelves next to his desk. Pirate Island, Space Land, a castle. Then I leave Brad's room and close the door behind me. I shuffle my feet on the carpet to erase the footprints of where I've been and clear all evidence of my trespassing.

It's time I stop snooping around and actually do something with this rare occurrence of being left home alone.

I call Brody and tell him to come over. He has to take his little brother to a friend's house, and then he'll drive over here to Boca from Coral Springs. I have to call him into the guard gate and give the passcode. It's 2723 and spells out B-R-A-D on the keypad.

I take a long shower and shave my whole body in anticipation that something will happen. I'm not entirely ready, but I need to get myself together anyway. I straighten my hair and do my makeup. I put on a pair of red underwear that are booty shorts but look sexy, the hottest pair I have. I throw on shorts and a tank top over a push-up bra, a lacy red one from Victoria's Secret. The guard gate calls me, and I know Brody will pull up in a few minutes. I go downstairs and wait in my dad's den. I can see outside to the driveway. He pulls up in his white Honda, and I open the front door. He gives me a hug, and I ask if he wants anything to drink. He asks if I have beer. All we have are my dad's Heinekens, which he drinks only on special occasions, but I say no, because I don't want my dad to notice if one's gone missing. Brody settles for a bottle of water, and I grab one, too. My mom has a weird thing about reusable water bottles and refuses to let me have one. She always keeps dozens of cases of Zephyrhills in the garage, even though we have a water filter in our kitchen faucet. All my friends have cute water bottles that they bring to school, with stickers and stuff all over them, but my mom says those carry bacteria and will give me stomach problems or something. Leigh always points out that my bottles are bad for the environment, and I worry Brody might say something, too, but he doesn't. Hopefully he's not thinking it, either, and has other things on his mind, like me.

We go up to my room, and he's brought *Rushmore* for us to watch on my TV. He says it's his favorite movie. I worry that Brody may think my room is too girlish or babyish, especially with the giant tree painting on the wall, so I've already decided I will lie and tell him it's the room I've had since I was a baby. It's true I haven't updated the layout much since sixth grade: my bed is in the corner, a daybed with a white, flowery-patterned railing around it that matches my floral bedsheets and comforter. I have a couch against the wall that faces my TV, which is part of a light-colored wooden entertainment unit. My desk is in the other corner, with my pink swivel chair. Then there's the white bookcase, the picture frame that's a gumball machine on my wall, my closet in the third corner, and my bathroom. The door is in the final corner and opens into the room, which is really annoying because it blocks my corkboard wall of pictures.

The couch pulls out to a bed—this is where Jensen usually sleeps because she hates sleeping in the same bed as another person—and I've set it up with blankets and pillows so we can watch the movie. I keep sipping my water because I'm nervous that my mouth will get dry. Then I get scared I might have to pee, so I stop drinking. A few minutes into the movie, Brody starts making moves. He kisses me, and his lips are big and nice, like candy fish. He runs his hands all over my body and takes off my shorts. He stares at my red panties.

He lays me down and kisses my neck, starts moving my

underwear over with his hand, and sticks a finger into me. It feels good, and he asks me how it feels, so I say good. He keeps going and gets deeper, tries two fingers, and I back away a little, so he goes back to one. For a second it feels like I have to pee really bad, so I stop him.

"What's wrong? Am I hurting you?" He has to catch his breath.

"No, I just feel like I have to pee or something."

"That means you're going to come." He smiles. "Let me keep going."

He continues, and it doesn't feel good anymore. It feels like I'm going to pee, but then it subsides and it just kind of hurts. It feels like pressure. It feels medical. A few minutes go by, and then he stops. He doesn't seem like he expects me to do anything back. The movie's in a different place, and I'm not sure what's going on. He holds me, and I see my shorts on the arm of the couch above us.

I lie and tell him my parents are coming back at 10:00 p.m. so he has to leave. It's just starting to get dark when he drives away. I think I want to lose my virginity to him. I've already gone this far.

I spend the rest of the night making Kraft macaroni and cheese and writing my English essay, like a good kid.

At school the following week, I'm walking to meet Brody at our usual place and time when Joey Fratinelli corners me in the stairwell. He runs his hand up my skirt to my thigh and tells me to kiss him. His eyes are so green.

Joey and Brody are friends. I see them playing Hacky Sack after school sometimes.

"I like Brody," I say, turning my head.

"Brody's dating Hannah. Are you stupid?"

"No" is all I can say.

"You're so stupid. He's in love with her."

Joey runs away and slams the door to the stairwell on his way out. I can barely move, so I decide not to meet Brody at all. I know the only thing to do is to ask Hannah to her face.

The next morning I get to school early and go to the 500 Building, where the sophomores hang out in packs. Hannah has short orange-blond hair and wears a lot of eyeliner. She's drawing something in a notebook when I walk over to her. She probably has no idea who I am, but I need to know. Brody's never early, so I know he won't be around.

"Hi. I know you don't know me, but I have to ask you something."

"Uhh, yeah?" Hannah looks up from her drawing. There are a few girls around her who have the same kind of punk style. They scatter and leave her alone with me.

"Are you dating Brody MacIntyre?"

"Yeah, for like two years. Why?"

I start crying and run back to the 400 Building and into the bathroom. Tomassi happens to be in there, and I ask if I can use her phone. I suppose the sight of me crying is enough, because she hands it over without asking for an explanation. I dial my mom and ask her to come get me, and she asks why. I tell her I left an assignment at home, and she says she'll bring it to me so I don't have to leave. I hang up on her and she calls back right away and says she'll come in an hour. I hand Tomassi back her phone and thank her. She's fixing her braid in the mirror. It's hard feeling like everyone is at peace when my world is a disaster.

I get called out during my second hour, English, which I actually like, but I need to get out of here. My mom's waiting right outside the office, in the hallway.

"What's wrong?" she asks, and I immediately begin crying. "I know you didn't leave anything at home—that's not like you. I think this is about a boy."

I don't respond. I just cry and stand in front of her.

"You can't let whoever this is do this to you. You have to be strong. I'm not taking you home. You have to get through this."

"Mom, please!" I yell in the hallway. I don't care how loud I am or who hears.

My mom crosses her arms and looks around the hallway. She knows she can't win this one. She takes me with her, and I sleep the whole ride home.

"This is the last time I'm doing this," she says when we pull into our garage.

I take my bag upstairs and immediately press EJECT on my CD player. I try to tear the CD in half, but it's too hard. I try cutting it with scissors, and that doesn't work, either. I keep trying to tear it, and eventually I fold it in half and it shatters. Shards of CD are all over the carpet, and I have to pick them out and throw them away before my mom sees. I cut my hand in the process and put a Band-Aid over it. I take a nap and sleep through dinner. When I finally go downstairs, there're only a few soggy raviolis left, and they're cold. I eat them anyway.

Upstairs, Brad is playing *GoldenEye 007*. I stop in his room. The medals he's won from various scholastic competitions hang over the kicking figures of his karate trophies. I love the way the golden plastic legs kick in the air at imaginary enemies.

"Do you know anything about boys?" I ask.

"You're too young for that stuff," he says, without looking away from his game. His character has a sniper rifle aimed at his opponent. He's in "the Facility," my favorite level when my brother lets me play with him.

"I'm fourteen!" I say, defending myself.

"So what's wrong with boys? What did they do?"

"They're just mean," I say, and sit down on the floor with my back against his blue bed.

"Kick 'em in the balls," he offers. I watch my brother kill people and win, and it makes me feel better.

The next day, I wait outside Brody's first period, geometry, in the 500 Building. My heart races when I see him walking toward me in his blue-and-white-striped polo. He's smiling and unaware of what's happened, what's about to happen, of what I know. He tries to hug me and I push him away.

"You broke my heart," I say, and walk away without looking back. I think about how I lost my chance to have sex; how Hannah might never find out the truth about me; how good Brody was at kissing; how maybe it wasn't supposed to hurt, what he was doing to me at my house; how maybe I do deserve better; how my mom would be proud of how strong I am right now; how Jensen doesn't know any of this. *Rosenberg showed me how to block someone on Instant Messenger, so I did that to Brody and felt better after. Joey got expelled for starting a fire in the bathroom with a cigarette and toilet paper. I never told Jensen about the whole Brody fiasco, because nothing really happened, anyway, except that I had to lie about never having been fingered. It was an easy thing to lie about, because I figured it would happen again soon, hopefully.*

SIX

A new kid transfers to our school in the beginning of December. The weather is still nice, but all the kids bring sweaters to school. If you're a senior, you're allowed to wear the sweatshirt of whatever college you're going to on campus. But we lowerclassmen have to wear navy-blue knitted cardigans or our school's hoodies, which are thick and hot and too big for our bodies.

The new kid is Max Green, and he just moved from New York, so there's an instant connection. We meet at an assembly where a guy talks to us about not smoking marijuana. He wears a fedora, and it's hard to take him seriously. Max and I sit next to each other by chance. He's wearing a white polo, and I like his blue-green eyes. He has a nice smile, and we make fun of the assembly the whole time. He says he's never tried weed, but if anything this guy makes him want to do it more. That's the thing about telling kids not to do something: it just gives us more reason to go against the powers that be. We always want what we can't have; even if it's bad for us, even if we don't end up liking it, we want it.

Max is in all regular classes, so it's hard to see him during the day. But he says he wants to get to know me better, and he calls me at night using the school directory. His mom got one for him so he could make new friends. We talk for hours every night on the phone and ask each other questions and wait for the answers. It feels so good to wrap my phone cord around my arms and legs, unwrap it, rewrap, and repeat, until I tell him I have to go to sleep. During these phone calls, I realize I'm boy crazy, a phrase I heard on the show *Bug Juice*, when a curly-haired girl named Stephanie said it once. She always talked about which boys she wanted to hook up with at socials during her confessionals, and when she said "boy crazy," I knew that's what I wanted to be. I love the boys in my school, the way they wear their shorts low, and how they carry their backpacks on one shoulder. I love how they smell of weed and musk, or sometimes their father's cologne, or just sweat. I love their full lips and wet tongues and their mischievous glances and the way they want to touch and feel us girls, our bodies, and find out what it means to be a man, which usually happens for most of them in their friends' bedrooms on weekends or during truth or dare at a birthday party.

I want to kiss Max so bad and be his girlfriend, but my friends don't think he's cool enough. At lunch, we sit at our usual table, just feet away from the snack stand and far enough from the teachers' table that they never hear our conversations. Brittany Gottlieb argues that it might not be good for me to date Max because he's new and doesn't have a lot of friends here yet. He might cling to me, or try to use me to get popular. Brittany Rosenberg says Max is really sweet, and she doesn't get why it'd be bad. She has history with him and says he asked to borrow some paper and was really nice about the whole ordeal. "He looked me in the eyes when he said it," she recounts. Brittany Tomassi, being new herself, tries to stay neutral on the subject, but she does shrug and says he seems nice while sipping her Arizona Iced Tea. Kenzie thinks none of us should date anyone our own age. "You should always date a guy at least two years older than you, because they actually know what they're doing," she says, sucking on a green Blow Pop. Leigh nods in agreement with everyone.

I turn to Brittany Jensen for her opinion, but she's focused on Brittany Rosenberg's double-chocolate Entenmann's donuts. Rosenberg always brings two and usually gives one of us the spare, and I can tell Jensen wants it today. Her parents give her money for lunch, and she already had a slice of pizza, but she loves those donuts. If I'm the one who gets chosen for the donut giveaway, I usually wrap it in a napkin and give it to her.

Rosenberg grabs Kenzie for a tampon change and leaves her food on the table. It's annoying how they always have to announce it, but at least Tomassi doesn't have her period yet, either, so I'm not too upset. I'm still waiting for a reply from Jensen. Suddenly she grabs the donut and eats it. Gottlieb and Leigh laugh hysterically. Tomassi and I look at each other in shock. Jensen puts a finger up to her chocolate-covered lips, signaling us not to say anything upon Rosenberg's return.

"How's it taste?" Tomassi asks, half disgusted and half still laughing.

"So good," Jensen says, crumbs falling all over her white polo shirt. "She never would have given it to me. I had to take it, just this once."

When the girls get back to the table, Rosenberg hesitates and looks us up and down.

"Okay, who ate my donut?" No one responds. "I was going to give it away anyway! What the heck?"

The whole table then stares at Jensen, who's still chewing the last bits of the donut.

"I ate it!" she exclaims. "And I'm not even sorry!"

"You're a bitch, Jensen!" Rosenberg yells, and walks away from the table. I think she wanted whoever ate the donut to be anyone else besides Jensen. They've never liked each other, not since Rosenberg came to our school last year. Jensen thinks Rosenberg's parents are weird, and they are, and Rosenberg thinks Jensen is mean. They only tolerate each other in groups, like when Rosenberg's parents took us to Universal Studios in Orlando last year over Christmas break, or when we all attend birthday parties for one another. You'd never find them at a mall together, though, or a one-on-one sleepover.

Jensen doesn't react to Rosenberg, and I'm still waiting for my advice.

"What do you think about Max?" I ask her as she takes Rosenberg's napkin and blots her mouth clean.

"I just don't understand why you have to make everything about a guy," she says. There's a smudge of chocolate on one of her front teeth.

It hits hard when she says it. I don't think being boy crazy is a bad thing. It's what we all talk about all the time. Our purpose for getting dolled up and coming to school each day is that a boy might like us, kiss us, talk to us, ask us to go on a date to the movies or to walk around the mall or to go to the park in his neighborhood and lie in bed with him until he tells you you're beautiful. Jensen rarely talks about guys, but I just think she's shy, not as open about it as the rest of us. I know she's kissed guys at parties and this one kid, Vince, at camp, who she always talks about because he's British and she has a thing for English guys, but otherwise she keeps quiet.

"I don't make everything about guys," I say. The bell rings, and kids start to leave the lunchroom. I have PE with Jensen next, so we continue walking together out the side door, down the way to the gym.

"I just don't want you getting obsessed with him, like you always do."

"That's not true. I'm not obsessed. It's not, like, affecting my life! I'm in all honors and I still get all As and I have friends and I do stuff all the time."

"Good for you." Jensen opens the door to the gym and lets it close behind her. She walks into the locker room, and I follow.

I watch her change into her PE shirt and shorts. We're both wearing the same push-up bra from Victoria's Secret that we got together at the mall last weekend. Hers is mint green, mine pale pink. A part of me wants to tell her that Rosenberg is right, that she is a bitch, a donut-stealing bitch. I'm afraid of what'll happen if she's mad at me. I see the way she yells at her parents. I see the way she doesn't care when they yell back. But I'm pissed this time. Before I can even say anything, Jensen starts in.

"I don't even get why you're so worried about guys, especially Max Green. Guys like you. You know that. You're just fishing for compliments."

"Fishing for compliments?"

"Yeah, you do it with my parents all the time, too, telling them what grades you got and awards and whatever."

"They ask me!" I say, which is true. Jensen's parents are always asking me about school and how I'm doing. But they do push it and make things uncomfortable, because their own daughter gets Cs and Ds while I get all As. "Why can't you be more like *her*?" they'll ask, and honestly expect an answer. But doing well in school is nothing to feel bad about. Aren't we supposed to want to do well, so that we can have a high GPA and get into a good college? Last year I told Jensen I couldn't come over because something I made in art class got put in a local art show and my mom was taking me to see the exhibit. "You're so annoying," she had said then, and that's when it started to get on my nerves, this hatred for my doing well, being good, excelling, while she pretty much stayed the same.

"You don't have to indulge them, though. Just say, 'Good, good, great, whatever,' and move on. It's just . . . conceited."

"I'm the *last* person who's conceited! I cried, like, three times doing my makeup this morning."

"You just care too much about that stuff." Jensen's already dressed and moves to the bench to put on her sneakers.

"Why is it bad to care?" I ask.

"It's not. But it's bad to care too much what everyone else thinks."

"I'm sorry your parents like me."

"Don't be a bitch," Jensen says.

Sometimes I feel like Jensen doesn't care enough about what other people think: the way she eats whatever she wants and never thinks to choose a healthier option, the way she laughs during assemblies or important announcements on the intercom, the way she lets her bra straps show or wears colorful bras under her white shirts, the way she bites her nails down to the cuticles, the way she burps and farts and thinks it's funny. And then I think I love her for those things, the way she is just herself, her true self, always.

Just then our coach comes into the locker room. I realize that we're probably late for PE and start to worry.

"What's taking so long, girls?" She folds her arms over her chest.

"Sorry," I say, knowing Jensen won't even attempt to respond to her. "We were just talking about something important."

"As if I give a tiny rat's ass!" Coach says. "Get out there now or I'll give you both conditionals!" She storms out, the big blue doors of the locker room swinging behind her.

It's silent for a moment when she leaves. I'm genuinely nervous about getting a conditional, even though it's just a piece of paper that your parents have to sign, so I start changing out of my uniform fast. I look over at Jensen, who is laughing, silently. I stare at her, as if to say, *What is it? What's your problem? Let's go!*

"*A tiny rat's ass!*" Jensen repeats. We both break out in a fit of laughter, harder than I've laughed in a long time. Jensen bends over the sink, laughing so hard she starts to cry. I slide down the row of lockers to the floor and try to catch my breath. The rest of the week is spent recapping the story to the girls, to my mom, to anyone who will listen—except we leave out the part about the argument, of course.

SEVEN

*M*y mom takes me to Party City before school the day of Brittany Tomassi's birthday. It's a week before Jensen's, which is annoying, because that means I'll be back here in a week, doing the same thing. When it's someone's birthday, you have to bring them a balloon. If it's your best friend you bring a few, sometimes a tiara or a sash, maybe even cookies or cake at lunch as well. I like Brittany Tomassi. She's from New York, like me. She's stylish, she's sweet and caring, pretty, and her mom and sister are cool. Her sister is older, a junior at our school, and always wears her hair in beach waves. Her mom looks like Kate Hudson and loves to take us shopping. The thing about the balloons, though, is that you're supposed to get something stupid, not just a plain HAPPY BIRTHDAY balloon. The more random the balloon, the better. The more ridiculous, the greater the reaction from the birthday girl.

My mom waits in the car while I peruse the selection on the wall. Among the Ninja Turtles and Hello Kitty balloons, I find one that's got the stork from *Dumbo* and reads IT'S A BOY! It's not that funny, but it's weird, and I think it works. I ask the cashier lady to blow it up for me, and she ties a blue ribbon to secure the helium inside. My mom rolls her eyes when she reads the balloon.

"I don't understand you girls," she says, and continues the drive to school.

I get out of the car, and the blue balloon pops out behind me. I'm excited to see Tomassi and what she's chosen to wear on her free dress-down day—you're allowed to wear whatever you want when it's your birthday.

I walk by the 500 Building and see Hannah Abrahams staring at me from afar. I keep walking with my head down, and she approaches me with two other girls. They're punk also; one of them has no eyebrows and the other has on headphones, with her hair covering them. I stop walking and hold my balloon like an idiot.

"Are you wearing your red underwear today?" Hannah asks. I'm so embarrassed I could die.

"No," I say, trying to be strong.

"You're a little slut," Hannah says. Her friends laugh, and they all walk away in the other direction. I keep going, but I can feel a lump in my throat. I know Hannah is just jealous. That's what my mom would say if she even knew about any of this, which she doesn't, but it hurts to have an older girl think badly of me. I just want everyone to like me all the time, and I guess it's not possible, especially in high school.

I see Tomassi outside the 300 Building. She's wearing tight boot-cut jeans and a floral long-sleeve top. Her hair is perfectly straight, and she's wearing a little bit of mascara. She looks amazing. She's already got a small bouquet of balloons, and I walk over to give her mine. She laughs when she sees it and gives me a hug. I say, "Happy birthday," and step back to read the rest of her balloons. Someone actually got her an IT'S A GIRL! balloon, and I don't feel so special anymore. The rest are pretty normal; there's one telling her she's OVER THE HILL. That one is probably the best and will be her favorite.

After school, Jensen and I have a volleyball game, and then we're going to sleep over at Tomassi's house and get breakfast with a bunch of girls in the morning, a sort of brunch birthday gathering. I hate games, because I never get to play much. I know I'm not good at sports. I'm only doing it so I can put it on my record for college. My mom agreed that I should do some more extracurricular activities, so I joined the junior varsity team, where everyone who tried out got a spot.

I usually get subbed in for one rotation, sometimes half a rotation, and I mostly try to stay out of the way while I'm there. After I get tagged in, I pull up my kneepads and tighten my ponytail, even though I know nothing is going to happen. A tall girl on the other team spikes the ball downcourt to my section, and I don't make it in time to bump it back to our setter. I fall on my knees and realize I didn't pull up my left kneepad all the way and now I have a court burn right on the spot. I go back to the bench when another girl tags me out. Jensen is still in—has been the whole time.

Sitting on the bench, I realize this is her place to shine, on the court. She's just naturally good at sports, anything athletic. I quit gymnastics because of her. I was the best in my level until she started coming and was able to do everything I was able to. She did it with ease, whereas I was calculated.

I pull down my kneepads and press my bottle of yellow Gatorade against the burn. It hurts, and I have to wait until the game is over to ask for a Band-Aid. I think about quitting the team; I hate it anyway. I hate how running in practice makes my lungs hurt, how I can't eat any real food until I get home, can't start my homework until much later. Why am I here if I'm not good? There's no point. I know I'm good at school: that's my place, not here. I'd get up and walk away if I didn't have to wait for the game to end, since Jensen and I are leaving together. Tomassi will be getting out of soccer practice around the same time, and her mom is taking us all back. I watch Jensen jump to spike an incoming ball. She gets enough height to hit it over the net, something I can only do once every so often in practice, definitely never in a game, and it lands on the floor on the other side. The point ticker goes up one for our side, and everyone cheers. I sip my Gatorade and give a halfhearted clap from the bench.

Tomassi has the most pairs of jeans of anyone I know. She has about sixteen pairs. Jensen and I sift through her drawer, unfolding the soft legs of each one, some embroidered, some with lace, some with intentional rips that cost extra. We are allowed to choose one to wear at her birthday brunch this morning, and we love each of them. Jensen has a bigger butt than I do, and my legs are much slimmer, but somehow we

both fit into the jeans that Tomassi wears, the ones she has to
ration now for dress-down days. It took her a while to understand the benefits of having a uniform—how it makes the
mornings easier, how it causes less competition among us. She
still wears a big, puffy scrunchie on her forearm in protest, still
dons elaborate headbands, still pays a dollar for every dress-
down day so she can show off her New York wardrobe.

The dynamic of three girls, especially three Brittanys, is
always interesting. And by "interesting" I mean bad. It doesn't
go well for one girl. This time, that girl happens to be me.
Tomassi and Jensen stayed up much later than I did and had
some kind of revelation that they both love sports, both don't
like Rosenberg, both don't really care about boys. Those were
the vague conversations I heard as I turned onto my side and
pretended to be asleep. I drifted off as Tomassi tried to convince Jensen to join the soccer team. Jensen said something
about how the varsity volleyball coach wanted to speak with
her about practicing with them, moving up from junior varsity
to varsity, something I was unaware of. I'm scared she'll actually get the spot, but also relieved; in that case I won't have to
watch her anymore, silently compete against her and lose every
time. She'd be the only ninth grader on the team. Maybe it'd
be harder for her, or maybe she'd still shine.

Jensen picks a blue-green pair that I actually think are the
ugliest ones, but they're the tightest on her ass. Even though
no boys are coming to the brunch, we still want to look good.
I pick a pair of destroyed ones with an embroidered butterfly
on the left hip. It's a bit childish, but they fit great and go well

with the tight black tank top I'm going to wear. I pull up the jeans, and one of the strings of fringe catches on the burn on my knee. It stings like crazy.

"Crap!" I yell. Tomassi and Jensen turn around, both of them at the mirror scrunching their hair. Scrunching involves taking a shower, letting your hair dry a little bit, then taking hair gel and scrunching it up into curls until the hair becomes curly and doesn't move. You can't get a brush through it. This doesn't look good on me because I have too much hair—I've tried it. Tomassi has a lot of hair, too, but somehow she makes it work. My hair is already straightened, and I decide to keep it that way for the birthday brunch. I might opt for a headband, depending on if I can borrow one from Tomassi's collection.

"What's wrong?" Tomassi asks, curling her eyelashes with a purple curler.

"I got a court burn yesterday during the game. The jeans scraped right over it."

"You barely even played." Jensen laughs, her head tilted to the side over the sink, covering every strand of her hair in gel that smells like berries.

"Do you really think Max Green would just use me to get popular?" I ask, to change the subject.

"Are we popular now?" Jensen asks.

"Well, we're not losers," I say.

"Your group definitely needs some shifting," Tomassi adds, moving on to painting her lips a deep mauve color. The tube smells like vanilla bean. "You two are the best, obviously, and Kenzie is cool, Gottlieb is okay, but Rosenberg and Leigh are just lost causes."

"I don't even know how this whole group got started," Jensen says.

"Well, it was always the two of us," I say. "The Brittanys, since fourth grade. But then it just kept growing, and I think it really solidified at fifth-grade graduation, when we all cried on the dock . . ."

"And in sixth grade, when we all had lunch together . . ." Jensen continues. "But I think Leigh is turning into a pothead and Kenzie is turning into a slut. Rosenberg is pretty boy crazy, too."

It stings almost as much as the stupid court burn to hear her say this again, although at least this time she's not talking about me.

"Tomassi, is there anyone you like in our grade?" I ask, fishing.

"Hmm, I don't really think so. There was a boy in New York I liked a lot, but we only kissed a few times."

"As a dare?" I ask.

"Ha! No, like, a real kiss."

"Have you ever done more?" I press, and Jensen looks back at me like I'm asking too much. I shrug, and we both wait for her response.

"The most I've done is kiss, and guys like to grab my butt." Tomassi turns around and shakes her butt at us, smiles, goes back to doing her makeup. We laugh.

"Have you ever smoked weed?" I press on.

"No, that stuff is dangerous. I agree, Leigh is becoming a pothead. So gross. You know, guys don't like it when girls do that stuff, either. It's not . . . clean. And as for Max, I think he's okay. A boyfriend should be someone who treats you right, no matter their status."

I sit in the front when Tomassi's mom drives us to brunch. Tomassi and Jensen sit in the back, whispering, laughing, complimenting each other's asses in their jeans. *I kept my borrowed pair for a long time, and when I finally tried to return them to her a few months later, Tomassi said I could just keep them. They were too "babyish" for her, is what she said. I wore them to at least three dress-down days.*

All the girls come to brunch except Leigh, along with a bunch of Tomassi's cousins and some neighborhood friends. Her older sister arrives late with one of her own friends. They are both wearing high-low dresses with heels. They look beautiful, their makeup light and perfect, and their hair in those beachy waves. I want to be them. I want to wear the right thing all the time and get guys and have a best friend who doesn't think I'm too boy crazy.

I keep going to the bathroom to pull down my jeans and look at the burn on my knee. It hurts to sit for too long with the denim pressing against it. I should have worn a dress or a skirt. Everyone orders salads for some reason, and I do, too, even though I want pasta. Everyone drinks iced tea, but I have a Coke. I don't understand why everyone is trying to be such a lady. Tomassi's mom keeps asking if I am okay. At one point I almost cry in front of her and excuse myself to the bathroom again. I don't want to be there; I'm not in the mood to have a good time.

When my mom comes and gets me, Jensen decides to stay, instead of our original plan to leave together. She and Tomassi end up having another sleepover, and Jensen is convinced to join the soccer team. They happen to have practice on the off days of the varsity volleyball team, which she is *also* asked to join.

I quit volleyball because I hate it. I know I could try harder to improve and play more, but I don't want to. The truth is, I want to go home from school every day and call Max from my room. I like to bring the receiver over to my desk by the window, sit on the roof, and talk to him while I look out at the lake. Sometimes I miss calls from Jensen because Max and I talk for so long. Sometimes we talk all night.

EIGHT

*A*t Jensen's birthday party, Kenzie goes missing, vanishing in her low-cut orange top and bedazzled jeans. I'm in a green bustier top and my favorite Brazilian jeans, black with lace-up ankles. I just got my hair dyed professionally for the first time, and I'm not sure if it's the right color. My mom finally let me do it, because I told her I wanted to look more like her. I've always admired her blond locks—that, and Sophie Pollack in science lab said my brown hair looked mousy, like I needed highlights. It's kind of brassy blond now, but I like that it's different because it stands out.

No boys I like are here, so I tune in to the drama between Brittany Jensen and Kenzie. Apparently, the last anyone saw Kenzie, she was with Jensen's brother, Matty. Jensen is furious and wants to send out a search party to find her. My parents are here, eating crab cakes while everyone else shimmies and twists on the dance floor. They'll wonder where I am, but it's my job to accompany Jensen on her mission. She's in a tight cream-colored dress that makes her butt look big, but that's in now, it's a look, and we told each other we look great when we arrived at the venue in separate cars. She also just got her nose pierced and is wearing a diamond stud in her nostril. Matty took her to the piercing parlor where his friend works and let her get it done as an early birthday present without telling their parents. Jensen says her mom likes it, though, that it makes her nose look cuter and less big, so she's allowed to keep it as long as she wears a clear stud for school. I imagine how grateful she must have been to Matty for the gift, and how all that grace is now absolutely out the window.

Jensen storms from the party room and down to the outside deck of the Hillsboro Beach Club. The club is a collection of white bungalows where people can rent rooms for the weekend, for a month, for a summer. Inside is all beach-themed: wicker chairs and paintings of birds, glass vases filled with shells. It's an eyesore. But the pièce de résistance is the lighthouse at the end of the inlet. It has a white base and a black top, and its light flashes a bright beam that can be seen by boats from very, very far away, according to Jensen's dad.

Jensen's parents are members here, and we sometimes come together on the weekends during warmer months. Tomassi came with us last weekend, and we took pictures on a disposable camera of us in the ocean. We all wore tankinis and screamed our heads off each time a wave crashed over us. After that, Jensen told me she thought Tomassi was getting annoying, that she was sick of her and needed a break. "It's okay if she comes to my birthday, 'cause it's a group, but I can't deal anymore. At soccer she always wants to do drills together, and I can't *always* be with her." I nod and agree.

It's December, but it's warm, still humid enough to make

Jensen's tight curls unravel into loose waves. The light of the lighthouse spins, illuminating her face every twenty seconds.

"Let's look on the beach," she suggests. "They're probably having sex."

We find Kenzie and Matty on the beach, passing a bottle of Captain Morgan between them. I've seen smaller versions of that bottle underneath Matty's bed when we've played video games in his room late at night. Jensen once showed me what a condom looked like: Matty had one under his stained black pillow.

Kenzie looks a little drunk, and Matty is smoking a cigarette.

"Ew!" Jensen screams in a whisper.

"Don't be a bitch, Britt," Matty replies. Kenzie grabs his biceps, and he pretends not to care. The whole thing is unfolding. It's obvious that they hooked up, or were about to, and we're spoiling it. I am happy it isn't happening. I want it to be me standing on the beach with an older guy. Not Matty, but someone who knows what they're doing, because I don't.

Kenzie and Jensen have been walking to English together every day, sharing a Diet Coke and a pack of Oreos. I'm always jealous of this, but, then again, I like walking alone and not sharing my snack. Sometimes I see my brother walking to his senior seminar and drinking a Sprite. He doesn't look at me, but I know he sees me and watches me as I walk to my language arts class. Brad couldn't be more different from Matty. One time when Matty dropped off Jensen at our house, they sort of sized each other up. They're both shorter than most of the other upperclassmen, but Matty is wild and Brad is calm. Matty acts out and Brad holds it all in. *I wouldn't know which was worse until later.* It kind of reminds me of the way Jensen is able to say what she feels and I'm not. I'm always holding in my feelings. It's especially hard at school, when everyone walks with such purpose and I'm left to wonder why I'm even there.

It was on one of their walks that Kenzie taught Jensen how to give a hand job. Jensen reported back to me that you're supposed to rest your hand on a guy's thigh for a while to see if anything's happening and then spit on your own hand before you go inside the pants. I wondered why Jensen even cared to know how to give a hand job, but I was grateful she told me the details anyway. I'll take what I can get.

"Want some?" Matty extends the bottle toward Jensen, and she scoffs, then grabs it and takes a big gulp.

"Are you finally gonna get a car this year so I don't have to drive your ass around?" Matty says.

"I'm fifteen, you idiot!" Jensen screams back. "And you never take me anywhere anyway."

"But Kenzie's sixteen," Matty says as he looks at Kenzie, who is almost falling over.

"No she's not! We're all fifteen now, except her." Jensen points to me.

"Whatever," Matty says. "Whatever you say, birthday bitch."

But I've stopped paying attention. I'm imagining being out here alone with someone else, getting undressed, feeling the salty breeze on my whole body, letting a person do things to me, and enjoying them. I can hear Jensen's dad running toward us, sand squishing under his boat shoes. I'm happy that he's coming to break up the drama. Sometimes it feels like no one is watching us, the way we find ourselves in spots to make our own decisions. But it also feels like we're too young to do so, even though it's all we want, to be able to cut our own bangs, kiss boys in public, pierce our own ears. Her dad looks more concerned than angry as he approaches us. I think about how he always got Jensen's Subway order wrong, how I'd end up sharing my half and eating some of hers, which had too much mustard or too many onions. I can tell he just wants to see that we're all okay. He wants us to come back to the party he probably paid so much for, but we run anyway, because that's what kids do.

We split up and race back to the party room. Matty takes Kenzie through the parking lot and into the main entrance. Jensen sticks with me, and we run through the halls of the hotel. We jump over empty room-service trays and discarded beach towels. We stop at room 113 and press our ears against the door. When we were younger, a kid told us this room was called "Bloody Cheerios" because a baby was murdered inside while eating cereal. We believed him when he said the carpet still had blood on it, stained forever and ever. We once chased boys down these same hallways and went into the kids' club to watch music videos on MTV. We walked out farther than we were allowed, climbing on the rocks and watching the lighthouse light spin and making up stories about buying a house here and sharing it, living here together, having kids who would be friends, best friends, like us.

We make it back to the party room, and my parents are up and dancing, and so we join them. Jensen's dad walks in, and her mom points at us. They join us, and we all dance to "Celebration" by Kool & the Gang, a song everyone knows, even the kids. They must figure that their girls are still girls, and we figure, since it's Jensen's birthday, they'll let us off the hook. When the chorus comes on, we all sing and hold hands, twirling each other, dads and daughters, mothers and best friends. Our hair is a mess. My spaghetti straps won't stay up, and I let them fall down my shoulders as I move.

Jensen invited Tarek Mendel, who goes to her sleepaway camp. Lately she can't stop talking about how they'll both be CITs, counselors in training, together this summer. She's shown me pictures of him: curly red hair, messy, dirty, and kind of chubby, but cute. I don't understand her type. She seems to be attracted to older men, British guys, or lovers of the great outdoors. Tarek never shows up, though, and I wonder if Jensen is upset. It's the first time in a while she's brought up any guy, and even though she swears they're just friends, I know she has a crush on him. I know she wanted him to come but would never admit that someone could hurt her. She doesn't seem hurt, the way she dances and holds hands with her dad, and I wonder if maybe it's just the shot of rum she had that's making her forget she's a girl who has feelings, a girl who wanted a boy to come to her fifteenth-birthday party. *Matty was kicked out of the house a year later, after he was caught with stuff worse than rum. He moved in with one of his friends. Our junior year, he picked us up late from a party, and there was a girl with him, in the passenger seat, crying. "Don't cry, dry your eye," he said to her, and it became an instant inside joke. I always wanted to go into his old room and look at all the stuff he left behind: go through his drawers and look at his movies and see if maybe he left any weed. Jensen never wanted to, though. She didn't talk about him much after he left, but she* developed a sacred respect for him. It was like she understood that what he'd done was wrong, but he was still her brother and she wished he was still around.

Matty eventually got his boating license, and now he takes tourists out snorkeling in Key West. He married a Vietnamese woman, and they have a daughter whose name means "star." Jensen is holding the baby in photos. She's an aunt, and I'm happy that she and Matty have reconnected.

It's funny to see Matty as a dad after all these years. I remember him at Jensen's house when we were in middle school, jumping off the roof into her pool, singing some rap song with bad words at the top of his lungs. When it got dark, he held glow sticks in between his fingers and showed us how to rave. He would dance all night, even after we fell asleep.

NINE

*N*ew Year's Eve is a week before my birthday. I'm the last one to turn fifteen, and I can't wait. I still don't have my period. Waiting by the bathroom door while all the girls change their tampons is just part of my daily routine at school. I start to wonder if I'll ever get the damn thing. Jensen taught me how to use a tampon during PE one time. She said it'd be good to practice, so I'd know how to do it when the time came. She told me how to angle the cotton tube back and up inside of me, farther than any boy has gone besides Brody. I said I felt nothing once it was in and secure, and she said that was good. She said sometimes it feels wrong, like a sharp pinch, and then you have to take it out and start over or deal with the pain for a few hours.

Jensen and I always spend New Year's together, usually with a trip to Orlando or a sleepover at one of our houses, hopefully hers. But I manage to get sick over Christmas break. We spend Christmas Eve at her house; her parents cooked seafood pasta with three different kinds of fish and wrapped presents all day and the night before. Jensen's mastered the art of wrapping, and I help her rip and stick tape on her packages as she works. In the morning I help her unwrap her gifts: a set of nail polishes in an assortment of Christmas colors, a new straightening iron, a gift card to Sephora, and a Coach purse just like Rosenberg's but white. Kenzie has it, too, in black. While Jensen is opening her gifts, her dad pulls out another wrapped present from under the tree and hands it to me. To my surprise, it's another Coach purse. Red, my favorite. The best part is that it matches Jensen's. I'm nervous she'll be mad at her parents for getting me such a nice gift, but she's excited, and we both scream, hold the bags on our shoulders against our bodies, and pose like fashion ads.

We went to church the night before, where, even though I'm Jewish, I accepted Communion at the altar because I was hungry. It was Midnight Mass, and I was so bored. I didn't understand anything the guy was saying, and Jensen looked just as unenthused. I wore a long-sleeve T-shirt and a long skirt, to look appropriate. After the service, in the parking lot, Jensen's dad congratulated me on becoming a Christian. I stood there, stunned, until he slapped me on the shoulder and told me he was joking. When we got home, Jensen asked her mom to read us the Christmas story she read every year before bed, but she said we were too old. Jensen thought she was joking, but she never came into Jensen's room to read to us. We fell asleep waiting for our story that never showed up.

I start feeling sick the next morning as we're finishing with the presents, and I realize no doctors' offices are going to be open because of the holiday. My mom picks me up and says she'll look in my throat when we get home. I fall asleep on the drive and wake up at the stoplight before the turn into our neighborhood. Mom follows me upstairs with a flashlight and says she sees white on my tonsils. I tell her I just want to sleep, my body hurts, and I'm out from 11:00 a.m. until the late afternoon. My parents order Chinese food, and I don't want any, but Mom forces me to eat wonton soup. I fall asleep again shortly after, on the couch, while watching *A Christmas Story*. I hear my mom tell my brother to pick me up and carry me upstairs to my room, but he says I am too big.

The next morning, we go to the doctor's office where my cousin Liza works. I'm in and out of sleep on the drive, and when I'm not sleeping I'm complaining. I'm so tired, and my throat hurts. There are two sections in the office: SICK and WELL. I've never had to come here and sit in the SICK section before. My mom was a nurse and thinks she can handle most of our ailments at home. I usually just eat a Get Better Bear and call it a day. But my mom says if I need antibiotics we have to go to the doctor for that.

"Maybe it's mono," Liza says. She's in scrubs with Winnie the Pooh chasing after a balloon on them. Her hair is in a braid, and her ears are pierced all the way up and down. I want that so bad, but it'll never happen. I couldn't even handle my tragus.

"What's mono?" I ask.

"Don't use your voice!" my mom yells.

"Mononucleosis, sweetie. It's the *kissing* disease."

Kissing disease? I assume it means you've kissed too many people, which isn't really the case for me, but maybe I got it from Brody.

"Is that a real thing?" I ask.

"Stop talking!" my mom yells again.

"It's not really from kissing." Liza laughs. "But it's common among teenagers, because you guys are swapping spit all the time. It's not a big deal if that's what it is. Dr. Price will just do a blood test and find out. It's like a virus—it goes away on its own. But you'll be out of commission for a few weeks."

"Blood test?" I hate blood tests. I hate the idea that blood is leaving my body. It makes me feel weak and dizzy just thinking about it.

I get called into a room and wait for Dr. Price. He's not my usual doctor, who's currently on vacation on some island, but he's the only doctor here at the office over the holidays. He's tall and tan and wears glasses and has a weird mustache. My mom sits in a chair while I'm up on the table. She takes off one of her flip-flops and scratches her leg with one toe. I'm so nervous I could die.

"Liza thinks you have mono, but we need to test before we can call it that," Dr. Price says, holding my file and perusing it.

"How do you test for it?" I ask.

"It depends on how many boys you've kissed," Dr. Price says, not smiling.

"I don't. I haven't." I stick up for myself. I don't want Dr. Price to think I'm some kind of ninth-grade slut. "I used to get strep a lot as a kid, and I think that's what this is. Can't you just test for that?"

"You have all the symptoms of mononucleosis. Your glands are swollen, you're running a high fever, you're fatigued. I'm ordering a blood test."

"I'm not fatigued. I'm just tired. I was up past midnight on Christmas. I went to Midnight Mass."

"Are you *nervous*?"

"Nervous? No. I just don't think I have mono."

Dr. Price leans out the doorway and calls for a nurse.

"We have a reluctant mono test in room four," he shouts. I begin to cry. My tears are hot on my face, and I try to wipe them off quickly, but they keep coming. I don't want a blood test. I'm not a slut. This is Brody's fault. Well, it's my fault. I can't have mono. It's not right.

"It's just a blood test," my mom offers from her chair. "I've had much worse."

"Like what?"

"I once had a root canal with no anesthesia. Oh, and my migraine headaches, those are worse than any pain on Earth." Mom always offers these tales of woe, and I wonder if she's actually trying to comfort me or just make me feel bad for being such a baby when it comes to modern medicine.

"I don't like blood tests," I say, still crying.

"It takes two seconds," my mom says. Dr. Price enters the room again, and Liza is with him.

"Don't cry, sweetie," Liza says, and begins cleaning my arm with alcohol solution so she can take blood.

"There's really no need to cry. It's just a simple test," Dr. Price offers, and I won't look at him.

Liza pricks me with the needle, and I watch the dark purple blood drain from my arm into a glass tube. I feel myself get weak, but I know I have to be an adult about this or else Dr.

Price will only have more ammunition against me. He leaves the room again, and I'm alone with my mom and Liza.

"Dr. Price called me a whore," I say to the room.

"No, he did not!" my mom says. Liza laughs.

"He implied it. He was trying to say I kiss everyone, and I don't."

"He's much better with little kids," Liza offers. "He might not know how to handle teenagers. You'll be too old to come here soon anyway."

Liza leaves to get the test results. I slide off the table and sit on my mom's lap; she doesn't expect me there and is surprised by my weight on her. She laughs a little at first, and then pets my hair and gives me a kiss on the head.

"You're my baby," she says.

"I'm not a baby anymore," I say.

"Then stop crying."

"He shouldn't have said those things. Just because I'm tired . . ."

"He's an idiot, okay? He doesn't have bedside manners with girls your age, you heard Liza."

Liza walks back into the room, and apparently I don't have mono. I'm too upset to gloat, and she has to swab my throat to test for strep, which I *do* end up having. She gives me a shot in my lower back. She grabs as hard as she can so I don't feel the needle. I feel it, though, and it hurts, worse than the blood test. I get a prescription for a bottle of pink liquid antibiotics that I have to drink two teaspoons of twice a day for a week. I don't get pills because I can't swallow pills yet, an adult skill my brother and I both lack.

We stop at the supermarket on the way home to pick up my prescription and some snacks that I'll be able to eat for the next few days. I get Jell-O and Cool Whip, chocolate pudding, and Campbell's Chicken & Stars soup. But I don't really end up eating any of it. I mostly sleep and watch *SpongeBob SquarePants* on Nickelodeon, floating in and out of consciousness. I dream of being underwater, hot water that burns when I try to breathe in, and of Krabby Patties that taste like pink gummies.

I know I'll have to call Jensen and tell her I can't come over for New Year's Eve, but for now I live in my room in layers of clothing, trying to sweat out the sickness, starve the infection, and sleep away the tiredness.

There is a hiatus from phone calls with Max Green. I haven't heard from him all break, and I've been too sick to notice, too self-involved to care. But now that I'm feeling better, I wonder where he went. I call him on New Year's Eve. I'm still considered contagious and can't go out, but nothing can be caught over the phone, except feelings, I suppose.

His mom answers, and it sounds like they're having a party. When I ask if I can speak with her son, she tells me to hold on and I wait. A few minutes later she comes back on the line and says he's not able to talk, but he says Happy New Year. It sounds like a lot of crap, and she wishes me well, and we hang up. *Your son is an asshole,* I want to say. What's he so busy doing that he can't talk to me? Wouldn't he care that I almost died of strep throat? I was so sick and he didn't even know. I imagine him drinking with his dad outside, by his pool, in

West Palm Beach. Kids from the neighborhood he doesn't usually hang out with, girls in silver sequined dresses and boys in shirts and ties, all crowded around the pool and drinking alcohol, but it's okay because they're with family, because it's New Year's Eve. I imagine his mother looking out at the scene, how she doesn't want to take her son away from such a good time, or maybe she did tell him and he waved me away, the girl from school who was popular but not popular enough. I start to think maybe Gottlieb was actually right for once. I wonder what Jensen would say.

My parents are downstairs, waiting for the ball to drop on TV. They said not to come down but to call for them if I need anything. My brother is at his friend's house for the night. I never really know what he's up to when he goes out, but he's a senior and can pretty much do whatever he wants. When he first got his license, my mom would wait in Dad's den and sit by the window until he came home. He was never once late for curfew, but she didn't understand why he wanted to be gone in the first place. I think it's about not having to ask: you just go, you just go and do what you want, because you can, because you have a car and a piece of plastic that says it's legal for you to be out there on the road. I used to worry, though. What if something bad did happen to him? What if he didn't come home and no one knew where he was? I still wait up for him in my room and listen for him coming up the stairs, shutting his door behind him. Sometimes I'll go into his room and play *Mario Kart* with him or just sit while he plays a game I don't understand. I just want to be with him, and since he got that plastic card he's been gone so much. It's not his fault, though;

he's just growing up, and someday I'll have that freedom, too. My mom has since stopped waiting for him by the window in the den, but I know she's relieved to hear the garage door open late at night when he comes back to us.

When I check my tonsils in the mirror, they're still white and patchy. I've been confined to my room, and I'm starting to go stir-crazy. The house phone rings, and I run to get it, but my mom's already picked up downstairs.

"You shouldn't be using your voice," my mom says on the line, and I'm not sure who's calling yet, so it's embarrassing.

"I'm fine!" I whisper-yell. "Hang up."

She hangs up and I wait.

"Hey, hey, hey!" Jensen says, doing her best Fat Albert impression. I laugh.

"I can't do that right now 'cause of my throat!"

"What are you doing?" she asks.

"I just looked at my tonsils in the mirror."

"What do they look like now?"

"Partly cloudy."

"Ew."

"What are you doing?"

"I'm at Thea and Christos's. They're banging pots and pans. It's awful."

I look at my alarm clock, next to my bed, and it reads 11:30 p.m. "It's not midnight yet," I say.

"They're old. They want to go to bed soon. And they keep telling me to get in bed if I won't grab a sauté pan to bang on."

"I saw them up late one time when we slept over there. It was pretty wild."

"They're a rowdy pair indeed."

"True. What are your parents doing tonight?"

"They went to some party in the neighborhood. I didn't want to go, so they dropped me off here. I didn't want to put on a dumb dress and talk to fancy people."

"The fancy people—sounds like a good book."

"Yeah, you should write it. What are your parents doing?"

"They're watching the ball drop. I don't get it. What's so great about a ball? What does it even mean?"

"It's, like, the ball of time, like Father Time's balls dropping."

"I hope my mom lets me do something for my birthday."

"She will. You always worry and then nothing happens."

"Sometimes bad things happen."

"Yeah, but they're never really that bad."

We stay on the phone until midnight, and after the magic of the New Year subsides, we continue to talk about absolutely nothing for a while. I don't tell her about Max, and she doesn't tell me about how much she hates her parents. We don't talk about the other girls or the many boys who have disappointed us. We don't talk about love or sex or how bad it hurts to feel such a gaping void in our teenage hearts, one that hungers for love and sex, to be loved, to be sexed, to feel something real and not imagined, to be outside of ourselves, or to truly come into who we're supposed to be. For this short time on the phone, Jensen fills the void. She's my best friend and I am hers and we have each other, without doubt, without the slightest feeling that something bad might happen.

"Do you think we'll be friends forever?" I ask.

"I hope we don't end up like two old ladies at the supermarket who meet in the dairy aisle. 'Agnes, is that you?' And then the other is all, 'Debra, I haven't seen you in ages!' "

"Right there next to the milk."

"And the cheese."

"I wish I had some cheese."

"You shouldn't eat dairy when you're sick."

"I don't give a tiny rat's ass!" We laugh; it hurts my throat. "Anyway, it's on the up-and-up."

"That's good. I'm glad."

I hear the commotion of pots and pans and her grandparents arguing. I wonder where we'll be next year for New Year's, if we'll celebrate together. I decide that maybe it's better if Max and I don't talk anymore. *When he switched schools the following year, it was nice not to have to see him anymore, to wonder why I wasn't good enough, why it hadn't worked out. He married a thin Jewish girl he met in college, and they look more like brother and sister than lovers. I wonder if he breathes in her ear at night while they sleep. I wonder if he realizes I was the one who first gave him a chance.*

It's a new year, and I can leave him, among other things, behind.

TEN

We attempt to savor the last few days of winter break. Jensen invites me over for a barbecue that her parents are hosting. I have one more day of bubblegum-flavored antibiotics, so it takes some convincing for my mom to let me go.

Everyone's out back when I arrive at Jensen's house. Her parents spent all of last summer remodeling their backyard so it would be perfect for parties, and it is. They have an outdoor tiki bar, a grill, and a huge, restaurant-regulation refrigerator for entertaining. Jensen is drinking something with a yellow umbrella sticking out of it.

"Try it," she says.

"What is it?" I ask.

"Amaretto sour. It's delicious."

"I think I'll have to pass. I don't want to infect you, as a courtesy."

"Oh, right. I forgot you were plagued. Also, my mom's on her, like, tenth glass of wine, so just don't *indulge* her, ya know?"

"How's your dad?"

"Right behind her, at glass number nine. But he made Key lime pie, so there's that."

Jensen's mom is grilling her famous barbecued chicken. We sit outside, in the backyard, even though it's a little too cold for a barbecue, but I'm still happy, sitting there on the lounge chair, watching Jensen feed scraps to Lucky, who's doing fine. She isn't jumping on me; she knows better.

"Fifteen is right around the corner," Jensen's mom says to me. She has a glass of red wine in her hand. It's only just after noon.

"Yep," I say trying to take Jensen's advice and be short with her parents. I see her eyeing me while she bites into another chicken wing covered in sweet barbecue sauce.

"There's Key lime pie for dessert, if you girls are interested."

"Yes!" Jensen says, not even finished with her lunch yet.

"Would you like some, too, honey?" Jensen's mom asks.

"No, thank you," I say. "I'm kind of full right now."

"That's why you look like you do, and why my daughter has a big ass!" She laughs.

There's a pause. Then Jensen gets up and storms into the house. I'm frozen on the lounge chair, Lucky panting next to me, but there's no chance I'll muster up the courage to feed her another scrap. Jensen's mom is already back at the tiki bar, refilling her glass. Eventually I get up and go to find Jensen inside. She's upstairs, in her room, setting a volleyball to herself over and over again.

"I thought you wanted pie," I say, flipping my head over and putting my hair into a messy bun, trying to be casual, even though I know how bad what her mom said was, how cruel.

I try to push away my thoughts that maybe this is about me somehow.

Jensen doesn't answer. I've never seen her like this before. She keeps playing with the stupid ball, setting it higher and higher. All of a sudden, she spikes the ball down and at me, and it hits me in the head, hard. She laughs. I run to the bathroom mirror and already see a bump forming.

"Why did you do that?" I yell.

"Oh my God, it's a ball, you're not going to die."

"Yeah, but you hit me. Like, on purpose."

"I thought you'd hit it back or something, but I guess I should have known you're not very good at sports."

I spot a photo of us at a gymnastics tournament from when we were in fifth grade on her desk. We're in hideous leotards, mine purple and hers blue, our hair in braided ponytails, and Jensen's giving me bunny ears behind my head. I'm smiling like a doofus, and she is, too. I feel so far away from that moment. I know Jensen is upset about what her mom said, but she didn't have to be mean about it. Jensen goes to her closet and takes out a pair of Rollerblades and a hockey stick.

"What are you doing?" I ask.

"I'm going to see if my neighbors want to play street hockey. But you probably shouldn't come, because you're sick or whatever."

I walk downstairs and go out to the backyard. Her dad hands me a slice of Key lime pie. I eat it and wait for my mom to pick me up. I tell her I'm feeling sick again, and I can tell she's mad. I pretend to fall asleep on the ride home.

I don't hear from Jensen the rest of the week. No calls, no

instant messages. But I figure all will be well for my birthday in a few days. She usually calls me at midnight on the day of, but, no, not even that. I'd hoped she just needed to cool down; now I'm not so sure.

I fail my permit test. I didn't know who had the right of way at a four-way stop. I didn't know the protocol for parking uphill, downhill, on any type of hill. A kid from my history class, Kyle Schwartz, is also at the DMV and sees me fail. He doesn't say anything to me, but I watch him move toward the photo area to get his permit as I walk away crying.

I wanted to get my permit on my actual birthday, but now I've ruined it. Rosenberg, Tomassi, and Jensen had all gotten their permits on their actual birthdays. I remember the day they all pulled out their permit cards in the bathroom of the 400 Building. We had left lunch early to check our hair and makeup, and all the girls who were already fifteen pulled out their cards to compare pictures. I couldn't wait to have my card, too, to be able to slide it in and out of my wallet at a moment's notice, to be a part of that elite club.

It even rains on my birthday, right after I fail the test and climb back into my mom's car, crying. I refuse to go to school permit-less, and my mom refuses to take me home. She tells me to lie, to say I couldn't get an appointment or that it was taking too long, anything to clear my name of a failed permit test. Kyle Schwartz poses a problem, though: He is such a little shit, always causing the type of unnecessary drama that high school freshmen thrive on. He's smaller than the other boys, and it was his insecurity over this that probably made him tell the kids in our grade that Amanda Wharton gave Richie Davis a blow job in the stairwell during Homecoming. He tried to hook up with her in sixth grade on a field trip to Washington, DC. She said his penis was too small, even though she didn't see it. "I felt it," she argued. "It was smaller than my dog's dick." Then there was Abby Lampbert, who claimed he tried to finger her during a pep rally, unsuccessfully. It seemed that his rejections made him lash out at the female population, and though he never tried to hook up with me, I was a girl and he would likely assume I was a bitch.

When Kyle Schwartz walks out of the DMV, my instinct says to get out of the car. I tell my mom to hold on, and I pull my hood over my head and run to him, desperate and frantic. He's smiling and showing his dad his new ID card when I reach him.

"Please, Kyle," I say, "I beg of you. Don't slander my name."

"Oh, because you failed your permit test?" He smiles and puts his ID in his pocket.

"Jensen told me not to study. It's not my fault."

"Is this one of your classmates?" Schwartz's dad asks.

"Yeah, but we aren't friends," Schwartz says. I realize it's true, we aren't friends, and he'll never cover for me. My life is over. Everyone will know I'm permit-less.

"That's not very nice," his dad says. "And I'm sure, if you want to keep this a secret, that Kyle will do that. No one should have to be embarrassed about these sorts of things."

Just then I notice my mom's gotten out of the car, too, with

her umbrella. She pieces together what's happening and introduces herself to Schwartz's dad. They apparently know each
other from a while back, some field trip they both chaperoned
for us in middle school. The parental bond seals the deal, and
Kyle agrees not to say anything.

"Do you think Kenzie would ever go out with me?" Kyle
asks, a last request.

"She has a boyfriend," I say. "Sorry. And thank you for not
telling anyone about this."

We get back in the car and drive to school. A part of me
still worries whether Kyle will say something, but I also know
my mom would make his life hell if he did. *Kyle never stopped
being mean to girls in high school, but at least he didn't tell on me that
day. I occasionally wondered if I should thank him, but that would have
meant thanking him for not being an asshole. I was so scared every time
I saw him in the hallway, that secret looming, the look on his face like he
might let it slip. But I got my permit two weeks later, after scheduling
another appointment and actually studying the stupid book.*

My mom drops me off right before third period, and I feel the
dumbest I've ever felt in my life. I am fifteen today. It's supposed to be the greatest day of my existence so far. I'm wearing
acid-wash jeans and a red off-the-shoulder shirt that's made out
of spandex material and is so tight I had to stretch it over my
head to get it on. I have on white Nikes with red laces; Jensen
has the same ones with blue laces, up a half size. No one knew
I'd be coming in late, but I assume they carried their balloons

and other gifts to their first two classes, setting them in the corner of the room, eagerly awaiting the time they'd see me in the hall and wish me a happy birthday.

Second period ends, and everyone rushes out of classrooms. I stand by Mr. Greggor's door in the 400 Building, where Jensen has biology. She walks out of the room wearing her over-size varsity volleyball windbreaker and a navy skirt with our matching shoes. She's talking to a kid named Joshua Sherman, who has white-blond hair, like hers, and wears his uniform super baggy. He's laughing so hard his face is all red. As they walk out, they begin playing some sort of tag game. Jensen touches Joshua Sherman on the strap of his backpack, then he lightly touches the collar of her shirt, back and forth. I've seen them do it before, and it's so annoying. It's like a variation on flirting, because they're either too shy or scared to actually flirt. Jensen doesn't see me. She doesn't stop walking.

"Hey!" I shout, following the two of them. Jensen turns around but doesn't stop moving. Joshua Sherman pauses, ready on his feet for an attack.

"I can't stop or he'll get me!" Jensen yells, darting across the hall, being chased. I realize she doesn't have any balloons, or a tiara, or a cupcake, a donut, anything.

"Did you forget my birthday?" I ask. It slips out, emotional, heavy, sad. Jensen stops in her tracks. Joshua Sherman tags her on the butt and she barely notices, lets him get away, off and down the hallway.

"I had to carpool with Jayce this morning," Jensen says. Jayce Williams is a junior who lives in her neighborhood. She does sometimes get a ride to school when her parents are away for business or on vacation without her and her grandparents can't make it, but I doubt that's the case this morning. It seems too random; it seems like an excuse.

"So?" I ask.

"So it would have been embarrassing to ask to stop and get dumb balloons for your birthday."

"It wasn't dumb when we did it for your birthday, or anyone else's."

"Maybe it *is* dumb."

"But did you even remember?" As I say it, I regret it, not wanting to know the real answer: That she probably did forget. That she probably doesn't really care. That she really is a bitch. I walk away before she can respond and head to the 500 Building, where Rosenberg has history. I want to catch her and ask for a second opinion, but by the time I get there the bell has rung and she's inside, in her seat. She can't see me motioning for her to come outside, to ask to use the bathroom, something. I have a pass, so it doesn't matter when I get to my own classroom. I take my time walking back to the 400 Building.

I get through my next two classes and eat lunch in the library, which isn't really allowed, but I tell the librarian, Mrs. Peterson, that I'm looking for a book to read. She's more than happy to help and suggests a book about a young girl in London who can't stop "snogging" boys and thinking about "snogging" all the time. I read the first twenty pages during lunch hour and decide to check it out.

It turns out none of my "friends" remembered it was my birthday or brought me anything. They all have excuses. The only ones who attempt to redeem themselves are Rosenberg and Tomassi. Rosenberg says she left cupcakes from Publix at home by accident. Tomassi draws me a card in fifth period that I end up throwing away. I tell my teacher I have a stomachache, so I sit in the nurse's office during PE. In seventh period, art, Todd Wexler asks me why I'm dressed down and I almost cry.

I'm embarrassed by my own birthday. I wish it wasn't even my birthday today, so it wouldn't matter that everyone forgot. It's too much to bear that no one remembered.

My mom comes upstairs and knocks on my bedroom door. I open it and she hands me a box full of various crafts.

"These are yours," she says. There are horrible crayon drawings of bulbous-looking people and collages of paper shapes badly glued to construction paper. There's a "book" I wrote from kindergarten called *The Queen Fairy Princess*, which is about a princess who orders a pizza to her castle and eats it.

"Why would I want this?"

"Because it's all of your artwork."

"Artwork?" I pull out a piece of blue construction paper with shapes glued to it. "This is artwork?"

"That was very good for your age!" My mom laughs. "I just thought you'd want to look through them."

"Why?"

"I just know things."

"What's that supposed to mean?"

"I'm your mother."

She walks out and closes the door behind her. The box sits

on my bed, and I decide to sift through it. I find my birth
certificate, prints of my baby feet in clay, a lot more very bad
"artwork," a few framed baby pictures, and birthday cards
from years past. I read through a couple of the cards, but none
of them speak to me in the way I want. The cards, from my
grandmother who lives in New York City, my aunt and uncle
who are down the street in another Boca neighborhood, and
my mom, are an endless string of promises that each year will
bring me luck, love, growth. Mickey Mouse holds a birthday
cake with five candles, Cinderella's shiny shoe sits covered in
glitter, Winnie the Pooh holds a lone balloon.

Then I find a Dr. Seuss book, *All About Me*, that I had when
I was seven years old. The book has a picture of me in a purple
dress inserted into the cover art—each kid was supposed to
make the book about them and ask a parent for help incor-
porating their photo into it. I wanted the book to have me
photographed in my favorite dress, and it makes me glad even
now to see myself documented in such a way.

The book had many blanks to be filled in, like eye color, hair
color, height, favorite food, number of pets, number of sib-
lings, names, dates, etc. But there is one page that asked for my
address. I had written my name, house number, street, city, state,
and zip code, and then proceeded to write below: *United States
of America, Planet Earth, Outer Space, the Galaxy, the Universe* . . .
And I wonder why I kept going, after I had already written all
I was supposed to. I must have felt the need to define myself,
to define my place in the whole world, at seven years old. I
remember feeling too old to have a book like that. Maybe I was
embarrassed about it and wanted to complicate the logic of the

book. Maybe I wanted it to mean more than it did. But reading it now makes me feel so small. I'm fifteen years old, but I'm not that important. I'm just a body, much smaller than any star in the sky. I'm only a person, just a girl.

I fall asleep in my clothes until my mom comes in again and says we're going out to dinner for my birthday. I tell her I don't want to, but she doesn't listen, and I end up leaving on my same clothes from school and going out with my family. My mom, dad, brother, and I go to an Italian restaurant close to home. My mom gets minestrone soup, and my dad gets a salad that he doesn't want, so I eat it, removing the tomatoes from my dish onto my mom's plate. Brad waits patiently for his dinner, not spoiling it with any appetizers. He seems really tired, but I assume it's from studying or something. His eyes are drooping, like he's stayed up all night. But when the food comes, he dives right in. I've ordered spaghetti and meatballs, my favorite meal, and I eat three pieces of bread. Two before dinner, one during. I dip the bread into my pasta sauce, and it's delicious. At the end of the meal, a waiter who is actually kind of cute brings me a slice of chocolate cake with chocolate icing and a candle. I blow it out and wish that someday I will matter to the whole world, that something good will happen to me. My dad helps me finish the cake, and I'm so full that I fall asleep on the ride home. I had forgotten it was Friday, and when I wake up the next morning at 11:30 a.m., I'm surprised at first by the prospect of missing school and by my mom allowing me to miss it. But then, slowly, I come to realize it's Saturday, and I turn on cartoons and watch *SpongeBob SquarePants* while I eat a bowl of Cinnamon Toast Crunch with milk.

There is a small amount of peace before I realize my parents didn't get me a birthday present, which causes an argument with my mom that lasts all night, the both of us crying, yelling, crying even more. Eventually we retreat to our rooms. Later, my mom comes into my bedroom with a printed-out picture of a Tiffany necklace that she promises is in the mail, on the way. She apologizes, saying she had planned to get me a gift when I had a party, and I tell her I'm sorry for being a bitch.

ELEVEN

I get a note in my locker from Stephen Fraber. He's in my grade but is unpopular. Naturally, there are certain kids at school who are favored. They are usually the richer kids, the kids who have famous aunts or uncles, the kids who fly to Turks and Caicos in private jets, the kids who spend summers in Europe. But sometimes they are the troublemakers, the kids who maybe don't have as much money, but what they lack in funds they make up for in mischief. They talk back to teachers and sell weed on campus. They wear their uniforms however they want to, sagging their pants or rolling up their pleated skirts until you can see their underwear from behind. Or maybe they become known for something that happened to them at school, like when Marissa Katz got caught cheating on her Spanish test. Her teacher, Señora Dolores, caught her and lifted up her skirt in front of the whole class to prove she had written the answers on her thighs, which she had. But Señora Dolores got fired, and Marissa Katz was only given a warning. There are many levels of fame one can achieve at our school; even being a Brittany counts toward boosting our reputations.

Stephen Fraber plays soccer, which works in his favor; the other girls have clearly disapproved of my choices in love interests. He has a few friends who are less than desirable, like Eddie Sullivan and Jerry Ferguson, who are perpetually getting busted in class for playing *Snood* or watching porn on their laptops. They're pretty goofy, but I don't care, because there's something about Stephen that interests me. I've decided I'm in a phase where I don't care what anyone else thinks of me except my parents, who are basically in charge of me. I walk through the halls at school with a different kind of stride. I'm learning not to give a shit, as they say.

The note asks me if I want to go to the movies. Stephen requests my home phone number and leaves his locker number on the bottom of the note. I write down my number and slip the note back during fifth hour, right after lunch. I tell him to call me tonight.

It's cold for January, still cold enough to wear my sweatshirt all the way through the school day. It's my brother's, actually, one of his old ones that I borrowed and never gave back. It's a navy-blue crewneck with a white-and-gold eagle emblem on the chest, our school's mascot. The Eagles. It always makes me think of the Eagles' song "New Kid in Town." My dad used to play that song a lot in the car when we were younger. I liked how it was about a new person in a new town and everybody liked him for just doing nothing, it seemed. Maybe I didn't fully understand, but it made me feel good to know that guy had a good life, and I imagined myself in the song, walking around school like I owned the place, being popular, being liked by everyone, having it be that easy.

I haven't really been hanging around the girls much, but I notice Jensen is getting closer with Kenzie. They hang out a lot, and I don't see why Kenzie even likes her. Kenzie likes guys, and Jensen only likes weirdos like Joshua Sherman and teachers. I'm supposed to have my annual birthday sleepover with all the girls this weekend, but I don't think I'll invite the usual people. Things are kind of off now, and I don't want to further upset the generalized chaos between fifteen-year-olds. Last year my sleepover sucked, anyway. We watched a movie called *But I'm a Cheerleader*, which ended up being about a girl who figures out she's a lesbian instead of what we actually thought it'd be about: cheerleaders. The girl *was* a cheerleader, but that wasn't what the movie was about. None of us were even cheerleaders, but we liked the idea of girls who were.

No one asks about the sleepover. It's been a week since the mess of my actual birthday, and I'm sure they all think I'm doing nothing to celebrate. It's sort of unspoken that I'm mad at everyone, so when I call Rosenberg to invite her over on Saturday, she's pleasantly surprised.

"I thought you weren't going to do anything," she says.

"I didn't want to, but it's my birthday. And I know the day's already passed, but I think I should celebrate the big one-five, you know?"

"Who else is coming?" she asks, and I hear one of her dogs barking in the background.

"I'm only inviting you and Tomassi."

"Is Jensen on your shit list?"

"I just want to keep it small."

"Don't get me wrong—I'm glad she's not invited, I can't stand the bitch. But she's, like, your best friend."

"She's not *not* invited. I just want a calm night. No drama."

"Gotcha. So what else is new?"

"Not much." I don't tell Rosenberg about Stephen. I'm not close enough to anyone right now to divulge that kind of information. I want to tell Rosenberg that I *am* mad at Jensen, that it *did* hurt my feelings when she not only forgot my birthday, but told me it was downright stupid. I want to tell her, tell someone, everything that happened, but if I say it out loud, then it'll be true; Jensen will be a bad friend.

Rosenberg tells me about this kid Milo Vance, who lives in her neighborhood. He's a sophomore, but his brother Mitchell is in our grade. There's a whole clan of them, descending in age, but Milo is for sure the most popular. They talked at lunch one day or something, and now they're friends. Rosenberg has no fear, which is why I really like having her as a friend. She'll talk to any guy, no matter what her hair or makeup looks like, no matter what stupid outfit she's wearing, and they seem to like her. She's great at befriending the older crowd and gets invited to a lot of parties she's not allowed to go to. Her parents are definitely the strictest of all of the parents in our group. But somehow they let her drive their golf cart around the neighborhood, and, unbeknownst to them, she rides over to flirt with boys in various houses.

"They want us to come over one night," Rosenberg says.

"For what?"

"Like, to hang out."

It's amazing to me how much Rosenberg has changed. When I first knew her, in middle school, she had this thing where every time a new member of our group went over to her house, they had to jump in the pool with their clothes on to prove their friendship to her. I remember hearing about this and not believing it or understanding it, but when my day finally came and my parents drove me over to Rosenberg's house for our first sleepover, she took me out to the pool on her house tour. First I saw her bedroom, the closed door to her older sister's bedroom, her movie room, the kitchen with the marble island that looked exactly like my family's kitchen, her parents' master bedroom, her garage with a second fridge stocked with juice and Gatorade, a backup generator for hurricanes, her parents' black Range Rover, her two dogs, three cats, and one bird, and then, finally, her backyard.

The pool was not heated and had a few straggling leaves in it from the last rain. It was designed with two circles that flowered out from one larger circle, almost like Mickey Mouse's famous ears. I remember I had straightened my hair that day and really didn't want to submerge it to appease Rosenberg. But as we stood there at the edge of the pool, she made me raise my right hand and solemnly swear that I would always be her best friend, forever and ever, no matter what. She had a towel ready and waiting on a lounge chair for me after my plunge. She stood with her arms crossed, smiling, in her glasses that had a blue tint in the lens, making her look a lot younger than she was. And I jumped, because that's what you do when you want to be someone's friend, someone like Rosenberg.

"Okay," I say now. "I'm in."

"I'm more interested in Mitchell than Milo. Is that weird?"

"Cradle robbing?"

"Oh my gosh, Mitchell is so cute. He *looks* eighteen."

"Yeah, but he's fourteen?"

"About to be fifteen."

"But we're fifteen *now*. God, fourteen sounds so young."

"I know, right? Like a baby. But, seriously, he's turning fifteen in, like, two months. He's about to age any minute now!"

"I feel like anything younger than fifteen is just weird."

"You've been fifteen for a week."

"I've grown up a lot this week, though."

Stephen Fraber calls shortly after my phone call with Rosenberg ends. He sounds nervous but manages to ask if I want to get dropped off at his house on Friday night and see a movie with him. His mom will take us, and she won't stay, he promises. She'll simply drop us off at the movie theater and pick us up when it's over. My mom agrees to this as well, and it's settled. The main issue is figuring out what to wear and how to style my hair without the help of any of the girls. My mom wants me to wear a skirt, which is ridiculous since we're going to the movies, where we'll be sitting the whole time and it'll be uncomfortable, but she says for a date that's what you wear. I guess it is a date—my first date, since no parents will be present—and it's a real outing, not like hanging out at someone's house and playing truth or dare.

I keep my date a secret all week, and when Friday rolls around I start to panic. I try to convince my mom to let me wear jeans, but she insists that the skirt looks better.

"Jeans look sloppy. You want to look nice. And can you part your hair on the side? Maybe curl it? It looks so good curled."

"It takes forever to curl!"

"Then blow it out and fluff it up. I hate when it's stick-straight like that."

"I like it like this."

"It looks so good fluffed up, though."

"Mom! I don't want to be fluffy. I want to be pretty."

"You're beautiful either way. I just like it fluffed up."

"Oh my God."

I settle on a white skirt from Abercrombie & Fitch that I got a year ago and never wear and a navy-blue tank top with lace on the chest. I wear a denim jacket and Converse sneakers. It's way too cold to be wearing what I'm wearing, but I want to look good. I wear a push-up bra and I feel like it works. I hope Stephen tries to kiss me tonight, maybe even more. Maybe we'll go back to his house after, and his little brothers will be sleeping, and his parents will let us have time alone in his room, and we can do stuff. I get more excited and nervous. My mom tries to take a picture of me, but I don't let her.

On the drive to Stephen's house in Coral Springs, I think about the girl in the snogging book. What is it that makes someone "boy crazy"? Is it bad that I want a boy to like me, maybe even fall in love with me, want to spend time with me and get to know me for who I really am? Do I even know who I really am? The girl in the book is smart, like me, and she's pretty, besides the fact that she over-tweezed her eyebrows because someone called her hairy and had to wait for them to grow back. In seventh grade, Spencer Wyatt told me I had sideburns, so I went home that night and shaved the sides of my face. It looked horrible and obvious, but I wanted to get rid of the baby hairs in front of my ears. The next day, he asked if I'd shaved my face, and I turned red but told him he was wrong and that I absolutely did not have sideburns. He said I was weird and walked away. They're still growing back funky. But I can relate to the girl in the book: Sometimes I do stupid, impulsive, slightly harmful things to myself because of what other people think. In the book, the girl's mom is her best friend, and sometimes I feel that way, too, that my mom is my only *real* friend. She's always been there for me, and although she has to take care of me and make sure I don't die until I'm eighteen, she really loves me, deeply, because I'm her daughter.

I always wanted to be like my mom when I was little. I clung to her leg as she vacuumed the house, lay in bed with her and watched her soap operas, sat in the front basket of her shopping cart on grocery runs. I loved everything about her: her hair, her eyes, the way she smelled like cotton and lavender, the skin on her arms, how it was soft yet her muscles were strong from carrying me. I wanted to be just like her. Now, looking over at her as she drives, mouthing the words to the song on the radio but not singing loud enough for me to hear, I wonder when my desire to be like her transformed, changed so that I'd rather be more like Kenzie or Rosenberg or even Katherine Bennington. They're so confident and beautiful, and sometimes I feel nothing like that; I'm a little ball of worry and fear and anxiety dressed in all the wrong clothes, my hair never fully straight, underdeveloped, a virgin, never tried drugs, barely a woman.

"If you're going to sing, can you sing louder, or just not sing at all?" I say, annoyed.

"I'm not singing."

"Yes, you are."

"If I want to sing, I'll sing. I don't need your permission."

"I know what you're doing. I can hear you!"

"Do you want me to just go home? I don't have to drive you all the way out to Coral Springs. I have other things to do."

"Like what? Watch *American Idol*? Clean? Help Brad with some school project?"

She stops short at a red light and turns the music all the way down. I realize I've just opened up Pandora's box, and I'm not even sure why. All the negative thoughts come rushing to me as I sit in the passenger seat, halfway to Stephen's house for my first date: *You're flat. You're ugly. You're not as pretty as Kenzie or confident like Rosenberg. You're not popular. Your outfit sucks. Your hair is stupid. . . .*

"Just because you're nervous doesn't mean you have to take it out on me," my mom says. "If you don't want to go tonight, we can turn around. And if your attitude doesn't change, we *will* turn around, and you won't go out for a month."

"I'm not nervous! You're just being annoying."

"How am I being annoying?"

"By half singing."

"You need to calm down." My mom laughs. She knows I'm being ridiculous, and even I know I'm being ridiculous at this point. I turn and look out the window. We pass into Coral Springs, where all the shopping plazas look the same. Beige buildings, signs with green block letters, doctors' and lawyers' offices, bakeries, coffee shops, banks, fast-fix repair stores, all the same string of stores, over and over again. It's greener here in Coral Springs, more swamp life and chances of alligator sightings, more humidity for some reason, too. I question my choice of straightening my hair. Maybe I should have fluffed it up.

We pull up to Stephen's house in a neighborhood where all the houses are two stories and painted various shades of beige: maple, caramel, brown, eggshell, cream, taupe. Stephen's house is caramel-colored. His mom's Jeep is in the driveway. I've seen him get picked up in it before, at school. He has two younger brothers, one in middle school and one in elementary, so he's always the last in his family to be picked up. I'm so glad I won't ever know what that's like, because I'm the baby in my family and I always will be.

My mom insists on waiting in the car until someone answers the front door.

"I love you. Call me if you need me to come get you earlier, and if not, I'll be here at ten o'clock."

"I thought you said eleven?"

"Ten."

"We'll see."

"Don't give Stephen this attitude. Men don't like women with attitudes."

I roll my eyes at her and get out of the car. On the walk to the front door, I step on the grass and immediately feel bad, like I should have walked around and used the driveway. I wonder if anyone will notice. Stephen's mom opens the door before I can even knock.

"Hi, sweetie. You look so pretty." She smiles.

"Thank you."

"Stephen's just upstairs. Stephen Ellis Fraber!" she yells.

Stephen runs down the stairs with his littlest brother, Grayson, chasing after him. His middle brother, Derek, runs out from the kitchen and grabs Grayson, slings him over his shoulder, and walks back into the kitchen area. Stephen slows down, relieved, and walks over to me. He's wearing a striped polo shirt that's not our uniform shirt and a pair of jeans with sneakers. I knew I should have worn jeans. His hair is gently spiked and he looks cute, cuter than he does at school. I'm excited that we might kiss tonight. It would be a good thing if that happened.

Stephen gives me an awkward hug and we head into his living room. There's an L-shaped couch with lots of pillows and blankets, and we sit. His mom brings out a plate of cheese and crackers and two glasses of lemonade.

"Mom, we talked about this," Stephen says, slapping his hand on his face and covering his eyes.

"Oh, I know, but I just want to make sure your guest isn't hungry or thirsty."

"I'm fine. Thank you."

"So polite! You picked a sweet girl, Stevie."

"Mom, please leave."

"Okay, honey, but we have to leave the house at six forty-five for the movies."

"Got it. Bye."

Stephen's mom exits the room, and Stephen takes his hand away from his face. He's so cute I can't stand it.

"That was hell," he says.

I laugh. "She's just being a mom. My mom was way worse, I assure you."

"What was your mom doing?"

"She was, like, half singing in the car on the way over here."

"Ha! My mom made me try on every shirt in my closet. And she wanted me to wear slacks, but I told her it's just the movies. I was wearing them until five minutes ago."

There's awkward silence for a few minutes. I hear his brothers playing. One of them makes the other cry. I assume it's Derek making Grayson cry. His mom yells, and the two spout back muttered apologies. It quiets again.

"What movie are we seeing?" I ask.

"Oh, right. Well. I didn't know if you liked scary movies, so the one where the guy's trapped in a bathroom and has to cut off his own leg—that was out. But I wasn't sure, so I got tickets for *Win a Date with Tad Hamilton!*"

"Cool. I wanted to see that. I mean, I want to see that. Good choice."

"Thanks! I mean, I'm glad you like it. Well, I'm glad you *will* like it. I heard it's really good. I mean, if we even watch it, ya know?"

I give him an uneasy smile and realize I should have done something sexy and flirtatious like grab his leg or wink, but I'm not savvy enough for that.

"No pressure, though. Whatever you're comfortable with. I was just hoping to get a kiss," Stephen says, and lightly puts his hand on my bare knee, which I realize I didn't do a great job shaving, so it's probably prickly.

"Let's just see what happens," I say, which is the best I can come up with on such short notice. I didn't know he would be so forward. I get scared, but I also know that he's okay not doing anything, which is good to know in case I chicken out. I want to do stuff; I'm just not sure how I feel about planning it out like that and knowing he does have some kind of expectation. I wish I could call Rosenberg, but no one knows I'm here. I kind of wish I was at home with Jensen, playing *Mario Party* in our sweatpants, eating popcorn and drinking a Capri Sun, but we hate each other right now. I look around the living room for a sign of comfort, something to take my mind off where I am and what I'm doing. I spot a family photo of Stephen with his parents and brothers. They're all wearing overalls and standing in front of a blue marbled backdrop. It's strange, but it comforts me that his family is normal, because they take photos at Sears. My family doesn't do this sort of thing, and that's how I know I'm unique. *Stephen is normal,* I say in my head a few times before returning my gaze to him.

"Don't look at that picture," he says.

"It's . . . cute," I offer.

"No, it's embarrassing. I was, like, twelve there. Grayson was just a baby."

"Your brothers are so cute."

"Everything is cute to you!"

"No."

"What am I, then?" he asks, and stares with one eyebrow up.

"You're hot," I say, uncertain of myself, of the statement, of what it even means to call someone "hot." I do find him attractive, but I don't know him that well, aside from the fact we had a science class together in sixth grade. During an experiment that involved a glass jar of water, I dropped the jar and it broke into pieces. Stephen proceeded to laugh and call me "butterfingers." But my teacher, Mrs. Silverstein, assured me that he was only making fun of me because he liked me, which in turn mortified Stephen and caused him to stop.

"You're, like, the hottest girl that's ever talked to me," Stephen says. It makes me happy, and uncomfortable, when he says this. I've never considered myself "hot" or "sexy" or anything like that. People usually call me cute because I'm short, but I've never been called "hot" before. He looks so excited, and I don't understand how he's so confident and able to say the things he's thinking. It seems like he doesn't even question himself before he speaks, either. I'm baffled.

Stephen's mom takes us to a shopping plaza where there's a movie theater and a restaurant right next door. She gives Stephen cash for dinner and says she'll be back after the movie to pick us up. Once her car pulls away I feel afraid about what's to come. What if I decide I don't want to do anything and he isn't okay with it and he makes a move anyway and it's weird? I'm stuck with Stephen now for the next couple hours, and I'll just have to see how it goes.

I'm not hungry, but he wants to eat at the restaurant. I don't tell him I'm not hungry, though. In fact, when he asks if I'm hungry, I say yes. I had dinner before I left my house, but I order chicken fingers and fries anyway. We sit at a table that has a swinging bench and sways back and forth if you want it to. Stephen uses his foot to rock our table, but he stops when the food comes. He orders chicken fingers and fries, too, and we eat the same meal. I only eat two out of the four chicken fingers and have to dip them in honey mustard to get them down. I drink a Coke and he dips his chicken in ranch and drinks a Dr Pepper. I've never had Dr Pepper before in my life. It's just not a drink anyone in my family drinks. We're a Pepsi family, but I actually prefer Coke. My parents let me have soda whenever I want. Stephen asks me not to tell his mom that we had pop—which is weird, that he calls it that. I'm not sure I can kiss someone who calls soda "pop." It's soda.

Stephen pays the check with the cash his mom gave him. At the theater, he picks up our tickets, and we have some time before the movie. Stephen leads me to the little arcade near the concessions stand.

"We have a few bucks left to spend," he says.

"I like racing games." I say this because they're the only kind of games I know. My brother likes racing games. He always plays *Cruis'n USA* anytime we're in an arcade. I usually opt for the grab machines, but I'm not about to admit I like stuffed animals to a guy who thinks I'm "hot."

"Cool, I think they have one of those in here."

We play a racing game that isn't *Cruis'n USA* but is very similar. We quickly make our own individual cars—choose manual or automatic, the color, the build—and a map to race on. I motion for Stephen to choose that part. He picks an easy level that takes place in a futuristic city, probably because he thinks I'm going to be bad at the game, when in truth I'm really good at video games. All those years of watching my brother, learning the rules, seeing how he played the games of his youth— it's seeped into my brain, and I'm confident that I can win.

We push START and the race begins as bikini-clad women wave flags in front of our vehicles. My red car thrusts out ahead, and Stephen takes second place. There are five laps, and I maintain my lead for most of them, until a ghost player in the computer knocks me off course and into the city's ocean. I lose time getting rescued, and Stephen gains a lead that he keeps until the race is over.

"You know, I'll be able to get my license soon," he says, rubbing it in my face that he won. The bikini girls bring a large gold trophy over to his car. The animated characters are excited, and the screen goes black.

"Oh, like your permit test?" I ask.

"No, like my real license. I already have my permit." Stephen pulls out his wallet and presents his permit card. He's smiling too big in his picture. I hand it back to him.

"I'm turning sixteen in March," he says.

"Oh," I say. Stephen turning sixteen in two months is an absolute bonus for his cause. The girls would definitely approve of my dating a guy who has a car and can drive.

"I'll have to use the family car until I can afford my own, but it's still gonna be pretty cool."

Family car. Bummer.

"I want to get a Mustang, all black, pimped out and everything. I can't start working at my dad's office until I turn sixteen, though. But it's gonna be sweet!"

Black Mustang. Hot.

"How are you already turning sixteen?"

"I got held back in kindergarten."

"You couldn't color in the lines?"

"Ha! No! I found out I have really bad ADD and the school thought I just needed more time or something."

"Oh. Sorry."

"Don't be sorry. I'm pumped I'm getting a car before anyone else!"

"Good point."

We make our way to the theater, and Stephen leads us to the very last row. The theater is full of families, couples, small children, rowdy teenagers. Stephen didn't ask if I wanted anything to eat or drink during the movie, and I don't because I'm so nervous, but I usually get popcorn and a slushie. Jensen and I always share a large tub of popcorn, and she gets a mixed-berry slushie and I get a Coke slushie. She always lets me hold the tub as long as she's allowed to reach over and take as much popcorn as she wants. She knows I like to hold the tub. I try to shake the thought of her out of my head and focus on Stephen and *Win a Date with Tad Hamilton!*, which is about to start.

During the previews, I tell Stephen I'm going to use the bathroom, and I find my way out of the dark theater. I check my hair in the mirror; the Coral Springs humidity has puffed it up a little bit in the back, so I run my hands under cold water and smooth it down. I reapply my lip gloss, then wipe it off with a paper towel, realizing that if we do kiss he's not going to want lip gloss all over his lips. I stare into the mirror in the bathroom and tell myself that if Stephen tries to kiss me I'll let him. It'll be okay. I've kissed before, and I'll kiss again. If it happens, it happens.

Next to me, a mom is helping her young daughter wash her hands because she is too small to reach the sink. The mom is holding her up by her bottom, and the little girl is rubbing her hands together under the water, making them clean. I feel bad for being mean to my mom when she was just trying to help me and be nice to me. She's been through all this stuff before, dating and drama. It's hard for me to picture her stuffing her bra and talking to boys, hoping to get kissed. But it happened. And I wonder how much of it she remembers, how often she thinks about it. I wonder how much of it will matter to me when I grow up. The little girl plops down onto the floor, and her mom holds her little clean hand as they walk out of the bathroom.

I remember, on a trip to the Cayman Islands when I was six years old, I started to worry about the day my mom would die. It came on suddenly, out of nowhere: I became obsessed with the idea that she was going to die one day and leave me alone on this Earth. I couldn't imagine a life with only my dad and brother, one where my mom wouldn't be there to comfort me through all of life's tragedies. I kept the fear to myself the whole trip, until the very last night, when we went to this crazy restaurant that had parrots flying around as part of their kitsch. Something about the parrots, their brightly colored bodies flitting around the room, the way my brother didn't even look up from his Game Boy and my dad was so focused on his steak, made me feel an immense pang of doom in my little heart. I burst into tears.

My mom took me to the restaurant's bar, away from the birds, and I finally told her I was upset because she was going to die. She told me that, yes, it was true, but it wouldn't happen for a long time. She promised we'd live our whole lives together, that she'd always be there for me. She was young and healthy and I was young and healthy and we'd have plenty of time to be happy and live. The bartender slid me a glass of water with a circle of lemon in it, and I remember thinking how the lemon looked like the sun. I took it to be a sign that she was right, that I shouldn't worry about her dying because it wouldn't happen for a long time, that I should enjoy and appreciate her while I could. *I often had moments like this, moments of extreme, almost holy appreciation for my mom. These times ended with promises to be nicer, to be better. But the surge of promises would always get lost in the ebb and flow of daily trials, the emphasis placed on all the wrong things.*

I look in the mirror and wish I had curled my hair like my mom suggested instead of straightening it. My hair is so pin-straight and lifeless. I run my hands under the sink's hot water, and then through my hair, to rough it up—a big mistake. I flip my head over a few times to dry it, but two girls, younger than me, walk in, and I leave quickly, embarrassed. *Forgetting another juncture of awareness, as I so often did.*

I walk back to the theater and find Stephen with his arm around my seat, waiting. The previews end and the movie begins. The movie is pretty cheesy, but we both watch intently. Stephen's hand moves from the back of my seat to his own armrest and remains there for the entirety of the feature. I keep looking at it, willing it to go around me, and it does not. When the movie's over, we walk outside without touching and wait for his mom. We don't speak, and I feel like I did something wrong. There's been a shift in the night, and I realize how cold

I am in a skirt. I hug my denim jacket around me, and Stephen still makes no move to hold me or keep me warm. I wonder what the hell is going on in his head. He's so quiet I could die.

His mom asks us how the movie was, and I do all the talking. I tell her about the beautiful, quirky girl and how the nerdy guy is in love with her, but she wins a date with the celebrity hunk and has to decide who her true love will be. When we get back to his house, my mom is already there, and I'm glad. I hug Stephen goodbye and he waves, like an idiot. I thank his mom for everything, and she gives my mom an obligatory smile and a wave as we drive off.

I fall asleep in the car. I forget about how cold I am. I forget about my bad outfit choice. I forget about how Stephen said we were barely going to watch the movie but didn't make even *one* move on me. I forget about all of it and drift off, sleeping so deeply that, when we arrive back at home, I'm still dreaming as I walk in the house and upstairs to my room. I'm glad my mom let me off the hook on having to disclose to her any information about my date. I change into shorts and a big T-shirt. I take off my makeup and brush my teeth and get into bed. I don't want to think about any of it.

I dream I'm on a plane going somewhere far away. I'm afraid of the long flight, but I'm already on it. I'm not sure how long I've been up in the air; I suppose it's something like twenty-four hours. I start to walk the rows, and everyone else is sleeping. I find a stewardess, and she tells me to go back to sleep. I ask for a soda. She says it's not time for drinks, it's time for sleep. She guides me back to my seat, but someone is in it, sleeping. There are no seats open except at the back of the plane. She leaves me there, and I try to get comfortable, but the seats are smaller and upright and don't go back. All of a sudden my mom walks up to the row and sits next to me. I ask her for a soda. She says to rest on her shoulder until we land. I ask her where we're going, and she says home. I ask what about the trip, wherever we were supposed to be going. She says no, we're going home, just home. I lie with my head on her shoulder and look out the window. The night sky remains still and blue.

Rosenberg and Tomassi come over the next night for my birthday sleepover, and I confide in them the tale of Stephen Fraber. They curse his name, as do I, and we chant that he has "no balls." The night is uneventful; we do not talk about Jensen. We do one another's makeup, which mostly consists of Rosenberg applying way too dark a shade of eye shadow for both Tomassi and me but us playing along with it. With my teal-shaded eyes, I insist that there was something between me and Stephen. Tomassi says it's a shame, because he'll be driving in two months, just in time for spring break. Rosenberg says he's a "douche," because he had so many chances and messed all of them up. "I was right there," I tell the girls. They nod in acknowledgment.

Rosenberg has brought her laptop and tells us she's been using her webcam a lot. I'm not even sure what that is, but she shows us that you can video-chat with whoever you want as long as they have a camera, too. She sets up the device and says we should chat with Milo and Mitchell Vance. I think Milo is really hot. I've been watching him at school. We're in the same lunch period, and since the girls have all split up, I've had more time to check him out. He always wears the collar popped on his polo and his khaki pants cuffed at his ankles. His hair is long to his shoulders and is the color of chestnuts. He makes me think of Christmas. He hangs out with the popular guys and girls in his grade, like Chris Saul and Amber Goodman, all the beautiful ones. I agree to do the webcam stuff if it's understood that Milo belongs to me.

Tomassi is too shy to partake but says she'll watch from the sidelines. Once it's set up, Rosenberg calls Milo and Mitchell at home and tells them to go online. We're all wearing shorts and tank tops with spaghetti straps. Rosenberg and I both have our hair straight, and Tomassi has hers in pigtail braids. Tomassi always looks gorgeous, but in a more natural way. Rosenberg and I need to look "hot." When the Vance brothers come online, they're both wearing white T-shirts and cargo shorts.

"If we put on music, will you dance?" Mitchell asks. I can't believe how forward he is, but I guess it's good, since we've spent the last few minutes giggling at nothing and embarrassing ourselves.

"Sure," Rosenberg says.

They put on a rap song that I've only heard on the radio a few times, "P.I.M.P." by 50 Cent, and Rosenberg turns around and starts shaking her butt.

"Oh my God," Tomassi says, and covers her eyes. She sits on my bed in the middle of the room. I move to join her.

"Get over here, ya little shit!" Rosenberg yells at me while she continues to dance.

"No way," I reply.

"One moment, please, technical difficulties," Rosenberg says to the boys on the screen, and walks over to me.

"This is embarrassing," I say.

"No, it's sexy. They like it. Trust me."

"I'm not good at that . . . kind of stuff."

"Dancing?"

"Yeah, whatever."

"I can show you how. It's really easy. You just put your hands on your knees and move your butt. It kinda jiggles up and down . . ."

"Oh my God!" Tomassi says.

"Where'd you go?" we hear from the computer.

"One moment, please!" Rosenberg yells back.

Another song comes on, Chingy's "Right Thurr," and I get up, involuntarily. I just really like this song.

"She's coming!" Rosenberg yells.

"Only because I like this song!" I do the moves like Rosenberg showed me, and the boys seem to like it. The screen is pixilated and blurry, but I can see Milo smiling as I dance.

After a few songs, we say bye to the boys, and Rosenberg says she'll call them. They say we all have to hang out soon. Rosenberg, Tomassi, and I watch a movie and eat brownie sundaes that my mom makes for us. We fall asleep on the early side, and it's exactly what I wanted, a calm birthday without drama. It's not until Monday that Jensen finds out about the sleepover, but she doesn't say anything to me. That's how I know I'm completely screwed.

THIRTEEN

*B*rittany Rosenberg and I start having a lot of sleepovers. She always wants to make up songs or do some sort of dance routine when we are at her house. One night, she and I decide to drink from a random bottle in her parents' collection while they aren't home. We don't know when to stop, and we don't bother using juice or Cokes for mixers. Rosenberg gets naked and throws up in her tub, and when her parents get home I have to pretend we're both sick but that she is more sick. Her mom gives us raspberry-sorbet popsicles, and Rosenberg throws that up, too, fuchsia goop on her pillowcase. In the morning, I realize I went to bed with makeup on for the first time, and my eyelashes are caked with mascara. They feel like spiders.

Meanwhile, Jensen's been hanging out with Kenzie, which concerns me. I know Leigh has been smoking pot and she hangs out with Kenzie all the time, so they might rope Jensen into their ways. It's crazy that we all go to the same school but live so far apart from one another. Rosenberg lives all the way out by the Everglades in Weston, a solid forty-five-minute drive from Boca. Jensen and Leigh are closer, but Gottlieb is at least thirty-five minutes away in Coral Springs. And Kenzie lives near Tomassi in Parkland. *Our time in high school was plagued with many things: worrying about how we looked, how we dressed, how we acted, and what we said; obsessing over our grades; cramming for the PSATs; getting overlooked by our crushes; getting our periods in the middle of the school day. But none of us ever worried about our safety, about someone doing something so terrible and heartless to us, to our friends. It wasn't our school where it happened, but it was our community. The name Parkland has forever become synonymous with the truly horrible thing that happened there. You can't hear it in passing or say it casually or write it in a book without thinking about what those kids went through.*

And yet I can remember what it was like, riding in my mom's car when Parkland was just another city that one of my friends happened to live in—Boca Raton, Coconut Creek, Davie, Coral Springs, West Palm Beach, Hialeah, Pembroke Pines, Cooper City, Pompano, Deerfield, Parkland—just another place on the map.

Rosenberg's house is really big; she says it's classified as a mini-mansion. Her mom doesn't work, and her dad works from home. Her sister, Cassidy, is a slut, but her parents don't know. Only we know. She's always going out on dates and coming home super late.

Tonight, when the doorbell rings, Rosenberg and I run to look through the peephole.

"Oh my God!" I say.

"What? What?" Rosenberg asks.

"That's my brother."

"Are you serious? Oh my God, let's hide!"

"Don't you dare get the door, you little bitch!" Cassidy screams from upstairs.

Rosenberg and I hide behind the staircase so they won't see us. Cassidy opens the door, and there's Brad, standing there in an outfit I've never seen him wear, holding a single rose. Cassidy took almost an hour to get ready, so she must care about the date, I think. Rosenberg laughs and says the rose is corny. I whisper for her to shut up, and we watch as Cassidy and Brad leave the house. We run to her dad's office window and watch them get in Brad's BMW and drive off for their date. Maybe I've been so wrapped up in my birthday drama that I didn't realize Brad started dating. The only girl I've ever known him to have a crush on is Julie Cohen, back when we lived in New York. He was only twelve or so, but I remember his fondness for her, the way he doted on her, and how his eyes glistened when he was around her.

Brad and I both have a sense of romance, of romantic love we want to share with others. I saw glimpses of it in that script he wrote a while ago that I still haven't fessed up to reading. Maybe we inherited it from our mom, or maybe even our dad, but I respect that he believes in love so strongly, enough to bring a girl he barely knows a rose. In kindergarten, I once wrote Robert Jenkins a love letter on tiny paper in my smallest handwriting and rolled it up like a scroll to give to him. He said it was too small to read, and I was too embarrassed, so he just threw it away.

Rosenberg concedes that my brother's car is pretty cool and she hopes she'll date a guy with a nice car one day. We joke that if it works out between them we could be sisters.

We watch MTV in her movie room and eat kettle corn with pineapple juice. Rosenberg shows me this thing in her parents' room that they call "the roller coaster." It's basically a contraption for her dad's back, but it looks like a dentist's chair without a seat that flips you upside down. Her mom comes in and asks if we can find something better to do.

Rosenberg's told me about the golf cart loophole, so we get dressed up to go meet the Vances. She does my makeup, and it's too heavy again, but I don't care. I let her borrow a top that I brought, a navy-blue short-sleeve shirt with buttons, while I wear the same one but in green. She drives us around her neighborhood, and the night air feels good on our skin. Our hair frizzes in the humidity, and it may ruin our chances, but we keep on riding.

The Vance family is old money. There are four sons, heirs to the throne: Milo the oldest, then Mitchell, Merrick, and Melvin the baby. Milo and Mitchell ask if we want to play pool, and we say sure, so we play, and I enjoy rubbing the blue chalk against the cue stick. I like the way it feels, like erasing a whiteboard at school or snapping your fingers against a plastic bag to get it open when it's stuck together, a trick my mom taught me. Rosenberg takes us to the bathroom for a pep talk and asks me which brother I want. I confirm Milo, and she still wants Mitchell. It's settled. She fixes my hair by running her hands under cold water and patting down the frizz. I try and do the same to her, but I don't know what I'm doing, so nothing changes.

Milo is drinking one of his dad's beers, a Stella Artois, and offers me a sip. The taste reminds me of trips we used to take to the Cayman Islands, when my dad ordered Heineken and always let me try. I'd sit on my dad's leg, the one he would later have problems with, and sip what tasted like game-room coins. The Vances' parents aren't home, and I think about how my parents have been leaving me at home more and more while they help Brad find the perfect college, help Brad get to his competitions, take Brad for his therapy sessions. I guess I'm okay that everything has been revolving around him. It gives me time to find out who I am, what I like, what I want.

Merrick is being punished for getting a conditional at recess, and Melvin is supposed to be asleep in his crib. Instead, he walks in with a Paddington Bear stuffed animal hanging from his hand. Brittany Rosenberg rubs his cheeks and plays with him for a while. I sit on the leather couch and drink a cup of milk that was given to me. The Vance family doesn't have bottled or filtered water, only milk, beer, and tap water. Milo sits next to me and puts his arm around my shoulder. I don't want him to feel me moving, so I hold my breath for as long as I can. I wonder if my mouth tastes like milk.

Milo and Mitchell walk us out when it's time to go, and neither of us gets a kiss. We call them later from Brittany Rosenberg's bed and pass the phone back and forth between us, and they tell us things. Milo isn't sure if he likes me yet, but I take it as promising that he talks to me in a low voice and recaps his favorite episode of *The O.C.* He has blue eyes, and his hair swoops to the side. He doesn't smell like hair gel. He smells like the ocean and our prep school and getting out of a pool late at night and cologne and rain and bedsheets.

February rolls around, and I'm in love with Milo. We talk on the phone at night, but at school he ignores me. He's in the popular crowd, and I'm just one of the Brittanys. He hasn't asked me to hang out since the infamous night when we played pool. On weekends, he frequents Chris Saul's house parties. Milo's best friend is Amber Goodman; it seems weird that his best friend is a girl, especially the most beautiful sophomore in school, but whatever. He tells me about his adventures but never invites me. I wonder why until Rosenberg pulls me aside one day at lunch.

"So I got intel on your lover boy, Milo," she says.

"Tell me everything," I say. "Unless it's bad."

"Well . . ." Rosenberg says, putting her wavy hair up in a ponytail. She's wearing her glasses today, and she looks younger again.

"Just let me have it, I can take it."

"Famous last words," Rosenberg says. "I was hanging out on the couches this morning . . ."

"How did you get up there before school? Isn't it only for seniors?"

"Yeah, but no one said anything. Chris Saul told me to come up."

"Chris Saul? Who *are* you?"

"I have no idea. And he's not even a senior. He just gets invited up there because he has the best parties, which leads me to the good news."

"Oh, there's good and bad?"

"Always."

"Go on."

"We're invited to a Valentine's Day–themed party at Chris's house this weekend."

"Are you serious?"

"I know, right?"

"Well, what's the bad news?"

"Oy, okay. Well, according to Chris Saul, Milo and Amber have been friends, like, forever, but there's a rumor that maybe it's more."

"More?"

"Yeah, like, they've hooked up."

"Hooked up?"

"Like, have gone all the way."

"Jeez. Okay. Well, does that mean I'm out of the picture? I mean, we talk, like, every night on the phone."

"He might be playing you, though."

"What the *actual* hell?"

"Guys are assholes sometimes. But, from what Chris Saul says, if you're willing to have sex with him, or at least give him a blow job, there's a chance."

"I've never given a blow job."

"Me either, but at camp last summer we all practiced on water balloons. It's super easy."

"I'm willing to give it a try."

"Milo or the balloon?"

We laugh. Lunch continues at a dull roar: the banging of trays on tables, the drone of the ice machine, the hum of kids' voices. Jensen hasn't been sitting with us. Kenzie doesn't eat, so I figure the two of them are together, not eating, somewhere. Maybe Jensen took her mom's comment to heart. A part of me hopes she's okay, while another part of me wonders if now I'm the bad friend, if I betrayed her by not inviting her to my birthday, if I should have said something else, done something else, to make things right. But then I remember what she said, what she did, and I push the thought out of my mind.

Rosenberg opens up a compact mirror and applies foundation that's way too light for her already pale skin. Her face becomes a cake layered in makeup. She takes a tool out of her makeup bag and curls her lashes. I watch and marvel at her confidence. I wonder if some of it might be rubbing off on me. Since hanging out with her, I've changed a little. I'm no longer staying at home wishing I was with boys but instead going out and meeting them, even getting invited to sophomore parties. I wonder if I'll actually give Milo a blow job at the party or maybe even have sex with him and finally lose my virginity. I know fifteen is young, but I feel ready. He's a really amazing guy, and I think it'd be worth it.

"We have to plan our outfits," Rosenberg says.

"What does a Valentine's theme entail?" I ask.

"Here's another piece of bad news. It's a *mandatory* lingerie party."

Chris Saul lives in a mansion in St. Andrews Country Club in Boca, where homes are worth millions of dollars. The neighborhood has a golf course surrounding the development, tennis courts, swimming pools, and a fine-dining restaurant on its grounds. I've been here once before, for a play date when I was eight years old. I remember coming over to a girl's house after day camp and swimming in the pool at the country club and eating blue Pop-Tarts that made me sick.

Everyone at the party is on the way to getting drunk. There are bottles of alcohol all over the place, half empty on tables, in the hands of sophomore girls who take pictures on their digital cameras, and full ones being brought out of an underground cellar by Chris Saul himself. Chris wears a black tie with no shirt and silk boxers and a matching robe that remains open. Milo Vance is at his side in a similar outfit but in red instead of black. Milo holds up a joint for Chris to take a hit, then passes it to Amber Goodman. She wears a black lace bra with high-waisted black underwear and black patent leather heels. Her hair is curled, and her lips are done in red. She looks amazing, like a Victoria's Secret model.

I had to borrow stuff from Gottlieb. Her parents just moved from Coral Springs to a neighborhood in East Boca. Even though we're not super close with her, Rosenberg said we should use her house as a base of operations, since Tomassi is in Barbados with her family and we're not really speaking to Kenzie or Jensen. I'm in a white corset that Gottlieb got at the mall and that was too small for her, and I'm wearing it with a white skirt, the same one I wore on my disaster date with Stephen, but no one else saw me in it, so it doesn't matter. Tonight, I roll it up twice to look sluttier. Rosenberg wears the same sort of outfit but in black, something she borrowed from her sister. Gottlieb wears a pink silk baby doll, and we all wear black heels that make us walk weird.

It took convincing to get here, and lies, the kind of dialogue I wish to avoid with my parents, but it had to be done. My mom didn't want to let me go *anywhere*, not even to Gottlieb's for a sleepover, because I got a B– on my history paper, but my brother intervened on my behalf, saying it's not that important, just a grade, and there's plenty of time to make up for it with the rest of the semester. Sometimes, out of nowhere, Brad will be really nice to me. It feels like an unspoken connection, the brother-sister bond, as old as time, coming into play. He sees that I'm upset by something unfair our parents are punishing me for and swoops in to save the day, the older sibling, the stronger one, wiser, more adept at handling Mom and Dad and knowing just what to say to put them at bay. He'll smile at me from across the room, the small smile of knowing what a big favor he's done. I remember one summer when he went on a teen tour to Australia, he gave me a little pink felt bear with a red heart that had a safety pin on its paw. He told me if I missed him I could wear the pin to day camp or put it on my pillow and I wouldn't be alone. I used to rub the heart and hope he was out there having fun, meeting friends, thinking of me, his little sister.

At the party, we begin drinking immediately. It seems that Chris Saul has a thing for Rosenberg, and he takes her hand and brings us to his kitchen, where more bottles are opened. She points to a bottle of vodka, and he pours us all shots in tiny glasses. We drink. It tastes like spicy water and burns the back

of my throat. We take another, and another. Then he makes
Rosenberg a mixed drink, and Milo walks in with Amber. He
ignores me and pours Amber a refill, and she tops off her red
cup with orange juice. A screwdriver. I only know what that
is because it's what Debby, played by Uma Thurman, orders in
the movie *Hysterical Blindness*. It's one of my favorites. It comes
on late at night, and I watch as, over and over again, Debby
chases after someone who's not interested.

Amber tugs at her bra straps. She has a small chest, but the
boys don't really care because she's so skinny and beautiful.
She has green eyes and shoulder-length brown hair. She always
smells like gardenias when she passes me in the hallway of the
400 Building. About the only thing we have in common is that
she wears red high-top Converse, the same ones I own. She
ignores us and only speaks to Milo, who ignores us, too. I stare at
him and will him to look at me. Amber catches my gaze and turns
to walk out of the kitchen, waits for Milo, then leaves. I start to
feel buzzed and notice that Gottlieb is already extremely drunk.
Rosenberg can hold her own ever since her incident at home,
but I've never drunk with Gottlieb before. I assumed she could
handle her alcohol, especially in the presence of sophomores.

Rosenberg goes off with Chris Saul, and I'm left to navigate
the party with Gottlieb. I figure if I can get her to a bathroom
she might throw up and feel better, or at least we can reconvene for a moment. We find Chris Saul's parents' room, and I
shut the door behind us. He had mentioned something about
his parents being in Tokyo for business, but that if we needed
to use the bathroom and the other ones were full, we should
just come in here. The room is done in shades of burgundy and

gold and is so gaudy I could die. The bed is taller than me. I have no idea how Chris Saul's parents get in that thing every night. They can probably afford to have people lift and carry them to bed. They're so freaking rich. *It's only now that I can see that the money was relative. We were so lucky to be living how we were, in beautiful beige houses with pools and country clubs. Growing up, I never thought about violence or poverty or racial inequality; it was a shock to have my bubble popped, to realize everyone I grew up with was rich, not just Chris Saul. But back then it felt like that was how things were supposed to be. We thought life would always be green golf courses and sugar sand beaches, matching Juicy sweat suits and trips to the mall. We didn't know anything different.*

Across from the bed is a fake fireplace with framed pictures sitting on the mantel. I see a portrait of Chris and his parents from his bar mitzvah. He's wearing a white suit with a yarmulke and is holding a Torah, and his mother and father are standing behind him. He's cute in that picture, always good-looking. I probably would've had a crush on him if I knew him when I was thirteen. Until last year he lived in New Jersey, though. He moved here as a freshman but got popular so quickly because of his car, a white BMW, and the fact that his parents are always gone and he can throw parties. When I compare myself to him, my life feels smaller, less important. Chris Saul pops his polo collar and sometimes even wears two polo shirts to school. He wears designer sunglasses and bleaches the tips of his hair. He's like the front man of a boy band come to life right there, strutting down the hallways. It feels almost holy to get close to him.

I look over, and Gottlieb is lying on a lounge chair, but her eyes are open.

"You all right?" I ask.

"Yeah. I just wish Aaron was here."

"Well, he doesn't go to our school, so it's kind of unlikely he'd be invited, right?"

"I know. I just miss him. We don't get to see each other that much."

Gottlieb's boyfriend goes to a high school in Coral Springs where there's no dress code, no group of Brittanys, no snotty rich kids. When she met Aaron Roth at her summer job at Cold Stone Creamery, she begged her parents to let her switch schools so she could be with him. I remember feeling bad that she would immediately trade in her friends for some boy she'd just met. But I wondered if I'd do the same thing.

"We did it, you know," Gottlieb says.

"What?"

"We had sex."

"Really?"

"Yeah. A few times, actually. He was over last weekend to watch a movie, and my parents were asleep, and we just did it. He had a condom with him and asked if I wanted to and I did, so we did it."

"What happened?" I ask, and realize it's a ridiculous question, but I want to know everything.

"Uhh . . . it hurt the first time, but I didn't bleed, because I wear tampons. But then it didn't hurt the next time or the time after. He's done it before, with his ex, which is good, because he knows what he's doing."

"Did it feel good?"

"I don't know. It's different. I guess it's like when you kiss with tongue for the first time—you just have to get used to it. I just *really* like him now. I think I love him. And I think he loves me."

"I think I love Milo Vance," I say.

"I thought he was with Amber."

"I think it's just a rumor."

"I think I have to throw up," Gottlieb says, and runs into Chris Saul's parents' bathroom. I wait for her and fix my chest in my corset. I reach into it and try to push out my boobs so they look bigger and draw more attention. As I'm doing this, the door opens and Kenzie, Leigh, and Jensen walk in. Kenzie is in a black baby-doll dress that's made of all see-through lace, Leigh is in a small red skirt and a red bra with her hair in pigtails, and Jensen is wearing a tight white dress that doesn't really fit the theme of lingerie but looks good on her. She looks at me and doesn't smile.

"Escaping to the bathroom?" Kenzie laughs.

"Gottlieb's sick," I say, and realize I should probably be more concerned, but all I can think about is that Jensen is here and I'm here and we haven't talked and it's weird. I know she's only here because of Kenzie, who gets invited to all these parties because she's Kenzie, but it still bothers me. I wanted to be the one who got invited, and now it doesn't seem so special anymore, because we're both here.

"Oh no!" Leigh rushes over to the bathroom to check on Gottlieb.

"Who did you come with?" Kenzie asks, and I can tell she's a little tipsy by the way she's hanging on to the edge of the bed.

"Rosenberg."

"How the hell did she get invited?" Kenzie asks.

"She's with Chris Saul."

"'With'?" Jensen asks, and even though it's one word, one meaningless word, I'm glad she's talking to me.

"He likes her, I think."

"He probably is using her," Kenzie says.

"For what?"

"Because he knows he can get her to do stuff."

"Or maybe he actually likes her. She's been up to the upper-classmen's couches before school. They've been talking a lot."

"Oh, little one, you have much to learn," Kenzie says, and walks toward the bathroom. "Are you done in there? I have to pee and I need to keep drinking!"

Gottlieb and Leigh walk out of the bathroom.

"I didn't get sick, but I want to go outside," Gottlieb says.

"Yeah, yeah, let's go outside!" Leigh says. "Everyone's out there now anyway."

Leigh and Gottlieb rush out the door and down the stairs, Kenzie goes to the bathroom, and it's just Jensen and me. She doesn't have a purse with her. I know she hates carrying one. Whenever we used to go out together, she'd keep her stuff in mine, and I'd tell her she was only allowed to ask three times for me to grab something for her, like if she wanted gum or lip gloss, but it always ended up being more, and it was okay. I always gave in.

"Do you have any gum?" Jensen asks.

"Yeah, one sec," I say, reaching into my purse to grab a stick. I hand it to her.

"I heard about Stephen Fraber," Jensen says.

"How?" I say, surprised.

"He told me," Jensen says. "I have English with him, re-member?"

"Oh, I forgot about that."

"Well, he said he knew we were best friends, and he wanted advice."

"Advice about what?"

"You." She stares at me like I'm the dumbest person in the world.

"What did you say?"

"Well, he just said he didn't kiss you at the movies and was wondering if I thought he ruined everything."

"Oh my God, yeah, that was so annoying."

"Why? It means he likes you if he doesn't kiss you right away."

"Or it means he's not into me at all."

"I told him you'd probably like him more because he didn't kiss you, that you're the type to take things slow. That's what I *thought*, at least."

"You *thought*?"

"Yeah." Jensen snaps her gum, and it annoys me. "Maybe you're not the type to take things slow. Some guys actually don't like girls who take things too fast."

"How would you know?" I say, and realize how mean it sounds, but I also don't care. She should have told Stephen Fraber he's a pussy. She should have told him he's a douche and chanted "no balls," like Tomassi and Rosenberg did. She should have stuck up for me. Maybe she really doesn't want to be friends. "The only guys you ever talk about are old teachers, or Tarek, who stood you up at your birthday."

"At least I had a party."

"I had a party. You just weren't invited."

"You had a sleepover. There's a difference."

"Whatever, at least I actually go out on dates with guys."

"Maybe I don't want to. Did you ever think of that? I'd rather play volleyball and spend time with my grandparents and . . ."

"Smoke?"

"You know I haven't smoked."

"No, I don't. You hang out with Kenzie and Leigh; they both smoke."

"So? That doesn't mean I've tried it."

"Just because I hang out with Rosenberg doesn't mean I'm easy."

"I know you, though. I know you want to do that stuff. I know all you think about is boys and love and whatever."

"It's not whatever. It's important. And I don't get why you care so much. I wouldn't care if you dated a guy or smoked or had sex."

"I thought we were going to smoke together the first time." Jensen looks down, and I can't tell if she's sorry for all the things we've just said or if she's getting more ammo against me for the fight. "I should have just told Stephen not to waste his time."

"You're a bitch," I say, and it feels good and bad all at once. I feel like I'm watching myself say it, or someone else is saying it and I'd hoped they'd say it for a long time, but now that they have I feel sorry for them, like they've just made a big mistake.

"Who's a bitch?" Kenzie stumbles out of the bathroom.

"I am, apparently," Jensen says, and the bold girl I met in fourth grade is the one who stands before me. She's strong and scary and might even punch me in the stomach.

"Um, you're kind of a bitch," Kenzie says to me, "for not even inviting us to your birthday sleepover thing, but whatever."

"Let's go," Jensen says to Kenzie. Jensen's face is unreadable, and I can't tell if she's happy or sad, or if it's pure anger. I feel like anyone would be able to tell I'm afraid, like my fear is so easy to read. I can't believe I called Brittany Jensen a bitch. She's my best friend, *was* my best friend. I'm not sure what to think. Jensen and Kenzie lock arms and walk out of Chris Saul's parents' room.

I need to find Rosenberg. I need another drink. I hurry downstairs to look for her. I'm frantic, and my heart is racing. I'm so mad at Jensen. I'm so upset I could cry. I want my mom. She doesn't even know where I am. She thinks I'm at Gottlieb's house, painting my nails or watching a movie. She doesn't even know Jensen and I are fighting like this. I want her, but I also want to find Rosenberg. I check Chris Saul's room, and the door is locked. I think he locked it for the party, but he might be in there with Rosenberg. She could be giving him a blow job.

It seems like everyone's made their way outside, so I join them. Gottlieb and Leigh are dancing by themselves near the pool. The older girls are lying on lounge chairs, smoking cigarettes and drinking straight out of champagne bottles. Some guys are rolling blunts at a table.

A few couples hold hands by the edge of the property, the part that looks out onto the lake and the golf course. I watch them sway in the night. They are the promise of something other than fighting with my best friend. They are drunk and happy and kissing and touching. The palm trees look like fireworks above them. The night belongs to them. The party is the backdrop for their love story.

I spot Milo and Amber. They don't see me, but I watch them together. She sits on his lap and wraps her arms around his neck. He pulls her in for a kiss, and I die inside. The rumors are true. Leigh grabs me and tells me Rosenberg is with Chris Saul in his room. She asks if I'm okay, and I tell her yes because I don't want anyone to know what I know. Gottlieb joins us, and we share a bottle of champagne. We drink until Gottlieb's dad comes to pick us up. Rosenberg appears as if by magic, and the three of us get into the car. We don't say bye to Kenzie or Leigh or Jensen. We're giggling and sloppy, and Gottlieb's dad jokes about how we must be drunk. We don't try to hide it. We just are, and he lets us be. When we get to her house, he says to get our giggles out by running laps around the house. We take off our heels and our feet get wet in the grass as we do cartwheels and handstands and jumping jacks in the yard. It's after one in the morning. The party is still happening at Chris Saul's house. Parties are happening everywhere. Girls are fighting, getting their hearts broken, and doing all the things they're not supposed to do.

· FOURTEEN ·

Somehow it's arranged for Leigh and me to have a sleep-over. I've been eating my lunch in the library lately, keeping to myself as much as possible. But one day my mom comes home from the salon and tells me that she met Leigh's mom and they've made plans for us to get together.

I arrive at her house on a warm Saturday afternoon. Leigh wants to go swimming, and I haven't packed appropriately. She lets me borrow a bathing suit, a black bikini with pink stars on the boobs. She braids my hair, and we go into the pool. She's good at gymnastics. We do handstands underwater. We race from one side of the pool to the other. I keep winning, and it feels good to win. She's not upset, though. She just likes to play. There's a jungle gym in her backyard for her little brother, Bobby, who's at a friend's house, and we play on it in our wet bathing suits. Our bodies dry as we swing from the monkey bars and climb atop the wooden structure. Her family has a trampoline, and we jump and sit and bounce each other. Popcorn. We look like popcorn when we bounce. She asks if I want to smoke—her cousin Kasey is coming over and he always brings weed—and I say, "Sure." Jensen is probably smoking with Kenzie. It's okay, because I have other friends, but it's also not okay, because no one is like her.

Leigh makes us tea with two drops of honey and a sliver of a lemon. I'm surprised she knows how to use a knife. I don't know how to cut fruits or vegetables or meat or cook or clean. I am my mother's baby, and I don't know how to do anything that she does. Leigh lends me a sweatshirt, and we sit at the kitchen table and eat dates from a bowl. They're chewy and fat, and they remind me of being little in New York City and eating raisins at my friend Clarissa's house. I didn't like her very much, but I was there all the time. I was jealous of her, because she had a life-size playhouse complete with a kitchen. She was mean and made fun of me, and she loved those damn raisins.

I wonder where Leigh's parents are, but they work or they're out and they're not coming home. Kasey shows up. He's seventeen and a junior and drives a green truck, and he's a little wild-looking, a little rough, but he has blond hair and green eyes. He's cute, and Leigh says Kenzie tried to hook up with him once and it made her really mad, so I keep my distance. Kasey's eyes are red, and I know he's been smoking, and I'm nervous, because I don't really want to do it yet. I do, but I don't. I'm not sure how it'll make me feel, and what if Jensen really is waiting and I'm the bad friend and not her? So I try to make up reasons why I can't smoke—maybe I can feign a headache or a stomachache, but that's embarrassing, and I don't want to get picked up and go home early.

It's dinnertime, and Leigh says she doesn't feel good—she took one of her mom's pills and it's making her tired—and

Kasey rolls his eyes and says she does this all the time, and one time she had to go to the hospital and get her stomach pumped, and I don't remember anyone telling me that story, and I realize I don't know Leigh that well. Kasey puts her to bed; she's still in her bathing suit, and I worry about her, but he says she just needs to sleep, because the pill makes you tired. It's something you just need to sleep off. He tells me it's for people who worry, and I wonder if I'll ever need something like that because of how much I worry all the time. *Years later, when I went on Wellbutrin, Lexapro, Celexa, I found that none of them made me fall asleep, but they did make me quiet, make my mind quiet. The medications also made my ears ring, gave me nightmares, forced me to think about dying. After so many prescriptions, so many bad experiences with drugs, I felt helpless until I found the right thera- pist. It turned out I just needed someone to talk to. For me, talking helps more than anything.*

Kasey says we don't have to smoke if I don't want to, and I don't say anything. He takes my hand, and we go back to the jungle gym. He wraps his arms around me and picks me up and spins me around and says, "You're just a little thing, aren't you?" I want him, and I'm shy, and I'm melting, and I feel good and anxious, and I want him to keep holding me. Leigh is in bed, sleeping off her worries, and her parents won't be home until late, and Kasey is holding me.

Kasey grabs my face and says he needs to take me on a date before he kisses me, and I say, "This is kind of like a date."

"No, a real date," he says.

I look at him so dreamily. He leans in to kiss me, but then we hear noise coming from the house, so we run back, and

Leigh's parents are home early. I wake up Leigh, and she's as good as new and bounces downstairs and hugs her parents. Her mom is so blonde and beautiful, with fake boobs and expensive jewelry and tight jeans, and her dad is so handsome and wears a suit. They tell Kasey he has to go, and Leigh and I walk him out. He asks Leigh if we could have a moment alone. When she's skipped off back to the house, Kasey asks for my number, and I say it, and he repeats it back, and I smile. He says, "I'm going to kiss you on our date," and he drives off in his green truck. I walk back to the house and feel like the world has finally shifted, like anything is possible again.

Later, Leigh says she knows that Kasey wants me. "He'll be good practice," she says.

My mom wants to meet Kasey before he takes me out. She agrees to drop me off at the mall, where she can meet him in a public place, and then leave so we can have dinner at my favorite Japanese place. From there, we will go to the movies and hopefully have our long-awaited kiss. We only spoke on the phone once to plan the date, but I've been thinking about Kasey holding me, our eyes meeting as we climbed the jungle gym, the way it seemed like he wanted me so bad. If only we could truly be alone, then maybe it would happen.

I wear jeans this time, after much arguing with my mom, and a tight shirt that's low and shows off my cleavage, with an added push-up bra. My mom buys me a new pink handbag that's so small it fits only a lip gloss and a pack of gum. She drives me to the mall, and we wait in the car.

"How'd you meet this boy again?" she asks.

"He's not a boy. He's a . . . guy, or, like, a man. He's a junior. Leigh's cousin."

"How do you know he's not a serial killer?"

"I really don't think he's a serial killer."

"Son of Sam lived in my building. No one thought he was a serial killer, either. He was a nice guy. I saw him at the ice cream parlor once."

"Can you stop?"

"What does he look like?"

"He's cute."

"That helps."

"He has blond hair and green eyes, and he's tall."

"Everyone's taller than you."

"Well, he's, like, *really* tall. Like six feet or something. That's him." I see Kasey walking up to the restaurant. My mom puts on her emergency signal, and we get out of the car. Kasey is polite. My mom doesn't embarrass me. I feel like an adult.

My mom walks back to her car, waves, drives off. Kasey and I enter the restaurant. We order quickly and retrieve our individual stir-fry bowls, then walk through the line of vegetables and sauces. I make sure not to get any onions or broccoli, anything that will get stuck in my teeth or make my breath stink. Once we're seated, we eat mostly in silence. The restaurant is busy on a Friday night, and I remember the possibility of seeing the girls here. We frequent this place, and it's totally possible one or more of them might be here. I go to the bathroom in hopes of seeing one of them, anyone except Jensen, but it's empty, and I check my eyeliner in the mirror. There's only a minor smudge underneath one eye, so I fix it and return to the table. Kasey sucks on a toothpick. He says, "Let's get out of here," and I nearly die.

He drives us to the theater in his green truck. He drives past the regular lot and to the parking structure, where we go up to the roof. We park, and as I'm getting out, he takes my hand and helps me down from the seat. It's high. I think I'm in love. He buys tickets for *50 First Dates*. He says, "I know chicks love rom-coms," and I smile. I wonder when he's going to kiss me.

We sit in the very back of the theater, all the way up the stairs, where no one usually sits. The theater is half empty and is mostly full of couples and groups of teenage girls. I think about how this is a movie I'd probably see with the girls if I wasn't here with Kasey. I know Jensen wouldn't want to see it, even though people sometimes tell her she looks like Drew Barrymore. The previews start, and Kasey grabs my hand in the dark.

"Shit," he whispers.

"What?" I ask.

"I forgot to ask if you wanted anything."

"I'm okay. Thanks."

"I'm gonna go grab a slushie. Be right back."

He lets go of my hand, and I'm alone in the dark. The previews roll and I wait for Kasey. I pick at my cuticles and bite a spot on my thumb where one is lifting off the nail bed. It's a bad habit, one my mom has tried to stop forever. She's gone as far as to get me nail polish that makes you sick if you ingest it, but I got used to the taste and would lick it off anyway. Or one time she got me gloves for at night so I wouldn't pick, but I flung them off in my sleep. Nothing works to get me to quit doing it, but sometimes I can control it better than others. Not now, though; I'm too nervous, wondering what's going to happen once Kasey comes back.

Kasey comes back, and the movie starts, and he grabs my hand, and I lean my head on his shoulder, and he offers me a sip of his slushie, but I say no, and he drinks it until it's gone, and then the movie is over.

We walk back to the parking garage and up the stairs, and when we get to the car he pulls me toward him and kisses me. His tongue tastes like the color blue, blue raspberry, juicy and sweet, tangy.

"I didn't think you would kiss me," I say.

"I can't do it in the theater. That's tacky."

"Oh."

"You think I'm just some tacky guy who's gonna kiss you during a lovey-dovey movie?" He laughs.

"No. You're classy."

"You're pretty."

We kiss again, and the night air feels good. It's dark outside. The temperature dropped while we were in the warmth of the theater. I'm glad I'm wearing jeans, or else my legs would be cold. I shiver, but only because I'm so entranced with Kasey. He helps me into the truck and begins to drive.

"I think it's about time I take you home, so your parents don't worry," he says.

"When will I see you again?" I ask.

Kasey pulls over at the edge of the parking lot.

"I know we go to different schools, but I like you, so I guess

I can see you on weekends and stuff. Or, if your parents are cool with it, I could come over sometime, take you to the beach—I don't know. We can make it work."

I think about Brittany Gottlieb and her boyfriend, Aaron Roth, and how they go to different schools but they make it work. I think maybe Kasey could sneak over and take my virginity and we could get close and fall in love.

"I'd like that," I say.

"Cool. I'm glad."

We stare at each other for a moment, and then Kasey puts the truck in drive.

"Where do you live?" he asks.

"Woodfield Country Club," I say.

"What street's it on?"

All the streets inside my neighborhood have made-up names that don't matter once you're outside the subdivision. I know my mailing address, but I have no idea what street the country club's entrance is on. I haven't had my driving lessons yet, and my parents won't let me drive with a permit until I do. I don't really pay attention when they—or anyone else—drive. I just sort of drift off or imagine the way I'd like my life to be.

"I don't know," I say.

"What do you mean, you don't know?"

"I'm not sure what street it's off. I know my subdivision is called Bay Creek."

"Yeah, but what's the intersection?"

"I don't know."

"How do you not know where you live?"

"I've never driven there before."

"You don't have to drive somewhere to know where a place is. You just have to, I don't know, pay attention."

I can tell Kasey is mad. I try being cute to make it better, a tactic I've always wanted to try when a boy is angry with me. Especially since Kasey just established we're pretty much together, I know I have him wrapped around my finger.

"I'm sorry," I say, leaning over the center console and grabbing his arm.

"Me too." He pushes me away. "I think maybe you're a little too young to . . . to handle this."

"Because I don't know my intersection?"

"That says a lot about you. I mean, like, what else don't you know?"

"I know my address!"

"That doesn't help when you're in a subdivision! I need crossroads. I need something more. It just shows you're not mature enough to . . ."

"I am mature. I'm *very* mature."

"Yeah, I can tell from your little pink purse."

"That's mean. This bag is cute."

"It *is* cute. And *you're* cute. But that's the thing. I think you're too young for me. You should be dating guys your own age."

"I'm fifteen. It's not *that* much younger than you. Two years. That's it."

"I'm going to stop at a gas station and call one of my buddies, see where Woodfield Country Club is, and take you home."

"I don't want to go home."

"Well, you have to."

Kasey drives us to a gas station and gets out to use the pay phone. He nods while he talks, laughs a little. I sit in the truck and press myself deep into the seat, trying to melt myself into it. I'm so embarrassed. I've just blown my chances with the only junior who's ever looked at me. I could have lost my virginity to him. I could have smoked with him. We could have been just like Brittany Gottlieb and Aaron Roth.

Kasey returns to the truck and says he knows how to get there. We drive the rest of the way in silence. The lights are on in my house, and even from my seat in the truck, I can see my mom in the window of my dad's den, sitting there, watching, waiting for her little girl to come home.

FIFTEEN

Spring break falls on the second week in March. It's the first year my parents don't decide to drag Brad and me to the Bahamas. My mom asks if I want to take a friend and go to Disney World for a few days, but I'm so sick of everyone and I don't really want to do anything.

But once break starts, I realize this means I'm going to be spending the whole week in my room. When I was in sixth grade, my mom let me redo my bedroom. We hired a decorator and everything. I wanted it to feel like "Fall in New York," so we hired an artist to paint that dumb tree on one wall and hang a swinging seat next to my window. I eventually got scared of the swing, the way it moved and spun at night without anyone inside of it, so my dad took it down. There's still a gold hook in the popcorn ceiling, useless.

Now I hate my room. The artist thought it would be cute to paint some happy squirrels around the tree, a liberty he took that I did not appreciate. My mom thought it was cute, too, but I've since pushed my bed to the middle of the wall to cover them. There are three of them, and I hate them all. My room is so childish, and I wish it was simple and yellow like Brittany Gottlieb's room, or done in classy pastels like Kenzie's room. Jensen has had the same white wicker furniture since she was a baby, but her mom keeps promising that this summer, when she's off at sleepaway camp, she will redo the room. I just want a normal room, free of squirrels and foliage.

I'm into this old Red Hot Chili Peppers CD, *Californication*, that I stole from my brother. I listen to it over and over again on my stereo and lie on different pieces of furniture in my room—my bed, the floor, the couch where Jensen used to sleep when she came over. I think about calling her, and I almost dial her number but call Rosenberg instead. She doesn't answer. I go online and see that Stephen Fraber messaged me when I was "away." He says he's sorry about how the date went and that he just got his license and a car. He wants to know if he can make it up to me. I don't respond.

It's Monday, and even though I did absolutely nothing the first weekend of spring break, I'm tired all the time. My body has trouble getting up and moving. I just want to sleep. My brother has a college visit at the University of Miami, and my parents are going down with him for the night. They're not staying in a hotel, but they'll be back late, Mom tells me. They leave around noon, and I'm still in pajamas. I make myself a tuna salad sandwich, and it reminds me of Jensen, because that's her favorite. I'm still hungry after, and I think about making waffles, too, but I know I'll feel sick if I keep eating. Instead, I eat a Blow Pop that was in the cabinet for some reason. We don't usually have candy, but it must be left over from Halloween. It's grape-flavored, which sucks, but I eat it anyway.

There's an Indiana Jones marathon on TV, and I watch for a while and paint my nails. I see the love story unfold between Indy and Marion and admire her brazenness and how she can knock back all those drinks, how *she* seduces Indy and isn't helpless.

I call Stephen Fraber, and he answers on the first ring.

"What are you doing?" I ask.

"I just got home from a friend's house."

"Did you drive?"

"Ha! Yeah. I have a car now. It's not like your brother's Beemer or anything, but it's pretty cool. It's a Mustang, all black, but it's old. What are you doing?"

"Do you want to come over?"

"Right now?"

"My parents are in Miami with my brother, looking at the University of Miami. They won't be back till late."

"UM is amazing. Damn. I want to go there when I'm—"

"Do you want to come over?"

"Hell yeah. Like, now?"

"Yeah. How far are you?"

"From Boca? About thirty minutes, I guess, maybe more."

"Okay. I have to call you into the gate. See ya."

"Bye."

I rush into the shower to shave my whole body. We're definitely going to have sex. There's no way Stephen Fraber is getting out of hooking up with me this time. Even though I planned it, the thought of losing my virginity becomes real when I get out of the shower. I look at myself in my bathroom mirror and feel so young without makeup on or my hair done.

I look like a kid. By the end of the night, I'll be a woman. I'll have accomplished something big over spring break, something to be proud of, something worth telling the girls. I'm all ready for it to be over, for it to be a story.

I decide to wear something that's easy to take off. I put on athletic shorts made of sweatpants material that make my butt look good and a white T-shirt with no bra. I've never done this before, but I see it in the movies where girls have guys over and they sleep together. The girl is wearing a white T-shirt with no bra, and it's really sexy. The camera always shows the guy taking off the girl's shirt from behind and you see her back with no bra and there's just skin. That's what I imagine Stephen Fraber will do.

He calls at the guard gate. I let him in and finish getting ready. He rings my doorbell, and I hurry downstairs. I open the door, and he's standing there in jeans and a black T-shirt. He looks older—like, way older than he did on our last date, only a couple months ago. Sixteen looks good on him. I'm glad he's here. His car is parked on the street, right in front of my mailbox. It's getting dark and there won't be mail so it's fine.

"Come in," I say, trying to be cool and coy and not nervous.

He walks in, and we go to the kitchen for some reason.

"Are you hungry?" I ask.

"Not really."

"I don't have much food here. I have waffles, but that's more like breakfast than dinner. We could order a pizza . . ."

"Isn't that how, like, every single porno ever starts?" he asks.

"I wouldn't know. I don't watch porn."

"You've never seen a porno?"

"I mean, I've seen them, but I don't watch them," I say, which doesn't even make sense.

"I watch porn when I jerk off."

"That's cool."

"Do you ever do that?"

"What?"

"Like, touch yourself?"

"I'd rather someone else do that for me," I say, and I can't believe myself. Who am I? I guess I'm someone who wants Stephen Fraber to make a move on me already.

"I can definitely do that for you. Want to go to your room?"

I nod, and we run upstairs. I close the door slowly and lock it, even though no one's home.

"Have you ever done it?" I ask, as I get into my bed and take off my shorts.

"No, but I want to, with you."

He takes off his shoes and leaves on his socks. He walks toward my bed.

"Take those off," I say.

"My pants?"

"Yeah, those, too, but I meant the socks."

"Ha! Okay."

He takes them off and gets into bed with me. We start kissing, and he's actually the best kisser I've ever kissed. He doesn't use too much tongue, like other guys, and he leans to the left, which feels more comfortable to me for some reason than leaning to the right. He gets really into it and I feel him start to get hard. I can feel myself getting wet, so I tell him, "I'm so wet," because I know girls say that to guys and it turns them on even more. It works, and he gets even harder. He's rubbing up against me and it feels good and I think that sex will feel a hundred times better than this.

All of a sudden he takes off my underwear and smiles.

"What are you doing?" I ask, a little freaked out.

"I want to eat you out."

"Have you done that before?"

"No, but I know how to do it."

"How?"

"Porn. And my friend who's done it."

"Okay."

"It's okay?"

"Yeah. I've just never had someone do that . . . but I want you to."

"Okay. Let me know if it feels good."

He kisses in between my legs, and at first it feels weird, like walking into the wrong classroom after you take a bathroom break and forget what period it is. Then I realize I'm supposed to be enjoying myself, so I start moaning a little but not too much. But then it really does feel good. He's massaging me with his tongue, kissing me like how he kissed my mouth, but lower and more intense, more intent, more passionate. I start to get lightheaded and warm and my body tingles and my breath is uncontrollable. I feel myself tighten around him and what he's doing and I shiver and shake and push him off me.

"You want me to stop?" he asks, and wipes his mouth with the back of his hand.

"Something just happened."

"Did you come?"

"What?"

"Like, have an orgasm?"

"I think so."

"Did it feel good?" he asks, smiling with eyes so big.

"Yeah. It felt amazing."

"Holy shit. That's awesome. That's so hot."

I smile, and I know it's about to happen. He takes off his jeans and I pull off my shirt. He kisses me and grabs my boobs and then takes off his shirt and I feel his chest against mine and he's in his boxers and I'm completely naked and I'm ready to have sex with Stephen Fraber, I'm ready for him to take my virginity and for him to lose his to me and for us to do it. I hear something that could only be a violent thunderstorm rising to the peak of its fury in a matter of mere seconds, or the unmistakable sound of the garage door opening.

"My parents are home!"

"Shit!"

We both get dressed as fast as possible. I succeed because I have a lot less clothing to put on, but Stephen only makes it to his top half because he can't find his socks and my mom is knocking on the door because it's locked. I throw his clothes into the bathroom.

"One sec!" I yell.

I put my hair in a messy bun and straighten the bedsheets and answer the door.

"Why is your door locked?" Mom asks. I'm still eyeing the room for a pair of socks when I realize that she doesn't know someone is here. Stephen parked in the street, so his car could belong to anyone—someone else who parked mistakenly in front of our house. It happens all the time. A neighbor's problem, not mine. But then Stephen comes out of the bathroom, and I see he's wearing his shoes without any socks.

"Hi," he says to my mom.

"Oh, I didn't know Stephen was coming over. Why didn't you tell me?" she asks. She doesn't even seem mad. "What are you doing?" She surveys the room but remains smiley and upbeat. I wonder if she can tell I just had an orgasm—like, if there's some mother-daughter energy pulsating through the room and she knows her little girl is not so little anymore. I sit on the bed and feel Stephen's socks under my butt.

"We watched a movie, but Stephen's about to leave, because it's getting late and all," I say.

"Yeah. I have a curfew, so I gotta get going."

My mom picks up my school bag and moves it to my desk. While she does this, I reach under the covers and fish out the socks and toss them to Stephen. He shoves them into his pockets and shrugs at me.

"Sorry this place is such a mess," my mom says to Stephen, and her eyes return to me. "I'm always telling her to get her crap off the floor and put everything away. Does your room look like this, Stephen?"

"No. It's much worse."

"Jeez Louise! Your mom lets you get away with that?"

"All right, well, I'll walk Stephen out," I say, to break the tension. Stephen follows me downstairs as I skip steps and race to the door. We walk to his car, and it's dark out. The whole world seems different now. It seems so easy for two people to have each other like that, to know sex is possible, fathomable. I feel older, more mature, cooler. I go to give Stephen a kiss, but he says he probably tastes like me. I tell him I don't care, but he gets into his car anyway and drives off. I stand out there for a few minutes longer. I want this feeling to last. It's cool to have done something like that with a guy. It feels like an accomplishment, a step up on the ladder of growing up.

When I get back inside, my mom asks why I didn't tell her I was having company. I say I thought I told her, and even though we both know I'm lying, she lets it go. What's done is done, and a boy was at our house without her permission. Maybe she wants to believe that nothing happened, that we just watched a movie and he had his arm around me, because we're still kids in her eyes. Maybe she wants me to be happy, and seeing me smile for the first time in a long time makes her happy, too.

I fall asleep thinking about Stephen Fraber going down on me. I replay it over and over and over again, until it seems like a dream I'm having. It's not until I wake up the next morning and my underwear is still soaking wet that I know it was real.

$\mathcal{M}$y English teacher assigned us work over the break, but I don't mind. I love reading, and it'll take my mind off obsessing over what happened and what might still happen and what my mom *thinks* happened with Stephen. We're supposed to read *The Outsiders* and write a five-page essay about what it means to be "an outsider." It's not until I go to read the book halfway through the week that I realize it's in my locker at school.

My mom drives me, and I'm praying the campus is open. There's a security guard at the gate, and he tells us the school is actually open for testing and that I can run in and go to my locker, but to be quiet and not disrupt the PSATs in progress. We pull up to the 400 Building, and I run inside. The hallway is the quietest I've ever seen it. No girls gossiping by the lockers, no boys roughhousing or talking shit, no teachers yelling at everyone to get in the classroom and sit down and be quiet. I'm glad no one's around, since I'm wearing an oversize pajama shirt underneath a hoodie and sweatpants with sneakers. My hair is in a messy bun, and I'm not wearing any makeup. I wouldn't be caught dead like this on a normal school day.

Someone comes out of the bathroom, and I hurry to my locker. I assume it's just one of the PSAT kids taking a break, but it's Amber Goodman. She's wearing a baggy sweatshirt and black leggings and slippers. She's holding her lower back with one hand and looks like she's in pain.

"Are you okay?" I blurt, and it comes out louder than expected since no one else is here in the hall.

She notices me immediately and smiles. "Yeah. Thanks. I got a tattoo yesterday, and it hurts like a bitch. Wanna see it?"

I nod, and she walks over to me. I can't believe Amber Goodman is actually talking to me. She lifts up her sweatshirt and peels off a thin layer of plastic wrap to reveal a hand with an eye in the middle.

"It's a hamsa," she says. "It's supposed to protect you from negative energies. The eye keeps away the evil eye. It looks gross now, but it should heal in, like, a week. Kinda stupid to get one now, because I can't go to the beach or swim or anything, but it'll heal soon."

"Cool."

"What are you doing at school?"

"Oh, I forgot my book for English and we have a project. What about you?"

"I get tutoring for math every Wednesday at this time, but I forgot about the stupid testing this week. My parents are monsters and make me go. I don't really care about math. What's the book?"

"*The Outsiders.*"

"I love that book!"

"You like to read?"

"Yes. Do you think I'm some idiot who has no interests or hobbies?"

"No, no. Not at all. I think you're, like . . ."

"Like what? A slut? Crazy? Psycho?"

"The coolest girl in school. And you're dating Milo Vance, so, like—"

"I'm not dating Milo Vance. He's, like, my best friend. Sorry, I've just been getting a lot of shit lately from my girlfriends because I'm hanging out with him and his friends a lot. They just don't understand that I get along better with guys. Girls cause so much drama, and I'm just over it."

"Yeah, that's kind of where I'm at now, too."

"I actually heard you liked Milo, but I didn't think it was true . . ."

"Where did you hear that?"

"From him. He said you guys talk a lot, but I didn't think it was true, because you're too smart for him. I love the kid, don't get me wrong, but he's . . . I don't know how to say it without sounding terrible, but . . . you're too good for him."

I'm shocked when she says it: Amber Goodman telling me I'm too good for Milo Vance. I wonder if she's only telling me that because she really likes him and doesn't want me to interfere or if she really means it and I am better than him and need to move on. Maybe she just feels bad for me.

"I'm serious," she says. "You're smart, and that's worth something. People think of you as the smart girl in your grade. You know how people see me? As a skank."

"I just can't imagine why girls wouldn't like you. My friends think it's *cool* if you hook up with someone."

"They just think I flirt with all the guys and sleep with everyone. And it's not true. I've never even had sex. God, don't tell anyone that. It's embarrassing, but it's true. I just don't get along with girls, because . . . well, my dad says because they're jealous of me, but I don't know, they're just bitches."

I try my best to keep back the tears. I'm reminded of calling Jensen a bitch at the party, when really I was just mad about the situation with Milo. None of this is really even worth getting upset over, but it hurts. It seems like even Amber has a hard time with it. I wonder if I should ask her for advice, but the tears start to fall before I can even speak.

"Are you okay?" she asks.

"I don't know," I manage to say, and look down, away from her pretty face. "It's just . . . hard." I begin to cry.

"Sweetie, it's okay!" She puts her arms around me and hugs me. I cry into her sweatshirt.

"Hey, what are you doing today?" Amber asks. "Do you wanna go to the mall and get coffee or something? I have my dad's car. We can just chill out and relax."

I really want to go and spend the day with Amber, but I remember my mom waiting outside telling me to hurry up.

"My mom drove me. She's waiting for me, actually. I'm sorry."

"Don't be sorry. Go be with your mom. I wish my mom was still around. You're lucky," Amber says.

I think about how hard it must be not to have a mom. I'm not sure exactly what happened, but I know Amber lives with her dad and her mom isn't in the picture anymore. There're rumors that she died, was murdered, left Amber's dad because he cheated on her, etc. But it makes me think about what it would be like if my dad had to be the one to raise Brad and me, since our dad commutes. He didn't want to risk trying to find work down south, since his paycheck was what kept our family alive. He explained to us that lots of dads commute to their jobs, but Brad had a hard time understanding this. I used to go with my mom every week, as often as I could, to the airport in West Palm Beach to pick up my dad when he returned for the weekend. I'd watch my parents kiss, and my dad would hug me, and I'd feel so special, like we were a happy little family. Brad said Dad was abandoning us, that he should be home to actually raise us, but I guess I just realized he was doing it to support us, so we could have nice things and go nice places. My mom was always the one to take us to our checkups and meetings, to Disney World and museums, to take care of us in that way, while my dad was solely responsible for putting money in the bank, loving us in that way, a different way. As I stand in front of Amber, I wonder what life would be like if it was the other way around, if I was in her shoes, our same red Converse.

"Thank you, Amber."

"I know I probably seem like a bitch, but I have feelings— we all do. Us book nerds gotta stick together." She smiles again.

"I hope your tattoo heals fast."

"Thanks, babe. I just have to stop picking at it and let it be."

I grab the book from my locker, and Amber walks out with me. My mom is waiting and gives me a look like, *What took so long?* Amber waves bye as I get into my car and she continues walking to the parking lot.

"Who was that?" my mom asks.

"Amber," I say. "She's nice."

I never spoke to Amber again in person, but I continued to see her in the hallways at school over the coming years. She always had a new boyfriend: the quarterback of the football team, the star pitcher of the baseball team, some older guy she met at a college party. When she graduated, she moved across the country, and I followed her life online. She went to school somewhere with seasons, and she enjoyed hiking in the snow and being in nature, the polar opposite of Florida. She fell in love with someone she thought she'd be with forever, but he broke her heart time and time again, until they split and she moved back to Florida. I saw her at the mall when we were both home for periods of time. We didn't speak, but we nodded at each other. Two girls who'd had a rough go of it. She eventually met the real love of her life, and they got married and had a baby, all within the span of one year. I "like" the photos, but when I go to write a comment, I never know what to say. I want to thank her for being kind to me. I want to tell her she's going to be okay even though she already is. Or maybe I still want her to tell me I'll be okay, like she did for me that day at the lockers. I want her to know how much it meant to be seen.

I start reading *The Outsiders* on the drive back home, and by the end of the day I'm almost finished. I keep thinking about Amber, though, and I wonder if she went to the mall and walked around alone with a coffee. I imagine that she did, and that somewhere out there she's having a nice time.

Kenzie calls me and invites me to a party in Coral Springs, which isn't far from where she lives in Parkland. She says it'll be the best party of spring break. I wasn't aware there were any other parties over the break, but I guess I wouldn't know, since I haven't gone out at all. I ask her if any of the other girls are going, and she says all of them are either grounded or away.

"Gottlieb got grounded because her parents found a condom in her trash can, Tomassi is in Cancún until Sunday, Leigh is also grounded for taking her mom's pills—again—and Jensen is in the Keys with her neighbors or something," Kenzie explains.

"What about Rosenberg?" I ask.

"Oh, I just didn't want to invite her because she's a little slut."

This is ironic coming from Kenzie, but I press on anyway. "What do you mean?"

"Well, I know you guys are friends or whatever, but I heard she had sex with Chris Saul, like, just to get popular. That's, like, not a reason you sleep with someone. I don't even think she likes him. They have nothing in common."

Kenzie usually hooks up with older guys, but maybe she does it because she really likes them. It's just weird that she's judging Rosenberg when she herself has done way worse. I also realize I'm a last-resort invite for the party, but it is a party, and I want to go.

"You in?"

"I just thought you didn't like me, I mean, after what you said."

"Oh, right. Well, I'm sorry I called you a bitch. I didn't really care about the sleepover anyway."

"Thank you," I say, thinking it might be the best way to accept someone's apology without adding to it and apologizing for something else in return.

"So. Do you want to go with me or not?"

My mom drops me off at Kenzie's house. I haven't slept at Kenzie's house all year, mostly out of choice. She has a wild reputation, and I'd rather have sleepovers at my house, where there's some kind of form and structure. Her parents are never home, and such is the case when I arrive early on Saturday night. My mom thinks we're having a normal sleepover. She trusts me, and it's starting to kill me inside. I almost want her to ground me or tell me what I'm doing is wrong so I can stay in my room forever. I've heard my parents say that my brother has social anxiety, and I'm starting to think I have it, too. I just have a hard time being around people, and I overthink things constantly. Sometimes even the lunchroom is too much to handle. But to be honest, eating alone in the library isn't so bad.

Kenzie says I can borrow whatever I want to wear tonight, since nothing I brought is "appropriate," which in this case actually means the opposite. I only brought jeans and plain shirts, but Kenzie picks out this pair of light blue Buffalo jeans that are too small on her and a gold V-neck shirt for me to wear. Everything is super tight, but it looks good. I'm wearing my favorite push-up bra, and it makes my boobs look huge. She wears dark jeans and a baby-blue top that shows off her cleavage, too. We both straighten our hair, and she asks me to do her makeup. I'm not really good at it, but she just wants me to pamper her. When I'm done, she says I didn't use enough eyeliner, and I feel really bad until she simply puts on more and then says I did great.

Since neither of us drives, Kenzie's boyfriend, Charles, is picking us up and taking us to the party.

"He's so annoying," Kenzie says, running the flat iron over her hair as I sit on her bed and watch.

"What do you mean?"

"Do you want perfume? You can grab one from my dresser. Just don't use the Juicy one—that's what I'm wearing, and we can't smell the same."

"Okay." I get up and walk to her dresser. There are at least twenty perfumes. The bottles are all different; one has a puff that sprays, one is in the shape of a girl's body, one is a bouquet of flowers where the flowers lift up and apart to reveal the spritzer. It reminds me of my aunt Elena. She has more than a hundred perfumes in the guest bathroom of her house. Every time I'm there, I open a new one and try it out on my neck, like she taught me. I find the Juicy perfume, and it smells so good, just like Kenzie always smells. It makes me wonder why she even has any other ones.

"Fine, you can use that one. It's the best anyway, I know."

"Thanks." I dab some on my neck. "Why is Charlie annoying?" I ask.

"Ugh. He just follows me around like a puppy dog. He always wants to hang out. For Valentine's Day, he made me chocolate-covered strawberries."

"That sounds sweet."

"Sweet if I wanted to gain ten pounds. I think I'm going to break up with him, tonight maybe. Do you think I should?"

"I mean . . ."

"It's nice to have a boyfriend, but I should be dating around, seeing what else is out there."

"I guess . . ."

"Although, Charlie is popular and gets invited to all the parties. But his friend Pierce Stein is such a hottie. It's so hard!"

The house phone rings, and the guard at the gate tells Kenzie that Charlie is here. She says, "Let him in," and I tell her I'm going to use the bathroom before we leave. I don't even have to pee. I just want to look at myself in the mirror and remember what it's like to be with a cool girl for the night, a girl who has all the options and choices in the world and doesn't even care. Kenzie will probably always be like this, I think. She'll always have everything. *Kenzie ended up getting into the most popular sorority in college, becoming a real-estate agent, and marrying the "perfect" guy. Her smile never seems real to me, though—like maybe it's just about checking off all the boxes for her. There's a light in her eyes that's missing. My therapist might call something like this a projection of self, but something about her life just feels fake to me, like it's all an illusion of happiness.*

"You can borrow shoes, too!" Kenzie screams. Her feet are two sizes bigger than mine, so I wear a pair of her mom's booties, only a half size too big.

We get into Charlie's car, and he kisses Kenzie on the lips. She's in the passenger seat, and I sit in the back, behind Charlie.

"Hey, babe," Charlie says, staring at Kenzie. "You look hot."

"Thanks," Kenzie says, pulling down the vanity mirror to

reapply her lip gloss, which is dark red and makes her lips look swollen. "Let's go, we're already late."

I look out the window, and the sun is setting. I watch the colors fade into one another and remember doing this when I was little. I loved watching the world go by without my having to do anything. I could just exist.

"What's going on with you and Jensen?" Kenzie asks, breaking the silence in the car.

"Nothing. I mean, I haven't talked to her. I don't know, I guess." Which is true.

"Last time I talked to her, she said you were a bitch at Chris Saul's party but that she doesn't hate you or anything."

"I was a bitch? She was! She—" I stop myself and remember that they're still friends and whatever I say to Kenzie will be relayed to Jensen. "I don't hate her, either. I miss her, actually. I just needed a break, I guess."

"It's good to take breaks from friends. Me and you took a break for a while, and now look at us!" I wasn't aware that Kenzie and I took a "break" from being friends, but I guess it's true. I had been choosing not to hang out with her because of her reputation, but she's really not so bad. She seems pretty understanding, actually. Maybe I was wrong. "You guys are best friends, though. It'll work itself out."

"Do you think I should make up with her?"

"Ha! She asked me the same thing."

Another party. Another kitchen table full of red cups and alcohol. A year ago I was still going to Boomers! to drive go-karts and climb the rock wall. It seems stupid to want those things again, simple things, kid things. I look at Kenzie, in her outfit with her hair and makeup, and wonder if this is what the rest of my high school life will be like, trying to get popular, trying to impress people. It feels like I have to try so hard now. I wish we could just be kids again, arm in arm at the fair, running, free.

Outside, kids are sitting around a circular table, packing weed into a hookah, calling greens, which means they go first, picking the order for how they will partake. Kenzie makes her way to the kitchen table and pours us two vodka-cranberry drinks. These have become my favorite, because they're easy to drink and taste like juice. Charlie goes to talk with some other older kids. Kenzie's told me before that he doesn't smoke and he hates when she does it, so she can't do it around him. She says it's cool if I want to, and I just tell her I'm good, no thanks, it's okay. It's mostly sophomores and juniors at the party, mostly guys from the swim team like Charlie, tall, skinny, lanky boys who like to party. Charlie has short blond hair and brown eyes and a six-pack. The swimmers are all in great shape. I see them practicing sometimes in the morning if I'm early enough when I pass the pool, walking to the 300 Building for English. I can't tell if they see me, because they're wearing goggles, but I stare anyway, in hopes they will stare back. There's something hot about swimmers: the way they glide through the water with ease, the way they breathe hard and fast, their bodies firm and muscular.

Kenzie disappears, which often happens, and I stand at the kitchen table and drink until I need a refill.

"What are ya so dressed up for?" Matthew Jarvis, a sophomore on the swim team, asks me. I suddenly feel stupid all dressed up, since most people are wearing shorts and T-shirts. Matthew wears a gray T-shirt with a flannel over it and cargo shorts. His calves are super toned, and his hair is curly and blond. He has green eyes. He's cute, but messy, but still cute.

"Kenzie dressed me," I say.

"I mean, don't get me wrong, it's great, but you little girls always come so fancy to these parties. We're just chillin', ya know?"

"Well, there's nothing I can do about it now."

"You could just take off your clothes."

I'm not sure if he's serious, but I begin to wonder what would happen if I just stripped in the middle of the party. Would anyone even notice, or care? Would it cause a scene, like in the movies, where all the other kids join in and we go streaking or skinny-dipping and hilarity ensues?

"I'm just kiddin', darlin'," he says. "Whatcha drinkin'?"

"Vodka. You?"

"SoCo. It's all I drink."

"Never had it."

"Wanna try it? I bet you'll like it. It's strong, smooth. Good shit."

"Sure. What do you mix it with?"

"Nothin'."

He pours us two cups of Southern Comfort from a big bottle that's halfway killed. I smell it, and it reminds me of the hydrogen peroxide I used to clean my infected ear piercing. We "cheers" our cups, and he shoots down the whole thing in one gulp. I take one sip and almost die.

"Come on, girl. It's not so bad!"

"I'll stick to vodka cranberry."

"Ha! Lame ass."

"I'm not lame. I just don't like SoCo. It's gross."

"You're just uptight. It ain't gross."

"Why do you talk like that?"

"Like what?"

"Country or something. Like Tom Sawyer."

"I guess you little Boca girls aren't used to a real man."

"I'm not a little Boca girl."

"Yes, ya are. Where do you live?"

"Where do *you* live?"

"I'm from Mississippi, but I bet you were born 'n' raised at the Town Center Mall. Prolly conceived right there in the Bloomies parking lot."

"You're such an asshole."

"Nah. I'm just being honest. You're the one puttin' on ten pounds of makeup, prolly got a push-up bra on, foolin' everyone here when you're just a little Boca girl."

"You're a dumb hick!"

"Aw, like I ain't heard that before."

"Why are you being mean to me? I didn't do anything."

"You offend my liquor, you offend me."

"That's so stupid. I'm allowed to have my own opinion. I'm not just going to like what you like, or pretend to like what you like, so you'll want to have sex with me or something. I'm not that desperate."

"Sure looks like ya are, honey."

Charlie walks over to us.

"Matt, can you chill?" Charlie says, stepping in between Matthew and me.

"You okay?" he asks me.

"Yeah. Where's Kenzie?" I ask.

"I was going to ask if you knew."

"You know where she's at," Matthew says.

"What's that supposed to mean?" Charlie asks.

"Where's Dave at? He can probably tell ya. Ha-ha!"

"You're such a dick, Matt. This is why you'll never make varsity."

"Oh no, my dreams are crushed!"

"Don't be a piece of shit, dude. Don't talk about my girlfriend like that. You can't even keep a girlfriend, bro."

"Piss off, man," Matthew says as he walks away from us, taking the bottle of SoCo with him. *A few months later, Matthew was sent to reform school. Two men came and got him in the middle of the night. They packed his bags for him and had to drag him out of the house. I thought that was the kind of thing that only happened in movies, but the rumor turned out to be true. I imagine it must have been hard for him to take orders, to listen to authority, to become obedient. I started to see there was a fine line between this kind of real danger and the kind of trouble I'd been dabbling in.*

"Sorry about Matt," Charlie says. "Ever since his ex-girlfriend cheated on him, he's just been a total dick to all girls."

"Thanks for standing up for me," I say.

"You don't deserve that shit."

"Thanks. I'm going to look for Kenzie. I kinda want to leave soon."

"No! You gotta stay. I promise, not all the dudes are like Matt."

"Okay."

"I'm gonna see if Kenzie's outside or something. Don't convince her to leave, please. I don't get to spend much time with her lately, and I really want to be with her."

"Okay. I won't." I smile, and Charlie goes out the sliding glass door.

I walk over to the stairs and slip off my shoes before stepping onto the carpeted steps. As I run up, I hear whispers and shushing. Then Kenzie flies out of one of the rooms and grabs me to turn back around and head downstairs.

"What happened?" I ask. We retreat to the downstairs bathroom, and she closes and locks the door behind us.

"You can't tell anyone," Kenzie says, putting her hair into a ponytail. She has dark brown hair, almost black, but with tiny, subtle streaks of blond from the sun. She's so tan, and it makes her brown eyes pop. She looks exotic, which is definitely why all the guys are in love with her. I notice a hickey on her neck.

"You might want to leave it down," I suggest, pointing to the spot.

"Oh, crap! Do you have concealer?"

"It'd be way too light—sorry."

"Let me see if I have some in my purse," she says as she digs into her black Coach bag. "Well, I guess you can figure out what happened."

"Who were you with?" I ask, and realize she doesn't have to tell me anything—it's none of my business. But Charlie is a good guy. He stuck up for me, and I'm curious why she would cheat on him.

"Me and Alex Abers have this . . . thing," she says, blotting dots of concealer on her neck and smoothing them out with her fingers. "We always make out at parties when Charlie is around. Alex says it turns him on. Alex always wins the four-hundred-meter backstroke, and that's *totally* Charlie's event. Charlie gets pissed and teases Alex that at least he has a hot little freshman, aka me. But I hate being objectified like that, so I do it to get back at him, ya know?"

"But Charlie is a really nice guy."

"Aw, do you have a little puppy-love crush on him?"

"No. But he was really nice to me just now. Matthew Jarvis was being a jerk, and Charlie stood up for me."

"That is really nice. I didn't say Charlie isn't nice; he's just . . . I don't know. . . . All guys are just . . . they suck!"

"I don't think that's true."

"Well, no offense, but you haven't had many boyfriends. I have. And I know what guys are like."

"What do you mean?"

"Most guys our age just want sex. And if they're halfway decent, they really do want you, like you as a person, but then they get possessive, like Charlie-boy. Or they just completely ignore you. Remember how upset I was when Theodore ignored me?"

"You mean Mr. Theo, in the history department?"

"Yeah. He ignored me 'cause he's married or whatever. But

I came to his room every day for free period and did stretches and let him see my underwear when I was doing backbends. He totally died over me, but he ignored me, because, well, he's a guy, and that's what they do sometimes."

"So . . . what are you going to do?" I ask, as Kenzie puts the finishing touches on covering up her hickey.

"I'm going to break up with him. But I'll do it after he takes us home, after you go inside. I won't put you through that."

I nod in support and try to fathom what it'd be like to have multiple boys wanting me at one time. I can feel myself getting lost in thought, on the brink of disappearing.

"And, by the way," Kenzie says, "can you please stop eating lunch alone in the library? It's not a good look."

We leave the bathroom and go outside to dance. Kenzie takes me by the arm and pulls me to the backyard, which has turned into a sort of dancing area. She swings me around, and her arms graze my body. Mostly only girls are dancing. I can barely even feel the vodka cranberries. My brother once told me something about how your tolerance goes up the more you drink, and I have been doing it more and more, so I guess that's what's happening.

Charlie and Kenzie reunite for a moment, and I stand and watch as they kiss and hold hands. Alex Abers stumbles outside, tucking in his button-down shirt, and he puts his arm around Charlie's neck. Matthew Jarvis is sitting in a lounge chair and smoking a cigarette, far away from everyone else, because most kids here think cigarettes are gross. Parties are so pointless. Nothing ever happens, or something big happens but then it just goes back to normal the next day. They don't mean anything. They don't change anything. In the course of a life, a party, all the parties, they don't matter.

"Let's keep dancing and burn off all our calories!" Kenzie yells, dragging me back to dance until we get tired, and then we leave. I fall asleep on the car ride home, and I can hear Kenzie quietly telling Charlie she wants a break. He keeps calling her "baby," and she keeps telling him to grow up. *Charles ended up moving to Los Angeles for college and then stuck around. He became a successful lawyer and dates a social-media influencer. The more I think about Kenzie and Charles, the more it makes sense that he wanted to be with someone who had a "perfect" life and was constantly showing off to the world to impress others, for attention, for validation. His posts are always generic and fabricated, punctuated by way too many advertisements. They're always going on wine safaris and taking trips to Spain. Charles is always posting about how blessed he is, how he's the luckiest guy on Earth.* Maybe, I think drowsily, growing up is something that's happening to us all the time. Every boy we kiss, every time we get our hearts broken, we grow up, just a little bit.

In the morning, Kenzie's parents are home. Her dad makes us granola and yogurt and calls it a "power breakfast." I usually don't eat breakfast unless it's Cinnamon Toast Crunch or my mom picks up Dunkin' Donuts. I definitely don't eat this healthy, ever, but I really like it. Her dad gets a work call and disappears to his office. Kenzie's mom comes home from the salon with her hair and nails freshly done. Her hair is dark, almost black, like Kenzie's, and is blown out and fluffy. Her nails are long and red and square.

"Look at my perfect daughter." She kisses Kenzie on the forehead. Kenzie smiles and continues eating her granola. Her mom pours a cup of coffee and sits down with us at the kitchen table. "Are you girls ready for school tomorrow?"

"Ugh, don't remind me." Kenzie slumps back in her chair and picks at her nails. "How come you didn't take me with you to get my nails done?"

"You were sleeping, and I didn't want to wake you up. But I made you a hair appointment for two o'clock. You can see if Jenny is free to do your nails after. Or maybe we can go a little early and see if she's free, but you have to get your butt moving."

"What time is your mom coming?" Kenzie asks, and seems annoyed. I realize this is rude, but I've just about had enough of her, too. I like her house and her food, but overall she's just kind of a brat.

"She should be here soon; she said by noon. I can call her again." I wonder if my mom would take me to the salon later if I wanted her to. Kenzie will look so good at school tomorrow with her new hair and nails, and I'll just be the same as before.

"I'm not getting it cut again, Mom," Kenzie says.

"Yes, honey, you need your ends trimmed. Just a trim. They're all ratty at the bottom. You need it cleaned up."

"Fine! But if they cut more than an inch, I'm going to die. Or kill someone. Or scream."

"You should really go into drama, sweetie. You're such a little actress."

"By the way, Mom, Charlie and I are taking a break."

"I was wondering if that love bite was from him."

"Ew, Mom!"

"Who's it from, then?"

"Alex Abers."

"Again? Charles will be very upset if he hears about that, you know?"

"Well, we aren't together anymore . . . until I feel like it again. He'll take me back anytime I want him to."

"Are you a little heartbreaker like Kenzie?" Mrs. Bedner asks, and I shake my head no. I continue scraping my bowl clean because it was so good, and I feel embarrassed because I'm not a heartbreaker. If anything, I'm the one who always gets my heart broken. It seems like Kenzie and her mom tell each other everything. I feel like my mom and I used to be that close, but once boys and drinking got involved, I got scared to tell her I was into those things. I thought she'd judge me. But it doesn't feel like Kenzie's mom judges her at all. She encourages her behavior, supports it.

When my mom picks me up, she doesn't ask if I want to go to the salon, but she does ask about my essay for Mr. Michaelson's class, and I tell her that it's done, I just need to print it.

Reading *The Outsiders* makes me wish I could run away like Ponyboy and do whatever I want. Obviously those boys were under dire circumstances, but the story makes me want freedom more than ever, even though it seems scary and dangerous.

I wonder why we have to read books about kids who grow up fast. Ponyboy was only fourteen in the book; I'm fifteen now, and the hardest thing I have to deal with is algebra. But maybe they want us to read this stuff so we can see that we don't have it so bad, that we go to a private school in a wealthy city and none of us will ever have to deal with gangs and murders and chaos. So I decided to copy Ponyboy and write my paper about all the stuff I've been going through with the girls lately. My story is about what it's like to lose a friend and to be the cause of that loss. In my paper, a group of high school girls traverse the halls in a pack. They become divided over issues of boys and family drama, and they end up at the same party, where a big brawl goes down. It's not as gory as *The Outsiders*, obviously, but the girls still have it out with one another. In the end, they all apologize to one another, because they realize they don't have it so bad and that they should do their best to get along. I hope Mr. Michaelson likes it. He's always encouraging us to be creative, to be ourselves. It's the first time I don't ask my mom to proofread my paper for me, and when she asks why, I tell her I don't need her help anymore, I'm old enough to do the work on my own.

SEVENTEEN

We get a schedule change on the first day back. Our first-period teacher presents each one of us with a sheet of paper folded in half with a list of our new classes. Our core classes are staying the same, for the most part, unless we are advanced or demoted from an honors course, but the ones that definitely change are our electives. My 2-D art class has been swapped for 3-D art, which is fine with me, because I prefer to sculpt rather than draw. I remember being humiliated in third grade when I tried to trace my hand to make a turkey and got caught and was scolded in front of the class.

What concerns me the most about my schedule is that my PE class has been changed to swimming. It *is* Florida, and the school *does* have an outdoor pool, but I don't want to swim. I don't want to wear a regulation one-piece bathing suit in front of boys my age who are expecting to see a filled-out chest and full breasts when I've got nothing going on up there. My parents have taught me that there's always a way to get out of something you don't want to do, and this *has* to be the case for swimming.

Throughout the day, the rest of the girls and I are in communication about our schedule changes. Despite all the tension between us, this qualifies for an emergency cease-fire. We reconvene at lunchtime to discuss our efforts. Kenzie will also be in swimming, but she doesn't mind and is actually excited about it, except that she has to get her hair wet. Tomassi is exempt from swimming because she's shadowing the school nurse and uses that time slot to follow her around and help sick students, something her mom wants her to do to help prepare her application for college. And Leigh gets to skip because of her ears, something about the water pressure, which I know is bullshit, because when I went swimming at her house recently she was more than fine. But it seems that Gottlieb, Rosenberg, and even Jensen will also have to endure swimming.

"If you just say you have your period, you don't have to go in the water," Rosenberg says.

"That is so freaking brilliant," Gottlieb says.

"But we still have, like, three months of school left," I say. "No one's period lasts that long."

"Well," Jensen says, "some of the days, we'll just *have* to go in the pool." She speaks to the group but makes eye contact with me for a minor second.

"How much trouble do you think we'll get in if we wear bikinis?" Kenzie asks. "Can't I just say I don't own a one-piece? I'm not about to go out and buy one from, like, Sports Authority or something just for this dumb class."

"It probably depends who's coaching," Leigh says.

"I think it's McGee," Gottlieb says. "And she's a total bitch."

"It might be Howard," Rosenberg says.

"From the science department?" Tomassi asks. "I'm so glad I don't have to deal with this. You all should really just pick up a work-study or something."

"I don't want to work under someone else," Kenzie says.

"That's not what Alex Abers said," Leigh says.

"Shut up!" Kenzie says.

"They can't make us swim today, anyway," I say. "They *just* gave us our schedules, and we couldn't have been expected to bring a bathing suit. They'll probably just tell us the rules and stuff today."

"True," Rosenberg says. "It's like the first day of school, sort of."

We are expected to be in our bathing suits sitting on the edge of the pool at 12:55 p.m. every day. Lunch ends at 12:45 p.m., so this gives us ten minutes to walk to the pool over on the other side of campus, change, pee, fuss with our hair, put our stuff in a locker, and realize we forgot to shave our knees. We swim in cloudy weather, a light drizzle, full rain, but not lightning. We do not swim if we have a sick note, an early dismissal, or our period.

Kenzie and Gottlieb have swimming at the end of the day, so at least it doesn't matter if they leave school with a wet head, but Rosenberg, Jensen, and I all have it together. After enduring one day of cold water and wet hair, we decide to take a stand. At twelve fifty-five, when our peers are lined up on the edge of the pool, we will, one by one, pull aside Coach McGee and tell her we have our period. This clears us for seven to ten days, during which we will watch the rest of the kids swim from the sidelines, do our homework on a towel, and stay dry. Although I don't have my period yet, I'm hoping Jensen won't rat me out. She and Rosenberg are the only ones who know I'm period-less. We discuss our tactics in the locker room before swimming.

"I'm supposed to get my period next week," Rosenberg says. "What am I supposed to do *then*?"

"Blame it on hormones," I say. "Just be like, 'It came back! What do you want from me?'"

"Ha! That's hilarious," Rosenberg says.

"McGee probably won't find it so funny," Jensen says.

"McGee needs to get laid," Rosenberg says.

"All right," I say. "Who's going first?"

"I'll go," Rosenberg says, "take one for the team."

"What if she gets suspicious?" Jensen asks. "I mean, we all have our periods at the same time?"

"I think that can happen," Rosenberg says. "Like, when a group of girls hangs out together all the time, they can sync up or something."

"How does that happen?" I ask.

"I don't know," Rosenberg says. "Bodies are weird."

"That sounds like a load of crap," Jensen says. "But I hope she buys it."

Rosenberg leaves the locker room, and it's just me and Jensen. We sit across from each other on two benches and stare at our shoes. Jensen finally looks up at me, and we make eye contact.

"Does it feel weird?" Jensen asks.

"What?" I ask.

"To fake your period?"

"Why does it even matter? McGee won't know I'm faking."

"That's the kind of person you are now? Someone who lies when they don't want to do something?"

"I'm not a liar."

"Yeah, you are. That's literally what you're doing."

"You don't have your period, either, right now. So you're a liar, too."

"I have it, just not right at this *moment*."

"That's still a lie. And why do you care so much, anyway?"

"You're right. I don't. Forget it." Jensen looks back down at the floor.

"Why did you even bring it up?"

"Because."

"Because why?"

"It smells like cat piss in here," Jensen says as she gets up and walks out. I guess I'm going last to tell McGee about why I can't swim this week.

A few minutes later, McGee comes into the locker room and asks if I'm not out by the edge of the pool because I have my period, too. I just nod, and she signals me to take my stuff and sit with Rosenberg and Jensen. They do their math homework, and I look over my spring break assignment. Mr. Michaelson wrote *Be careful, but nice job* underneath a big *A*. I write on a blank page of my English notebook, *I will get my period, I will get my period, I will get my period*, over and over again. The rest of the kids are swimming, and it actually doesn't look so bad. At least they're doing something, while I just sit here bored. It's weird that, even though the boys are shirtless, the girls still have to wear one-pieces or tankinis. No one seems concerned with that, though; they're just swimming. I write until the bell rings. I get splashed when everyone gets out of the pool, and my skirt is wet for the rest of the day.

The first week after break, I go to school every day anxious and excited at the possibility of running into Stephen—of starting the next stage of our love story. But fate does me no favors, and I don't see him. I start to wonder if he's ignoring me, that wonder evolving into fear that maybe he's doing it on purpose.

Over IM, he and I try to make plans, but it never seems to work out. He has to take care of his brothers, he's busy with friends, he's working on his car; it's always something. Eventually, one night on the phone, he tells me his family actually moved to Wellington Green over spring break. Wellington is only thirty minutes from Boca, but he changed schools, too. He's started attending a Christian school, because his parents felt like he was getting into trouble after he got his license. He confesses that he doesn't think long distance will work; it'll be too hard, even though he says he really likes me.

I start crying when he says this, but he doesn't seem to notice. I tell him I have to go and hang up the phone.

I wait for him to call back, or even to instant message with an apology, an explanation. But he doesn't reach out again. *I tried, but I never fully understood why he lied to me. I guess that sometimes that's just something that people do.*

One day in early April, Mom calls the school to say she'll be late for pickup. I learn this information in the form of a note during my last period of the day, 3-D art. I wonder if something happened, but the note doesn't say. My mom is usually first in line. I've always wanted her to come later, so I could stay with Brittany Gottlieb and Leigh, whose moms both work, to experience the in-between dimension of time when no parents or teachers are around.

Bus riders wait in the cafeteria until they can board their respective buses. They buy candy from the vending machine or churros from the snack stand, but it's not cool to be a bus kid. I rode the bus in elementary school with Jensen, but now I wouldn't be caught dead on it. The car-pool kids have to go outside when the bell rings and all the teachers leave. The big, heavy doors of the classrooms shut, and they make everyone head out and wait for their rides, but people find ways to sneak back inside. Brittany Gottlieb said that before she started dating Aaron, Tyler Gentz let her touch his boner one time by his locker. Leigh got fingered for the first time after school when band practice was canceled and the room was empty. I imagine the brass instruments keeping her company while some boy stuck his fingers in her pants, tried to do something to her without being precisely sure what. She said it didn't feel good, but I didn't believe her. That kind of stuff can be good if the guy knows what he's doing. Didn't she at least *want* to enjoy it? What's the point if you don't? If you don't want it again and again? And what's the point if you can't be the type of girl who knows how to make someone else feel good, too?

I'm really crazy about this kid, Jared Richman. Jared isn't popular, but he's not unpopular, either. If anything, he has a sort of troublemaker reputation. I've seen him carving his initials into lockers with the pointed end of a math compass. He's not afraid of getting a conditional or being sent to the dean, something that terrifies me so greatly I don't even like to think about it. We don't have any classes together—like Jensen, he's not in honors. But at lunch I always give him my Rice Krispies Treat, even though I want it.

I want to know what goes on inside after school, and today's apparently my chance, so I devise a plan to go to my locker and pretend I forgot something. I leave my backpack at the base of a small cabbage-palm tree and head inside. I immediately see Jared Marshall coming down the hall with Jeremy Weisberg and Jason Walker, his posse. He's wearing a navy-blue uniform polo and matching navy shorts. I don't like when people match the colors of our uniform, but I like the way the dark blue brings out his brown eyes and jet-black hair. He smells like cologne and hair gel. I'm really into that. When I see him coming, I take my hair out of the ponytail that I had from art because we were doing a sculpture project. I can feel a crease from the elastic band. I hope he doesn't notice. I tell Jared my mom is late picking me up, and he smiles.

He takes my hand and leads me to a classroom doorway down the hall like he knows where to go, like this is where he takes all the girls after school. No other kids are around. He pushes me against a wall and puts his hand on my chest and grabs. I push him away and say, "What are you doing?" even though I know. Jared asks, "Are you a prude?" I don't want it to be true, so I let him do it again. He does it for a few seconds and says, "I'm so hard," before he puts my hand on his pants. It feels hard in my hand. He stands there with his mouth agape, and there's a pause. I know he wants me to get down on my knees and give him a blow job, but I just can't. I want something like that to happen in the privacy of a bedroom, not in a hallway. I wonder if I should ask Jared if he'd want to hang out outside school or if we could at least maybe go to the band-practice room, but then he says, "Great, now I'm going to have blue balls," and runs away. I can hear the other boys laughing down the hall. Their sneakers squeak against the floor until the double doors burst open at the other end.

I walk back to the tree to get my bag and wait for my mom. A sixth grader I have art with is sitting under the tree with her headphones in. She's reading a book and ignoring a group of boys playing cards, some game with levels and attacks. I can't remember what it was like not to care what boys thought. I want to be able to sit and read or write or just do nothing. I want to wait for my mom and not get into trouble or be talked about the next day or wonder what everyone else is thinking when they think about me. I sidle by the girl and retrieve my bag, give her a nod for inadvertently watching it for me. She smiles and continues bopping her head to her music. I try not to cry. I stand on the curb with my face toward the sun.

When my mom pulls up, she says we have to meet Dad at a furniture store. She apologizes for being late but says we're in the middle of bargaining for a dining-room set—we don't currently have one, even though we moved to Florida six years ago. I'm quiet as she drives.

"Are you okay?" she asks.

"I'm just in a bad mood."

She laughs and makes a snorting sound.

"What?" I ask, getting mad.

"If I ask you about your day, you're mad, and if I don't ask you, you're mad, too. It's just impossible."

"You don't get it" is all I manage to say. She has no idea that I have just been felt up against my will and am trying to deal with it, that I am thinking about Jared, about whether he likes me or just wants to use me for play. She doesn't even know who he is and wouldn't understand if I tried to explain.

"Is this about Stephen?" she asks, and I want to kill her. "It sounds like you're playing this cat-and-mouse game with him, and, to be honest, I don't think it's fair to him. He obviously likes you, but you play so hard to get and are only interested when he's not—"

"I didn't do that!" I yell. "You have *no idea* what you're talking about!" My heart is racing, and I start feeling overheated.

I turn up the air conditioning in the car, and we continue the rest of the drive in silence. When we arrive at the store, my mom motions to the trunk, where there is a bag of clothes for me. She walks in ahead of me. It looks like it might rain all of a sudden.

I go into the bathroom at the furniture store to change into the shorts my mom packed so I wouldn't have to stay in my uniform skirt. I look in the mirror and lift up my polo shirt. My black cotton bra has two little cups and some padding inside them. My boobs are small, but I have them now; I have something. There's the possibility, whether I want it or not, whether I understand what it means. What the boys will do next is always a mystery. I reach under my shirt and grab my own chest. I feel cotton and sweat.

I'm asleep when I finally get my period. I don't notice it until the next morning, when I'm getting ready for school. My underwear is covered in dark red blood, and I throw them in my trash, wrapped in a wad of toilet paper. They were the ones that said TUESDAY, and I wonder if my mom will notice a missing day of the week when she does the laundry. I go under the sink and get one of the pads my mom bought for when the time came. But I don't tell her at first. A part of me thinks that maybe I don't *really* have my period, like it's just a mistake, not the real thing yet. But I can't wait to tell the girls.

It's finally warm enough to have lunch outside again. The girls set up camp on the picnic tables outside the cafeteria.

Kenzie's started drinking water with lemon, so when I

approach our group she's showing everyone the sliced-up lemons inside her water bottle.

"It helps you lose weight," Kenzie says, passing it around.

"I heard it's good for your skin, too," Tomassi adds, nodding.

"Guess what?" I say, interrupting but not caring. The girls turn their heads toward me. Kenzie looks annoyed. Jensen continues to eat her ham sandwich. "I got my period!"

"Mazel tov!" Rosenberg screams, then gets up to hug me.

"Now you can lose your virginity," Gottlieb says with a smile.

"I couldn't lose it before?" I ask.

"No," Gottlieb says. "It's, like, not possible if you don't have your period. You're not ready, or something."

"That's *so* not true," Leigh says. "That doesn't even make any sense."

"Well, I heard that somewhere," Gottlieb says.

"I'm so happy for you!" Tomassi says, grabbing my arm. "I got mine when I was in Barbados, but I didn't want you to feel alone."

"Yes!" Leigh says. "Congrats!"

"Why are you all congratulating her?" Jensen asks. "For bleeding out of her vagina? That's not an accomplishment. You guys are so dumb."

My heart drops when she says this. Jensen isn't excited for me or even happy that I'm a woman now. She knows how bad I've felt about being almost the only one without my period, and now I have it and she doesn't even care.

"First of all, we're girls, not guys," Rosenberg says. "And we're not dumb. It's exciting. We're excited for our friend."

"Yeah," Kenzie says. "Don't be rude about it."

"I'm not being rude!" Jensen says. "It just doesn't mean anything."

"Maybe not for you," Rosenberg says. "But just because you haven't hooked up with anyone since my bat mitzvah doesn't mean nothing good can happen for any of us. You're just bitter."

"My goal in life isn't to hook up with guys," Jensen says.

"We're not saying that," Tomassi chimes in. "But you can be happy for your friend."

"Are you guys this stupid?" Jensen says.

"Stop saying that!" Gottlieb says. "None of us are stupid. You're actually the only one not in any honors classes, so . . ."

"Yeah, but I also play more sports than any of you put together, so . . ."

"Which only makes us question if you even like boys at all?" Rosenberg says. "I mean, you *never* talk about guys . . . *ever*. What are we supposed to think?"

"If you are . . . you know," Leigh says, "it's totally okay!"

"Yeah!" Tomassi says. "My aunt is a lesbian."

"Oh my God!" Jensen raises her voice. "I'm not a lesbian! And I don't even care if you think I'm gay, anyway. We aren't friends anymore. Me, her, all of us. Can't you tell I've been spending less and less time with you all?"

"Then leave!" Kenzie says, and everyone else nods. I'm standing opposite Jensen as she pushes away from the table. Jensen stares at me for a moment. She looks at me like it was all my fault—not only the fighting, but all of it: the way we seem to crave guys' attention, how we hide the truth from our parents, the fact that we're growing up and she doesn't want to. She turns her head and walks away.

I try to remember the girl who saved me in fourth grade, the girl who wanted to be my friend. That time seems so far away now, as if that moment happened on a distant planet. I start to cry. I miss her so much, the old Jensen, who would do everything with me, no matter how dumb or silly. I don't understand why she's being like this. And I feel bad that everyone's turned against her now. I also wonder if I'm just emotional from my period. I feel a sharp pain in my stomach and bend over the picnic table.

"Aw," Kenzie says. "Cramps?"

"Is that what this is?" I ask.

"Yeah," Rosenberg says. "But they usually don't make you cry."

I stand up and go to the bathroom. I'm annoyed with everyone all of a sudden.

"Do you want company?" Tomassi asks, following me.

"No," I say, and continue walking.

Tomassi follows me to the bathroom anyway.

"What's wrong?" she asks.

"I don't really want to talk."

"Well, I think you need to. Usually when I'm like this, my mom says that's when I need to talk the most. Get it out. Don't keep it inside."

"I don't know why this is happening," I say.

"Which part?" Tomassi asks, boosting herself up onto the bathroom counter. I put my backpack on the floor and slink down next to it.

"The whole thing. My ovaries feel like they're at war, my friends *are* at war—I just don't know when things got so complicated."

"No offense, but all your friends are assholes."

"But you're friends with everyone, and you're my friend, right?"

"Of course. I wouldn't be sitting in this smelly bathroom with you if I wasn't your friend. But you have to know that this group of girls is a bunch of bitches."

"Then why are you in it?"

"Why are you in it?" Tomassi takes a deep breath and sighs. "This is the price you pay, having a group of girlfriends like this. We're all going to fight, make up, be best friends again. Trust me, it was way worse with the girls in New York."

"When will we make up? Because it seems like *never* right now."

"Probably when you least expect it or not until something else big happens, like when Rosenberg loses her virginity or something."

We laugh, and I hug her. *Years later, she came to one of my readings in Brooklyn. Her face was as bright and beautiful as ever, her hair still long and blond. She was in a winter jacket and had a copy of my book in her hand. She came in a little late and waited until the reading was over. We spoke for a while, and she told me how proud she was of me, that she envied how I was able to write about my experiences. She hugged me, and I was brought back to our friendship, the sweetness of it. Even though she broke apart from the friend group, I never held it against her. We were a lot to handle. In a way, she was too good for us, but I never hated her for that.*

She of course asked me about Jensen. I wasn't sure what to say, so I just told the truth—that I wished her the best.

Tomassi and I break apart. I take a square of toilet paper and fix my makeup in the mirror. The rest of the day, I deal with cramps and try to convince myself that it'll get better soon, that things will really start to change.

NINETEEN

Spring passes by so fast. It feels like there's no time some days. I wake up early for school, sit in class for seven hours, then come home, do homework, watch a show with my family, then go to sleep. I'm tired all the time, and I wish I could have a break—a day, a week—to just sit in bed and sleep. *This feeling re-emerged in college. I was walking home from class on a cold day when it started to snow, and I didn't have on the right jacket. The light made it hard to tell the time of day. Some of my friends were studying abroad, but I wanted to finish quickly so I could go become the thing I was meant to be. So I stayed in the Midwest, with cornfields and football games. It felt endless, infinite. I wanted it to be over, but the next day would come and it was still happening.*

Then, all at once, it was over. I didn't walk with everyone else at graduation but instead came home early and had my diploma mailed to me. It sits in my closet, and years later my master's degree would sit right next to it. Back then, my life felt like it was about to start, not yet at the important part, but now I wish I had been mindful of the world around me and noticed it as much as possible. I wish I had found joy in that instead of rushing through it.

I come home from school one day and find my mom has arranged driving lessons for me. I really just want to nap and write, but a tall man named Hank Garfield, whose last name happens to be the same as my favorite cartoon character, stands in the driveway. My mom tells me to get my permit and get in the car.

"Why can't *you* just teach me how to drive?" I ask her.

"We used Hank with Brad," she says. "You'll be fine."

"But I *want* you to do it."

"I can't deal with the attitude anymore," she says, and offers a hand to take my backpack. I give it to her and put my permit in the pocket of my school uniform pants. Because I have my period again this week, I'm wearing pants, the dark blue pair that's too tight on my waist but too big in the butt, so I have to leave them unbuttoned so I can breathe and I tug at them all day to keep them up. I put my hair in a ponytail and get in the driver's seat.

The car is rigged with an extra set of brakes on the passenger side. It's the ugliest car I've ever seen, bright orange, with HANK'S DRIVING SCHOOL painted on the sides. I hope I don't see anyone I know.

Hank shows me how to make turns, how to signal before I am turning, and then how to proceed to engage in an actual turn. He sort of looks like Luigi from *Super Mario Bros.* and smells like the soppressata my dad buys at the deli. He tries to make a joke about how he only uses the extra brakes on his students and his wife, but I'm actually pretty nervous and don't laugh. I stay quiet and do everything he tells me to. The lesson goes fine until we get back into my neighborhood. I attempt to make a left turn out of a subdivision, and the right wheel goes over a curb. The car rises and falls with a solid thud. I forget to pump the brakes and freak out. Hank uses his spare set and tells me to brake as well. I don't. I take my hands off the wheel.

"Get your hands back on the wheel!" Hank yells. "Ten and two!"

I sit motionless, in shock. The car is stopped in the middle of the road. Luckily, no one's around. It's a neighborhood road, so it doesn't count anyway.

"Can you drive?" I ask Hank.

"We're right around the corner from your house. You can do it."

"Was that bad?"

"It wasn't good," he says, then laughs. "It happens. Just take us back to your house."

"I'm really tired. I didn't want to do that last turn. I don't see why I had to. I was done. I could have just been done."

"When you get your license and you're in your own car, you can't take breaks when you're tired. I won't be there. You won't have other people to do things for you."

"I can do it, I just don't want to right now. I'm shaken up."

"You're fine. It was only a curb."

"I want you to drive." I start to cry.

Hank gets out of the car and comes around to the driver's side. He opens the door and we switch places. The drive back to the house takes less than a minute.

When we arrive, my mom is in the driveway with her checkbook. She pays Hank, and I wait in the garage. I overhear him say something about "a little hiccup" and how I could use a lot of practice. I sit on the carpeted floor. I think about how dumb it is to have carpet in a garage, carpet that gets run over and over by my parents' and brother's cars every day. Hank leaves, and my mom walks over to me.

"Get off the floor," she says.

"It's carpet."

"It's dirty."

"Then why do we have it?"

"Why couldn't you finish the lesson? Do you know how expensive it was?"

"I got scared. And I didn't ask for lessons to begin with."

"You need them. What's going to happen when you're out on the *real* road and you get scared?"

"I don't get why *you* can't just teach me."

"Because we fight all the time," she says, moving toward the door.

"No, we don't!"

"Just come inside. You need to start your homework."

"No. I need to talk to you."

She stands by the door and crosses her arms and waits.

"I don't want driving lessons. I don't want to meet with Hank again. I don't like him."

"You don't have to like him. He's just teaching you how to drive. You don't have a choice, unless you don't plan on getting your license. Now get up and go inside. I need to make dinner."

"Oh, you need to *make dinner*. What? You're going to heat up some meat sauce out of a jar and overcook the pasta? I don't want your dinner."

"Okay, then you don't need to eat."

"Why do you want me to be unhappy?"

"I don't. Why do you think I'm such a terrible mother?"

"I didn't say that!"

My mom starts crying, and I want to get up and hug her, but I don't. She's standing in the doorway to the house, and I'm still sitting on the floor. I pick at the rubber on the bottom of my sneakers. A piece tears off, and I ball it up in my hand until it disappears.

"Everything I do is wrong," she says after a while.

"No. Everything *I* do is wrong."

"I'm sorry you don't like my cooking."

"I'm sorry I said that. I just want you to help me with stuff."

"I help you with everything! I got you driving lessons, I help you with your papers, I make sure Brad helps you with math. . . ."

"No, like, my life."

"I ask you all the time about what's going on and you never tell me, or you lie, so I just stopped asking. I can only take so much."

"I'm sorry. I don't want to make you feel bad. I just feel like you'll judge me if I tell you stuff."

"I'm your mother." My mom sits down on the floor next to me. "I would never judge you."

"Yeah, you would."

"I guarantee you, whatever you tell me, I've done worse. I used to be a nurse, you know. I've seen it all. I wanted to ask about Jensen, but I didn't want to pry."

"I don't know what her deal is. She's distanced herself from everyone."

"Do you think she's upset because you've all hit puberty and she hasn't?"

"Mom, gross! What are you even talking about? She has her period, too, like everyone else."

"Getting your period doesn't mean you're just grown up all of a sudden. Growing up is about maturity, too. And that takes a long time to develop. Jensen doesn't seem as interested in boys as you are, as your friends are."

"But do you think that's bad?"

"To be interested in boys? No. It's natural. Just don't be too fast with them. There's no rush. I don't care if you kiss a boy once in a while, but I don't think you're ready for sexual inter-course yet."

" 'Intercourse'?"

"Please don't tell me you've had intercourse."

"No. I haven't. But no one calls it that."

"Good. Please don't be fast with boys."

" 'Fast'?"

"Moving fast—like, sexually." I see her pause. "Did you . . . move too fast with Stephen?" she asks. "Is that what happened between you two? You can tell me."

"No!" I say, even though it might be true. Maybe we did too much too soon and it scared him away, or maybe he got what he wanted and got bored. But he really did move, and for whatever reason that distance was too far for him to travel to me and make things work. "He moved to Wellington and switched schools."

"Oh," she says. "That's a shame. He was a nice young gentleman."

That's up for debate, but Mom presses on. "Maybe Jensen is just upset because she hasn't gotten those feelings yet," she says.

"I guess."

"She will, though, soon enough."

"How do you know?"

"Because you're at that age when these things happen."

"That's what Tomassi said."

"Tomassi is a smart girl. I like her."

"Yeah, she gives good advice."

"I can give you advice, too, you know. I'm your mother."

It would be years before I could have a normal, healthy conversation with my mom. I don't know when other girls learned how to do that, but for so long I couldn't. I think my mom always wanted to be my best friend, and when she saw me attach myself to Jensen and then boys and then men, she felt me pull away from her, not need her anymore. But the truth is that I will always need her.

For years, I would wish that I could call and tell her how I was feeling: that I didn't even know who I was in the garage that day, because my mind was all over the place. I would have so many therapists later on who told me about "boundaries," that I needed to speak up about what made me uncomfortable and learn to leave people, places, and things that weren't healthy for me. Of course, I didn't put this into practice right away, but slowly I became better at communicating how I felt. I started to treasure phone calls with my mom instead of dread them. When she visits me, we often go to museums. She loves to walk through the exhibits and look at the art, see the view, and stand with me. I hold her hand; I speak to her with lightness and ease where there was once heaviness and fear. I'm finally able to tell her I appreciate her after all this time.

"It's hard for me to talk sometimes," I tell her, my face covered in snot, as we sit on the floor of the garage. I take a deep breath and wipe my face with the sleeve of my sweatshirt. "I just come off like a bitch."

"It hurts my feelings when you say those mean comments. I know I don't work full-time anymore, but being a mom is a full-time job. Someday, when you have kids, you'll understand. I worry about you all the time, and I just want you to be happy. You can always come to me and talk to me about anything."

"I love you, Mom."

"I love you, too. You'll always be my baby."

I lean over and hug her, and she starts to cry into my hair. It's usually intolerable to see her cry, but now I sink into her even more, and we let each other sob.

Eventually we separate and stand up to go inside. My mom shuts the door behind us, and I head upstairs to wash my face. I stare at myself in the mirror. My eyes get really green when I cry, just like my mom's.

TWENTY

*I*n May, my brother receives a full scholarship for the premed program at the University of Miami. He's basically set for life. My dad flies home early to celebrate, and even though it's a school night, we decide to go out for dinner. I rush upstairs and take a quick shower, throw on a pair of jeans and a sweatshirt, and meet my family in the car.

We drive to Maggiano's. It's a huge Italian restaurant that's supposed to resemble a house with lots of rooms and lots of people. My mother has summoned my aunt, my uncle, two cousins, one cousin's long-term girlfriend, the other cousin's husband and their daughter, the long-term girlfriend's mom (who is a pastry chef from Hungary), and the mom's boyfriend (who lives in Puerto Rico but happens to be here now for some reason). My brother hasn't technically graduated from high school yet, but lots of kids seem to be celebrating graduation early. We're seated next to another party: a girl with platinum-blond hair, chemically straightened (I can tell), celebrating her graduation from Boca Prep, one of our rival schools. Their party is somehow bigger than ours, and it almost feels like we're competing.

The Boca Prep family has lots of children with them, little kids that they're letting run around in circles, dragging metallic helium balloons, in the shape of stars and graduation caps, by their weighted sandbags. One of the balloons, a royal-blue star, hits our table, and my dad elbows it away. The group of kids waits in front of him, ready for punishment, ready for scolding, and I don't blame them. They've crossed a line, entering the realm of parents, who may choose to yell instead of ignore.

"Hey, kids," my dad says. "Go play in traffic." They scatter.

"Mom," I whisper, and pat her leg. "Do you want to, like, say something?"

"Maybe we should move?" she suggests.

"No!" Brad yells. "This is fine. Let's just order. I'm starving."

The waiter takes all of our orders, going around the table slowly, painfully. Brad calms down once the breadbasket arrives. He eats six pieces of bread with a lot of butter. I have two pieces and a spoonful of my mom's pasta e fagioli soup. I try my dad's Italian wedding soup, too, and I like his a lot better. He offers me the rest, but I say no. He gets mad when I eat more mozzarella than tomatoes from the caprese appetizer.

"Finish your tomato," he says, eating the last of his.

I excuse myself to use the restroom. In the bathroom, the graduation girl reapplies her lip gloss, and another girl, a friend, plays with her hair, fixes it, even though it doesn't need fixing.

"What are you staring at?" Graduation Girl asks me; I'm just standing by the bathroom door, motionless.

"I need to use the bathroom."

"It's a free country," she says with a laugh, and proceeds to ignore me.

I think about Amber and how she'd probably stand up for me if she was here. At least I have a friend, somewhere out there.

Back at the table, we eat fast and get full quick; we need to take most of our meal home. The pastas and heavy sauces make me tired, but I manage to have another piece of bread and butter, which my dad scolds me for. My brother hasn't said a word all night and keeps falling asleep. When the cake comes, his head is on the table and he won't wake up. My food coma usually ensues mid–drive home, as I delicately slumber away in the back seat, but this is a new one for Brad. He must have had too much shrimp fra diavolo.

My parents begin whisper-yelling to each other, with my uncle getting involved at one point, then backing off. I don't realize how serious it is until my cousin Liza, the nurse, starts taking Brad's pulse. She lifts his head and his eyes are blank. I get scared for a second that he's dead. I hold my hands together under my napkin and pray that he survives whatever this is. My dad carries him to the car, and the bill is taken care of. My aunt shakes her head and rubs my back as we follow them, and I feel lost, like I'm left out of the loop of what's going on here.

When we get home, my mom puts my brother to bed and comes into my room. She says something about pills, pain-killers, taking too many. She says he must have gotten them from a friend at school. I wonder if he got them from Matty, but probably not, since he and Matty never got along. I think of Leigh and the night I saw her passed out from pills, but at least she was at home. My brother was in public. We were at a freaking Maggiano's.

It reminds me of when I was little and Brad used to get these horrible headaches, migraines, and I didn't know whether he was going to survive. I held conferences with my stuffed animals over whether or not I should venture to his room to check on him. Sometimes I thought it'd be best to knock on the wall connected to my parents' room and ask my mom what was going on, but other times I crawled on all fours to his room and made sure he was breathing, sleeping on his side in his blue blanket in the night.

Tonight, though, my mom begs me not to go in there. "He just needs to sleep it off," she reassures. "He'll be fine tomorrow."

"Is he in trouble?" I ask, not wanting him to be, but curious.

"Yes, but it doesn't concern you. Just get some rest."

I go to sleep, and when I wake up, it's after 11:00 a.m. and it's clear that Brad isn't fine, that he *is* in trouble, and that I'm missing school.

I spend the day in bed, wearing pajamas: an oversize shirt from the first bar mitzvah I ever went to and an old pair of boxers that I roll over twice so they stay on my hips. Brad sleeps most of the day but comes downstairs for some leftover shrimp late in the afternoon, wearing his L.L.Bean shirt with holes in it that he's had forever. No one in the house speaks. Dad does work in his den, and Mom watches TV in the master bedroom. Around 4:00 p.m., I stand outside Brad's room and wait for him to notice me.

"You can come in," he says. "I'm not dead."

"Okay," I say. I walk in and sit on the floor next to his bed.

His TV is on, but he's not watching it. He's painting a LEGO set with gold paint, and he's got his desk light on, focused in on his subject. His forehead is sweating, and he stops and takes a sip of Pepsi out of a Styrofoam cup before continuing.

"I can't believe we missed school," I say, trying to break the tension.

"It's really not a big deal," he says.

"I know, but Mom never lets us, and it'll probably, like, never happen again."

"I meant what I did. Everyone at school does pills—all the kids in my grade, at least. I just overdid it."

"Oh."

"It's not a big deal. I'm fine."

"I was worried."

"Don't be. I've done worse."

I stay in Brad's room for an hour, just sitting and watching him paint with the precision of a surgeon. Even though he says he's fine, I'm still worried. I want to do something for him, help him in some way, but I can't think of anything. All I can do is sit on his blue carpet and try to hold the room together. I suck in my breath and count to ten and let it out slowly. Brad doesn't say anything but keeps working on his LEGOs until I eventually walk back to my room and attempt to sleep. *There are fifteen years between then and now. There have been spreads of time when we didn't speak because he was using. There have been times when we talked every single day, like when I got my first teaching job and he stayed on the phone with me all night to calm me down because I was so nervous. Brad went to rehab, relapsed, moved in with a friend, moved home. Then it was another treatment center, another therapist,* more help, always. He finally got clean a decade later, an accomplishment that's greater than all the math-competition trophies and scholarship money put together.

On my wedding day, Brad flew to Los Angeles, rented a car, and drove out to the beach, where the ceremony was being held. He was wearing a white suit and looked as handsome as ever. After dinner, when friends and family gave speeches of congratulations, Brad stood up and moved toward the microphone. His speech was funny at first and had everyone laughing, but then he turned toward me and slowed down, started talking about our childhood together. He said it was his fault that we grew apart. He knew his mistakes caused me pain, but I never blamed him or made him feel bad about any of it. He thanked me for loving him through it all and for never judging him. I remember myself as a kid, sitting at the foot of his bed, watching him play all those video games, the way I always looked up to him and wanted to be as smart and cool as he was. I waited fifteen years to hear him say those things. I always felt like maybe I hadn't done enough to help him, or maybe I shouldn't have moved away from home and left, but the words he finally spoke to me made me realize that all I had to do was love him. He's my brother, and loving him is enough.

No matter how dark things got for Brad, he always came through for me.

TWENTY-ONE

I can't sleep, so I go online way later than I'm supposed to. I want to talk to someone. My parents have finally stopped arguing and fallen asleep, and my brother remains incommunicado in his room, so the house is quiet. There's a hum in the neighborhood where I live that vibrates through all the houses, like when the air conditioning kicks on or off and you notice it when you didn't before. All the houses are strung together on an invisible plane. All the Internets join up in a cloud above the houses. I picture these things I can't see and it makes me more awake, more full of longing.

My computer chimes with an instant message. It's Jensen. She asks if I'm awake, which I feel should be pretty obvious if I'm online, but sometimes people forget to put on their "away" status and aren't really there. I remember what my mom said, about how Jensen might be mad at herself for not having the same feelings as me, as the other girls, as everyone else. My mom also once told me that sometimes you have friends for a reason, a season, or a lifetime. I've always felt that Jensen is and would be one of my lifetime friends, and if that's the case, I should suck it up and talk to her. I can't let this end us.

What's up? I say.

You weren't at school today, she responds, fast.

I know.

You haven't missed a whole day of school . . . like . . . ever. I mean your mom lets you leave early to skip art or whatever but never a full day.

I guess she wants to know why. Maybe she missed me. Or maybe she's just bored. I quickly imagine a scenario where she lost a dare and had to be the one to sign online and ask me, report back to the group, but then I realize she's not really in the group right now. Maybe the whole group thing is over, done, and was just a phase. Some teenagers with nothing better to do, so we hung around one another until we outgrew the whole thing. Or maybe it's still happening and we just haven't figured out the logistics yet, the ways we stay inside of it when we're mad at one another, upset for our own reasons, wanting out. But it's impossible to escape, the pull of girlhood.

There's a good reason. I try to stay mysterious.

You don't have to tell me, she says.

I want to. It's personal though.

Like . . . family stuff?

Yeah.

Do you want to talk on the phone?

K but can I call you? I don't want my house phone to ring.

Okay. Call whenevs.

I sign off and sit at my desk. Do I even want to talk to her?

Yes. Do I want to give in that easily? I don't know. I don't want to go crawling back to her, but *she* messaged *me*. She obviously cares, if she wants to know why I missed school. Should I tell her? Are there some things you just don't tell the people outside of your family, even if they *feel* like family? My mom used to kiss Jensen on the head before we both went to sleep. Jensen had a crush on my brother until—well, I think she still might have a crush on him. She was there the first time a boy kissed me, she was there when I got my back handspring in gymnastics, she was there to defend me in fourth grade and ask me about where I was from and if I wanted to see her dogs after school. She took to me first, and no matter how weird I am sometimes, no matter how embarrassing it is that I get all As, no matter what color I want to dye my hair, she still wants to be my friend.

The phone rings once before Jensen answers. We're both silent for a minute, but then she breaks the ice.

"So, like, what happened?" she asks.

"Family stuff, like you said. Did I miss anything at school?"

"I don't have any classes with you anymore, remember?"

"Well, I meant, like, gossip or something."

"A sixth grader threw up in the cafeteria, so everyone pretty much ate lunch outside. You would have hated it."

"Oh yeah, that sounds terrible. Lunch outside sounds nice, though."

"Yeah. I sat with everyone. We sat in the grass, actually."

"You had a picnic?"

"Ha! Yeah, I guess."

"That sounds fun."

"Rosenberg was complaining about her grass allergy."

"Oh my God. Was it weird?"

"What?"

"Sitting with everyone?"

"It just kind of happened. Everyone was asking me where you were, because you never miss school."

"It sounds like you turned a corner or something."

"I'm sorry about your family stuff. My family sucks, too. That's why I'm always staying at your house."

"But you guys have a boat."

"Yeah, but if you put a bunch of shitty people on a boat, then it's a shitty boat."

"My brother took drugs at his own dinner party."

"Jeez. My brother's done all of that crap, though, as you know."

"Yeah. I just don't want him to die."

"He's not going to die. People do crazy stuff all the time, but your brother is so smart, and he knows what he's doing."

"He's, like, too smart sometimes."

"Definitely."

"Why are you up so late?"

"I couldn't sleep. I had coffee after school, and now I'm just . . . up."

"You and your coffee."

"What are you doing tomorrow?"

"Tomorrow? Oh, it's Saturday. Holy crap."

"Do you want to go to the mall?"

Jensen and I talk all night, until around 5:00 a.m. A while ago my dad told me our phone bill went from minutes to unlimited, so I don't feel bad. We talk about everything and nothing. I try to explain the plot of *The Outsiders* to her, since she didn't read it. She says all the guys sound like assholes, but I tell her they just wanted to protect one another, to do the right thing. She tells me about her soccer game and how two girls got in a fight that resulted in a bloody nose and calling the game. I tell her I can come watch her next game, but she laughs and says she would never make me sit through that. And my watching would make her nervous anyway. We mostly listen to each other breathing in between conversation and enjoy the feeling of coming back together, a remerging of friendship. When we finally hang up, I know I'll see her in a few hours, and I'm glad.

I wake up at 11:00 a.m. and ask my mom if she'll take me to the mall to meet Jensen. She smiles and says if I hurry we can be there by noon. I put on an outfit I haven't worn in a while, a jean skirt from Abercrombie and a yellow ribbed tank top with lace on the chest. I wonder what Jensen will be wearing, if she'll try to look as good as I'm trying.

My mom drops me off in front of the mall, and I don't see Jensen yet. I wonder if maybe her mom wouldn't let her come. Maybe she didn't even ask. My mom says she'll be back at four o'clock, which is more than enough time—too much time if I end up here by myself. She asks if I want her to wait until Jensen shows up, but I say no and sit on the bench until she drives away. I can't move, because we're supposed to meet here, but I don't want to seem stupid sitting here, doing nothing. I worry that maybe Jensen is going to stand me up, that the remerging friendship was just a ruse.

Then I see Old Mercy pull up in front of the mall. I stand up and walk over to it just as Jensen is getting out.

"Do you need money for lunch?" Jensen's mom asks her.

"No. Well. Maybe."

"Here's forty."

Jensen nods and puts the money in a white Louis Vuitton with rainbow letters all over it, a bag I've never seen her wear before. I immediately feel dumb wearing my same Burberry bag. Jensen's wearing acid-wash jeans and a white tank top, an outfit I'd normally have tried to talk her out of putting together, but now I don't dare say a word.

"It's so good to see you," Jensen's mom says to me.

"You too," I say, waving, realizing I haven't even said hi to Jensen yet. "Hi."

"I need new concealer," she says, grabbing my arm and escorting me into the mall. We hear her mom call "Bye!" from the car before we enter through the sliding glass doors.

We used to buy drugstore makeup, but now that we're older, high school, it's pretty necessary for us to shop at Sephora. As we walk into the store, I try to think of something I can pretend to need. She flits over to the Benefit counter, and I follow. Maybe if I let her lead she'll feel like we're having a good time. Even though I talked to her last night for hours and hours, I still feel like I need to prove myself for some reason, to solidify our friendship again.

Jensen tries a bunch of concealers on her hand, a series of stripes that range from white to tan. She has moderately fair skin, so I point to a shade closer to the whitish side of the spectrum, and she nods.

"Do you need anything?" she asks earnestly.

"I, uh, yeah. Lip gloss."

"You should really get lipstick. Gloss is kind of childish."

"I'm open to it."

"It's up to you. It's your face."

We walk over to Urban Decay and I peruse the lipsticks. They're all either purple or dark red, and I was hoping for a pink or something neutral. I don't need anything, but I have to buy something out of solidarity.

"Try this one," Jensen says, handing me a beige color I didn't see. I flip it over to see the name. It's called Flaunt.

"Did you pick this because of the name?" I ask.

"No! I just know you like plain colors."

"I actually really like this," I say, swiping it on my wrist to test. It shines, with just a touch of nude coloring.

"It's pretty and natural," she says, and I'm hoping she means I'm pretty and natural, too, not the fake skank she thought me to be just a few days ago. We head to the register, and Jensen goes first. She takes out one of the twenty-dollar bills her mom gave her and pays for her makeup, getting some change in return. I pay with a twenty my mom gave me this morning, stuff the change in my purse, quick and unorganized, not wanting to fall a second behind Jensen.

We go to the food court. I wait for Jensen to drift toward a place. She grabs a sample of sesame chicken from Manchu Wok, then a single tortellini from Pummarola Pastificio, then a falafel ball from the new Israeli place. Then she returns to Manchu Wok, orders orange chicken and fried rice and a Diet Coke. I order a small white rice and a regular Coke. I know she'll judge me for not eating a real meal, but I'm not hungry at all. I barely want the rice.

We sit in the middle of the food court, at a plush bench with a table attached. Jensen digs in, and I pick at my plain rice.

Jensen's head pops up from her meal. "We forgot the cookies."

"I'll go grab them," I say.

"Get me two," she says, and continues to eat.

I get up from the table and head back to Manchu Wok, where I grab three cookies from the cookie bin. When I turn around, I see a cute guy sitting with a friend at a nearby table. He has dark brown hair and blue eyes and is wearing white Converse, which I think are really cool. I think about going up to him, but I don't want to embarrass Jensen or mess up the way the day is going. He glances at me, and I smile but proceed to walk back to the table, where Jensen is waiting.

"Do you want to pick your two first or have me pick first?" I say as I throw the cookies down on the table.

"Those guys are looking at us," Jensen says, wiping her mouth with a paper napkin and pushing aside her tray.

"Oh, I didn't even notice," I say.

"The blond is my type, definitely," she says.

"You're calling dibs?"

"I haven't kissed a guy since, like, this weird kid at the Hillsboro Club kissed me a few weeks ago."

"Who?"

"Well, it was actually Tanner Martin."

"Your neighbor?"

"Yeah. He's so gross. But he, like, cornered me in the hallway and kissed me and I just, like, went along with it."

I think about telling Jensen about Jared, the awful grab-and-go in the hallway, but I want to keep things light, keep things about her.

"Was it good?"

"No. That's why I really need to kiss someone good."

It seems like Jensen did some growing up while we were apart, and I wonder if it would have happened the same way if we had been talking then, if maybe our friendship could have gotten in the way of it. Now it seems like we can become an unbreakable force, two girls who want to kiss boys, calling dibs on the ones we want, making it happen all on our own.

"Let's go say something," Jensen suggests.

"No, let's just look at them and wait for them to come over here. Guys should make the first move."

"Okay. That sounds good. How should we look?"

"Look at them, then look away, then back, then away. And just keep talking to me."

We glance over at their table a few times, until it's obvious that they see us. The boys get up and walk toward us.

"Hey," the blond says to both of us. "I'm Sebastian, and this is Ryan."

"Hi," Jensen and I say in unison.

"Sebastian, like the crab?" Jensen laughs.

"I've never heard *that* one before." Sebastian laughs, too.

"What are you doing tonight?" Ryan asks, mainly looking at me.

"We're busy," I say, and take another sip of my Coke. Jensen follows suit and takes a sip of her Diet Coke.

"Oh, we see how it is," Sebastian says.

"Well, maybe sometime soon we can all hang out?" Ryan asks, once again mostly to me.

"We'll see," I say. "Why don't you get our numbers and call us."

I pull out a pen from my purse and tear a paper napkin in half, giving one piece to Jensen so she can write her number while I write mine on the other half. Both boys take their respective pieces of napkin paper and put them in their pockets.

"What do you girls like to do?" Sebastian asks. I look at Jensen and let her answer.

"Like, movies, Boomers!—you know, stuff," she says.

"Boomers! would be fun. We would beat you so bad on the go-karts," Sebastian responds.

"I don't think so," Jensen says. "We go there a lot; we've had a lot of practice."

"Is that so?" Ryan asks, looking at me.

"You'll have to wait and see," I say.

After a while, the boys give us hugs and go off to roam the mall, probably to check out sneakers or electronics. Jensen and I go to Forever 21 but don't buy anything. Then we stop at the candy store and load up on sour gummies and malted-milk balls. She calls her mom and asks if she can bring a bag of clothes so she can sleep over at my house. We then call my mom to make sure it's okay, after the fact. My mom asks where we want to go to dinner, and it already feels like nothing bad has ever happened between us.

TWENTY-TWO

The school year is ending, and Kenzie and Leigh aren't friends anymore because Leigh smokes pot and Kenzie's become really straightedge when it comes to drugs. Anyone who doesn't smoke or do drugs draws a big *X* on their hands, and even though they're trying to do the right thing, the teachers tell them to wash it off. Brittany Gottleib spends all her time with her boyfriend. He broke up with her when she thought she was pregnant because her period was late, but they got back together when she finally started bleeding again. She's never around, but it doesn't really matter. We never liked her much anyway. Brittany Tomassi suddenly becomes really cool and starts hanging out with the popular rich kids. Her mom travels a lot for business, so when she's home alone she throws house parties that we're never invited to. She gets her hair chemically straightened and looks beautiful every day. Kenzie lives down the street from her, so they hang out sometimes. Kenzie's parents sell vitamins to Brittany Tomassi's mom. Kenzie says hot guys come in all the time with their shirts off, sweaty and asking for protein shakes.

Brittany Rosenberg kind of went off the deep end for a while, but then came back to us. Apparently she gave Chris Saul a blow job. He wanted her to blow him and Milo at the same time, and she asked me if it was a good idea, and I said I had never even blown one guy and wasn't sure how it would work. She says Chris and Milo have a very strange dynamic. They would "share" girls, as they called it, and she didn't like the idea of being used like that, even if she wanted to lose her virginity as soon as possible. "I think they might do stuff together—like, without girls, too," Rosenberg tells me. *The boys continued to have raging parties all throughout high school and even after they graduated, when they returned home for college breaks. I didn't attend another one, but sometimes Kenzie or Leigh would go. There were rumors that Milo got some girl pregnant after college, that he paid child support but didn't live with them. People say he's not openly gay but that if you catch him on a night out, it's obvious. I wonder why it's "obvious" when I couldn't tell. Rosenberg could, though, and maybe you had to be with him in that way to really know. I feel sorry for him; the rumors that haunted him in high school have continued following him long after. I wonder if he wishes people would just leave him alone and let him live his life. There were so many boys at school who felt they couldn't be themselves, who were closeted for so many years until they graduated, moved to big cities, and started over. Girls, too, pretending to be someone else until we felt free enough to break away.* Ultimately, Rosenberg says she should have just stuck with fawning over Mitchell. "I'm keeping it in my age bracket from now on," she jokes.

Jensen starts sitting with us at lunch again. She also starts asking for my history papers again and stealing Rosenberg's desserts. "You don't need these Oreos, you already got creamed!" Jensen says one day, and we all laugh, even Rosenberg. "At least she didn't steal Kenzie's SweeTarts," I say. Jensen gives me a high five for that one.

We start going to the bathroom after lunch together, just Jensen and I. We talk more about boys, who we should like next, what a penis feels like, that kind of stuff. One time we see Leigh in the bathroom. We watch her sniff something off the blue sink, and then she asks us for a tampon.

Jensen and I are in my mom's car one Friday after school. So is Dylan Kramer. Dylan's a drug dealer who lives in my neighborhood. Our moms met at our country club's pool, and when my mom found out Mrs. Kramer had a son who was new in town, she wanted to help him "acclimate." So, for the last couple weeks of school, he's carpooled with us, and we haven't said two words to each other. Sometimes my mom tries to make conversation, but he doesn't respond. He listens to rap on his headphones, and his shorts are always too long. He smells like weed all the time.

Jensen sits in the back seat with me, and Dylan is in the front. I ask if she wants to play a game—maybe the alphabet game, where we find restaurants and stores and street signs with letters from *A* to *B* to *C* and so on until we reach the end. We always have to wait for the La Quinta to get past *Q*. She mouths "no" and seems embarrassed that I asked.

My mom asks Dylan what he is doing tonight. He takes one earbud out of his ear and says he's going to a party at Brittany Tomassi's house. He must not realize that we used to be friends with her. "Are you girls going?" my mom asks, and we stare at the backs of the seats in front of us. "Can they go?" my mom presses, and Dylan looks confused and shrugs and puts his earbud back in. When we drop him off, his mom says that Dylan's older brother Harris is driving and that he could pick us up at 8:00 p.m. It is arranged that Jensen and I are going to our first real party *together*.

"How did this happen?" Jensen asks when we get upstairs to my room.

"Magic, or something," I suggest.

"We need to get ready!" she yells, and turns on my CD player. My Spice Girls CD isn't in position one, luckily, and Brad's Eminem CD is, so we play it and get ourselves into the mood to go to a party. We practice booty dancing, where we put our hands on our knees and swivel our butts up and around and around. She borrows a pair of my Brazilian jeans and a tight white tank top, and I wear another pair of very similar jeans with a black tank top that has GUESS printed on it. She is adamant about scrunching her hair, so I let her, but I know wearing it straight would be better. We both wear our Coach purses and kitten heels. She shows me how to put eyeliner on the inside of my eyelids—my "waterline," she calls it—and we both hope Kenzie won't be at the party.

"She's such a slut," Jensen says, and I agree. "And she stuffs her bra!" Jensen contemplates stuffing hers for the night, but I let her borrow a push-up bra instead. It's my favorite one, but I let her wear it, because it seems more important that she does. Maybe this will resolve the last bit of tension from our fight, if we both kiss boys tonight and have a good time.

We see Brittany Tomassi as soon as we walk in, and she takes us to her room. It's weird to be back at her house, even though it's only been a few weeks. She fixes Jensen's hair and lets me borrow a different pair of her jeans, the Buffalo ones that she got in New York. Kenzie is here, too, and we avoid her when she tries to talk to us, because she is drunk. Jensen is nice to her for some reason, and I just stare at her chest in her push-up bra and notice everyone has their boobs pushed up except me.

There are a lot of junior and senior boys at the party; we only know of them from fawning over their yearbook pictures or watching them play at football games. One named Demetri asks for Jensen's number, and I hear her say mine instead. "This way we can talk to him together," she says, but I'm not sure she understands that it may not be like that anymore. We have to grow up, grow apart, be ladies now and not dumb girls.

Dylan approaches us and says he is going to smoke a blunt and asks if we want to join. I say "No" right away, but then Jensen nudges me. "Why not?" she asks. *Why not, why not, why not*, repeats in my head, and I say "Sure" instead to Dylan, who leads us into the courtyard and sits us down on the steps. He and his brother roll the blunt, and a small crowd forms. Harris shoos some people away and is selective about who gets to stay.

"How do you know these girls?" he asks Dylan.

"They're the Brittanys," he says, and I realize we are the

last of our kind, a dying breed. Dylan shows us how to put
our lips on the tip of the blunt and suck the smoke deep into
the back of our mouths, how to pout a little and then let it out
slowly.

We feel it right away and lie down on the steps. Everyone
else in the circle smokes and then walks away, and it's just us
two. I feel like time has slowed down. I notice it's warm, but I
don't feel sweaty and sticky. My body has adjusted its temperature to the night, and I feel connected to the earth.

"Do you remember when you beat up Billy Millman?" I
ask, after a long silence.

"Ha!" Jensen laughs. "Yeah, why?"

"Why did you do it?"

"Because you're my best friend."

"You're, like, my person," I say.

"I know," Jensen says. "But it won't always be like that.
Someday we'll find other people."

"I can't imagine having a best friend other than you."

"Not just that. Like, boyfriends, then husbands. That's just
the way it goes."

"But what about this?"

"We're *not* going to end up like those old ladies who recog-
nize each other in supermarkets."

"Is that you, dearie?"

"Oh my, it's been fifty years!"

"Has it? Well, I'll be damned!"

Jensen looks up at the stars and then at me. She stares into
my eyes so deeply, like she wants to kiss me, or tell me some
deep, dark, incredible secret no one else has ever heard. I think

that if she tries to kiss me I'll let her. It'll be like a sign of love, of friendship—not forever, but for now, something we can remember having.

You cut your hair, you moved away, you made new friends, friends I couldn't stand. We grew apart. But I know you. You've always had so, so much love to give.

"I definitely feel it," Jensen says, and then I realize she's really high, and I'm really high, too. We laugh at nothing, and I can feel the little hairs on her arm sticking up, excited. We lie with our shoulders touching on the steps, closer than we've ever been, and stare up at the sky full of stars. It's only here that they're visible, far enough from the city, close enough to the swamp so you can hear the frogs croaking late at night. It feels like the middle of nowhere, and it feels so good.

• EPILOGUE •

*J*une in Las Vegas. Mom likes to walk everywhere. Dad doesn't, but we do it anyway. All anyone can talk about is Brad going away to college. It's so hot that my shorts stick to the back of my legs, and my hair is a mess. I forgot my straightener and have to blow-dry my hair if I want it to look normal. I give up after the second day and start wearing my hair in an obnoxious bun that Jensen calls "the Bell." You put your hair in a ponytail and then, on the second loop, you stop midway and let the hair flop into a ringlet that resembles a bell. I'm dying to talk to her; I haven't in four days.

Every morning, my mom and I go to the pool and I listen to my John Mayer CD, *Heavier Things*, all the way through. Half of the album I spend on my back to tan my front, then, at song number six, "Home Life," I flip. We get lunch from the pool bar at the Mirage, where we always stay every year, and I always order chicken fingers or a Caesar salad wrap with fruit on the side. Dad is in the casino most of the time, trying to win back the money the trip cost, and Brad travels from game room to game room but is required to have dinner with us every night.

Mom insists that we do at least one cultural activity as a family per trip. Last summer we went to this museum in the middle of the desert that had a circular room with all the stages of the big bang theory in little models. It showed how the continents came together—Pangaea—then separated. The stages were all placed next to each other, which made it seem quick, but really it took hundreds of thousands of years in between to break apart. It happened slowly but looked fast in the models. I remember thinking it would have sucked to be alive then, but I realized no one was alive then except dinosaurs. It made me wish I had paid more attention in science, but my teacher had scabies the year before and it was all we could talk about.

We're at a place on the Strip that has deals for activities and outings: you can see ten magic shows in two days for a hundred bucks, you can ride a roller coaster on top of the Stratosphere hotel. Brad sits on the steps outside the store while Mom and Dad are inside. I stand, too hot to sit, and lean against a newspaper dispenser. I'm so bored I could die. Mom comes outside for a second, and I decide it's now or never.

"Mom, can I please use Dad's phone?"

"I was just going to tell you, it's going to be a little while longer. It'll be worth it, though, because tomorrow we're going to see the Grand Canyon!"

"What's the big deal?" Brad asks. "It's just a big hole in the ground."

"It's history! It's culture!" she says.

"Mom, please?" I ask, again.

"Fine, but just for five minutes. He'll get charged if you go over his minutes, and he only uses that phone for work."

She goes back inside, and Dad comes out to where I'm standing. "I know Mom said five, but I'm giving you two." He hands me the phone with Jensen's number already dialed, as if he doesn't trust me to make a phone call.

"I've made phone calls before," I say, as he walks back inside.

I dial and wait. Jensen picks up on the second ring.

"Ugh, finally!" she says.

"I know. I was dying."

We're both silent for a second, letting the anxiety of not having spoken in a few days sink in. We normally talk to each other incessantly. We wait for a few moments to go by and then I break the silence.

"Did Sebastian call?"

"I'm not sure. I've been going to the Hillsboro Club every day with my parents. They always try to cram in time with me before I leave for camp. My mom lets me drink Amaretto sours, so it's fine, but it's so boring. I wish you were here."

"Are there any guys?"

"I kissed this one kid, Tony. He's like, my mom's coworker's son, and it was weird, but good, I think. What are you doing?"

"My parents are trying to get a deal on a tour of the Grand Canyon. I don't get what the big deal is—it's just a big hole in the ground."

We both laugh; then it settles.

"What if Ryan's been calling your house and you're not home?" Jensen asks.

"Maybe it's better this way," I say.

We continue talking about nothing, and I start to pace, then make a beeline for the parking lot, where I'm definitely not supposed to go. In the hot desert sun, I walk and talk to Jensen and press the phone against my ear. It's making me sweat, but I want to hear her better through the static. I look around for a cell tower to see if I can get closer to one. I wonder if it's been more than five minutes, let alone two, and I see the mountains in the distance and think about how far away we are from each other. I don't ask about the other girls. I only think about what I have to look forward to. I think about sophomore year and everything in front of me. I keep walking and talking to her on my dad's phone. We could talk forever, if only someone would let us.

ACKNOWLEDGMENTS

Thank you to my mom, Ilene Ackerman, who read the first draft of this novel, when it was something I had created by writing for an hour a day at the Starbucks in Studio City, California. Thank you for being my mom and for holding me through all the experiences I went through when I was fifteen. Thank you for bringing me chocolate milk every day after school and for being quiet when I didn't want to talk, for playing Billy Joel and Barry Manilow, and for letting me be who I needed to be then.

Thank you to my husband, Carl, my dearest one, for also reading the manuscript when it was just a stack of papers. Thank you for helping me see these girls cinematically through your eyes, for helping me find the moments of joy in the writing, for laughing at the funny scenes and crying at the painful ones. Thank you for loving me, no matter what.

Thank you to Alan Heathcock and my fellow participants at the 2016 Writing By Writers workshop in Chamonix, France. Thank you, Alan, for telling me that the collection of stories once known as *Boca Bitches* needed to be a novel, which is now this novel, *The Brittanys*. Thank you for prying open the door when we all got stuck in that lift before workshop and for teaching me that every story needs empathy, authenticity, urgency, meaning, and originality. Also thank you for being a badass in general.

Thank you to my friend Marianthi Hatzigeorgiou for being there then and now and for your Greek expertise, of course. To Erika Gallion for all the coffee dates and six-dollar lattes, for your sweet friendship, and for being my hype woman, always. To Rebecca Jensen for going through it with me— you know what I mean—and for letting me use your name for my narrator's best friend. To Casey Fisher for always answering texts and coming back to me with positivity and love. To Kelly Grzinic for the long drives, the cigarettes, the cookies, the yoga, and the appreciation for the beauty of life.

To Jo Ann Beard, whose novel *In Zanesville* heavily inspired me to write *The Brittanys*, my own version, my coming-of-age tale for my generation: Thank you for coming to FAU in the spring of 2015 and for your lessons that I will never forget. Thank you for your body of work, which has shaped my path as a writer and carried me through. Thank you for emailing back and forth with me when I was in the Redwoods, writing and crying, and you told me it would all be okay, that one day I'd be in your position because not so long ago you were in mine.

Thank you to the Wellstone Center in the Redwoods, where I wrote and cried, as mentioned previously, and where I took hikes with Sally the dog. But most important, it's where I learned to sit down for an hour a day and do the damn work.

Thank you to the city of Santa Cruz for being the love affair I needed. I hope to see you again someday soon.

To Anna Kaufman, my editor and guru, for your brilliance and your time, for listening to my Spotify playlists, for all the phone calls and oh my goodness all the emails, for teaching me how to celebrate each step of the way, for showing me how to strengthen my work, for illuminating my life in so many ways. I love working with you. Can we please have a fancy lunch when I make it out to New York?

To Mark Falkin, my agent: Thank you for believing in this story, for believing in me. I am so happy you have daughters and related to this book wholeheartedly, that you saw the need for these characters to live in the world, that you were pulled to it and helped bring it to life. Thank you for your revisions and your time and your sincerity. Thank you for our talks, which made me feel normal, or maybe we're both just strange—either way, thank you. Thank you for your readership, for your compassion, for your friendship. You rule.

Thank you to my production editor, Kayla Overbey; to my copy editor, Terry Zaroff-Evans; to my cover designer, Madeline Partner (omg!); to my text designer, Steve Walker; to my proofreaders, Hayley Jozwiak and Andrea Molitor; to my publicist, Julie Ertl; to my marketers, Lindsay Mandel and Annie Locke; to my social media team, Alexa Thompson and Erin Merlo; and to Daniel Novack.

Thank you to all the readers. I truly hope some piece of this story resonates with you, that you can think back on your teen years and find a way to love yourself through it all.